SLAUGHTER IN THE COTSWOLDS

Thea Osborne has just lost her beloved father and, with her faithful spaniel Hepzie, she retreats to her next house-sitting job, hoping to find peace and quiet to deal with her grief. As she settles down to two weeks of solitude her biggest challenges are jigsaw puzzles, and bats in the bedroom, but when her bossy elder sister arrives on the doorstep having witnessed a horrific killing, the rural serenity in Lower Slaughter is shattered. Investigating a murder while being a responsible house-sitter is no easy task, especially when you've got a dog-killer and a temperamental parrot on your hands.

SLAUGHTER IN THE COTSWOLDS

Slaughter In The Cotswolds

by

Rebecca Tope

Magna Large Print Books
Long Preston, North Yorkshire,
BD23 4ND, England.

British Library Cataloguing in Publication Data.

Tope, Rebecca
   Slaughter in the Cotswolds.

   A catalogue record of this book is
   available from the British Library

   ISBN   978-0-7505-3106-1

First published in Great Britain in 2009 by Allison & Busby Ltd.

Cover illustration by arrangement with Allison & Busby

Published in Large Print 2009 by arrangement with
Allison & Busby Ltd.

Magna Large Print is an imprint of Library Magna Books Ltd.

Printed and bound in Great Britain by
T.J. (International) Ltd., Cornwall, PL28 8RW

Another one for Liz,

celebrating 50 years of friendship

AUTHOR'S NOTE

As in previous titles, this story is set in a real village. However, the farms, houses and characters are all the products of my imagination. The Manor Hotel is an amalgam of a number of establishments in the area.

The lines on page 15 are from a hymn by John of Damascus.

CHAPTER ONE

They had automatically lined up in age order –
Damien, Emily, Thea and Jocelyn – along the
front pew of the little church. Their mother, however, interrupted the line, squeezed between
Damien and Emily, clutching tightly to a hand of
each. The pale coffin, which Thea had seen
recorded as being 5'10" by 16" on the undertaker's
card, stood on trestles only three feet away. Her
father lay inside, his hands folded tidily across his
stomach, his lips and eyes glued shut, his hair
brushed in a style it had never known in life. Only
the day before she had studied him for several
long minutes in the undertaker's chapel, fighting
to convince herself of the normality of death. But
there was no shaking the aching loss that arose
from knowing she would never again breathe in
his warm male smell, never again know the
special quality of attention that he gave her and
each of the others in turn. Richard Johnstone had
enjoyed fatherhood from first to last. He had
loved being a grandfather – the full complement
of nine grandchildren in a pew of their own across
the aisle from their parents could all attest to that.
Even Jocelyn's youngest, Roly, had insisted on
being included. Emily's three boys, a gangling
teenage trio, were behaving with unusual
decorum.

That Thea had arranged the funeral with her

daughter Jessica had surprised and unsettled some of the family. 'Surely you never want to go through that again,' Emily had said, reluctant to yield control. 'Why don't you let me or Damien do it? Or Mum. She's quite capable.'

'Anybody's *capable*,' said Thea impatiently. 'I'm just saying I know the routine with the undertaker and may as well make use of that.' Thea's husband, Carl, had died in a car accident, two and a half years earlier, and she would never forget the calm kindliness of Mr Williams as she forced herself to make a long list of irrelevant decisions about flowers and whether the dead Carl should wear his best suit for the occasion.

'Well I want to choose the hymns,' said Damien unexpectedly. When his three sisters and mother all stared at him, he flushed and flapped a hand. 'Don't look at me like that. I've been reading up on hymns, that's all, in the past day or two. There's something awful about nearly all of them when you look at the words.'

'Right,' said Jocelyn. 'They've all got God in them.'

Damien winced. It had been dimly apparent to them all that he had started going to church in recent years and involving himself in a weekly discussion group. Nobody had overtly referred to it, but it was dawning on them now that the crunch had finally come. 'Well it's just a short one,' he went on, producing a folded sheet of paper. 'I think it's part of something longer, but these ten lines say it all. See what you think.'

Thea took the paper and unfolded it. After a quick glance, she read the words in a self-

14

conscious voice, making the lines sound glib and obvious:

'Take the last kiss – the last for ever
Yet render thanks amidst your gloom;
He, severed from his home and kindred,
Is passing onwards to the tomb.
For earthly labours, earthly pleasures,
And carnal joys he cares no more;
Where are his kinsfolk and acquaintance?
They stand upon another shore.
Let us say, around him pressed,
Grant him, Lord, eternal rest.'

'Drat,' said Jocelyn. 'We were doing rather well until the last line.'

Thea looked at her brother. 'What's the tune?' she asked.

'No idea,' he admitted. 'I think it would work with the one to "Jerusalem". If not, we can probably fit it to something else we know.'

'I don't know any hymns,' said Jocelyn.

'Shut up,' Emily and Thea said in unison.

When Carl had been killed, Thea had let herself be persuaded by her father to bring the whole funeral to her childhood home, where her family could support her. It was only fifty miles from Witney where she and Carl had lived. His colleagues and relatives made no objection to travelling the extra distance, if that was the choice of the new young widow. Carl had been buried in the same churchyard that her father was now to occupy. The graves were four yards

15

apart. It was pleasing to think of them ending up so close. She suspected her mother eyed the plot with some wistfulness, seeing death as an easeful escape from the bother of being alive. Unlike her husband, Maureen Johnstone found it difficult to feel joy. There was always some worry, some irritation that spoilt it. 'Your expectations are too high, my love,' Richard would say. Thea had watched a thousand instances where her mother had nodded in rueful agreement, quite unable to do anything about it. People let her down and disappointed her. They forgot Mother's Day, or gave her presents that were the wrong colour or size, or neglected to ask after her welfare. Or they timed it badly, wanting her to join a celebration when they knew perfectly well she was consumed with anxiety about Jessica's choice of career or Emily's sudden loss of weight.

The interment was the usual awkward procedure, the horror of it obscured by the potential for farce. The sky was overcast but still the day was hot and the undertaker's men uncomfortable in their black clothes. The coffin was heavy and despite long practice, the moment of lowering, with its absolute need for dignity, gave rise to stress. When it had finally reached the bottom of the disconcertingly deep hole, the family shuffled their feet and threw glances at each other. 'Do we chuck soil onto it?' Jocelyn whispered loudly. Thea tried in vain to catch the eye of the funeral conductor who stood to one side, and then shook her head. 'Seems not,' she muttered. As at Carl's funeral she persuaded herself it was only in films that the practice existed, since no handy pile of clean dry soil stood nearby.

The gathering afterwards, which Thea always labelled a 'bunfight' to herself, was the usual jolly event, relief buoying everybody up. Two cousins materialised, sons of Richard's sister, not seen – at least by Thea – for a good twenty years. They had got fat and dull, both of them. Aged something like forty-seven and forty-nine, they seemed alarmingly old. Their own father had died five years earlier, and their position now as Top Generation seemed to have weighed them down. Brian was bald and Peter was grey and wrinkled.

Emily was slender and poised, holding a wineglass carelessly, sitting on the arm of her mother's settee. She watched her sons critically, now and then correcting one of them, or instructing her husband, Bruce, to do it on her behalf. 'Tell Mark to tuck his shirt in,' or 'Hasn't Grant had enough of those sandwiches?' Thea's older sister had always been bossy, maintaining a tight control over everyone in her immediate orbit. She had worked herself up through the Civil Service, despite according each son due attention in his early years, and keeping dozens of friendships alive with relentless emails and phonecalls.

Thea and her elder sister had seldom been alone together, all their lives. Emily had been nearly three when Thea was born, and six when Jocelyn followed. Somehow it seemed she had never quite adjusted to these additions to the family. There had been her and Damien, brother and sister, nice and normal, and then for some bizarre reason, her mother had produced the two extra girls. The family dynamic had been constructed and maintained by Dad, by the man who loved babies and shared himself out so effortlessly. But even he had not always managed to placate Emily, who shared some of her mother's tendency to dissatisfaction. Emily craved approval and respect, hating to be teased, forever suspicious of people's motives. 'Why didn't Dad take Grant with him to London last week? He took Jessica often enough when she was that age,' she would grumble to Thea, constantly watching for injustices and slights.

Maureen had arrayed the sympathy cards on a side table, where people drifted to look at them. The sentiments, added by hand inside the cards, were uninhibited. *Such a lovely man; Richard was always so helpful and patient with me; A good man taken much too soon; What a shocking loss!* But nobody uttered such thoughts out loud, not here in his house, an hour after burying him in the deep dark earth. Here they twittered and smiled and drank wine and forgot the man who had brought them there. Thea watched and grieved and inwardly raged.

'I had forty-eight cards,' said Emily, coming up behind her. 'I could have brought them with me, I suppose, but Mum wouldn't know who half the people were.'

'*Forty-eight?*' repeated Thea in blank amazement. 'How is that possible? I've had four.'

'Well, I emailed everybody in my address book with the news, plus work – I just know a lot of people.'

'I don't know how you do it.' Thea shook her head. It seemed almost indecent of her sister to outdo all the rest of them in such a way. Her cards undoubtedly exceeded the total received by the rest of the family. 'My mind boggles.'

Emily shrugged complacently. 'It's not so remarkable.'

'I'll have to go,' Thea said at three. 'I'm supposed to be in Lower Slaughter by now. Sorry, Mum, but it can't be helped.'

Her house-sitting commission was scheduled to run from a Friday for two weeks – a change from the usual Saturday. Not that it mattered to her: the days were interchangeable as far as she was concerned. Only the fact of her father's funeral on the day she had promised to take charge had caused difficulties.

Not lingering to bid goodbye to the cousins and friends, she kissed her mother, gave her younger sister a double pat on the upper arm, and left with a sense of escaping a situation that could only become more difficult as the hours went by.

The drive to the Cotswolds passed in a blur. The grey day would have been depressing in any circumstances, but on the day of her father's funeral it felt somehow fitting. The leaves had not yet begun to turn to autumn tones, and might not for another month or so, but the best of the summer was irretrievably over. Her insides felt heavy, turgid with endings. There seemed little to look forward to but worry and bother. Following this house-sit, there were two more already fixed: a September week in a bungalow in Stow-on-the-

Wold and an unusually protracted commission in Hampnett in January, which was definitely not something to look forward to. She had done her best to refuse, but the woman had offered to pay her such a high fee that she felt she had no choice. It would finance a decent holiday next summer, if she could survive the wintry uplands of that particular area without going insane.

'You're a fool,' said her 'friend' (she was never able to think of him as 'boyfriend' or 'lover' despite both labels being perfectly appropriate) Phil Hollis, uncompromisingly. 'You don't need the money. If you want a holiday, come to Greece with me and I'll pay for everything.'

Greece with Phil sounded fine, but she didn't like the idea of letting him pay. Even after a year's relationship with him, she clung to her independence. She still lived in her own Witney cottage, while he was in a Cirencester flat. They often went a whole week without seeing each other, and she was increasingly reluctant to make any changes to this pattern.

The house she was guarding in Lower Slaughter was old – very old in parts – low-slung and neglected. The owners were a dying breed – Cotswold born and bred, he a gamekeeper and she a former postmistress, her Post Office closed three years ago, and naught to be said about it. Retirement had been forced on them both, and in an effort to compensate for the shock, they were taking themselves off to their son in Hong Kong. They left behind them a motley collection of dogs and cats, as well as a gaudy parrot and a large cage containing five ferrets. 'I'll be bringing my dog with me,' Thea had said firmly. 'She's a cocker spaniel, very well behaved.'

Cedric and Babs Angell shrugged this off as irrelevant. 'Ours both be dogs,' said the woman, referring to the animals' gender. 'They ain't likely to mind a little bitch come to stay. Can't vouch for Ignatius, mind. He can be funny about strange animals.' Ignatius, it soon became clear, was the parrot.

Babs had introduced her to the bird with some ceremony. 'He belongs to Martin, our son, by rights. He brought him home one day when he was fifteen. Never would say exactly where he came from, but swore he wasn't stolen. That was twenty-something years ago now. Taught him all kinds of daft things to say – you'll hear most of them, shouldn't wonder. Turns your heart over sometimes, the way he seems to understand what's going on.' She scratched the feathers of the parrot's chest with a confident finger. 'He's a good old boy. Can't tell you how fond we are of him, after this long time.'

'How old is he?' asked Thea, with the inevitable house-sitter's worry that an animal might die in her care.

'No idea. Martin claimed he was just a fledgling when he came, but he seemed more than that to me, not that I ever knew anything about parrots. But they live sixty, seventy years, so he's in his prime.'

This visit had been a fortnight ago, after an initial quick meeting a month or so before that, while in Temple Guiting with Phil. The owners

21

had found most of her questions irrelevant and irksome. Routines, keys, visitors, phone calls – all were waved aside as minor issues. Past experience had taught Thea that there was almost certainly a central reason for employing her services that might not be instantly apparent. Given the feral nature of several of the animals, and the relative ease with which someone could have been asked to come in daily to feed them, there were grounds for wondering just what the point was.

The house was surrounded by a reduced acreage, remnants of a much larger farm. Cedric had bought the house and the vestigial two fields from the farmer who had been brought low by agricultural misfortunes. He told Thea the story, as if it had all taken place a week ago. 'Poor old Ralph, too stuck in his ways to keep up with the times. Silly sod sold up in a fit of panic, and regretted it ever since. Just missed the price boom. If he'd waited another year or two, he'd have got half as much again.' He smiled smugly, still glowing from his good fortune after ten years or more.

'Is he still alive?'

Cedric nodded. 'Got himself a nice enough place just beyond Moreton, market garden sort of thing. Never made much of a go of it, mind. Some people just don't have the right outlook to make a success of things – don't you find?'

Thea knew, in a vague way, that farmers detested selling any of their land. They hoarded and competed and mortgaged in an effort to hang onto every inch of their property. Like little heads of state intent on expansion, they glanced hungrily over borders and boundaries and dreamt of acquiring each other's forgotten corners.

'Poor chap,' she murmured. 'What happened to the rest of the land?'

Cedric's face darkened. 'There's talk of building on the Six Acre field. It's only a little way from the village, see – some bright spark snapped it up, on the off chance. Now they've got new houses going up in Lower Swell, there's a chance he'll get the go-ahead.'

Uh-oh, thought Thea. What am I walking into here? She looked to Babs enquiringly. The woman was in her early sixties, with curly white hair and a body the exact shape of a pear.

'Everyone got a letter from the Council Planning Office,' she said. 'They're applying to build ten new houses on the field. Can't see it, myself. Lower Slaughter's not Lower Swell. This is in all the books – famous it is, for the way it looks. New houses would stick out like sore thumbs.'

'Right,' Thea agreed. 'And surely–' Thea knew a bit about planning laws, as did most rural dwellers. 'I mean, that must be a change of use? There must be a County Plan that excludes it from development? Didn't Ralph put a restriction on it when he sold it?'

'Never crossed his mind, seemingly. Well, it wouldn't, him not being the sharpest nail in the bag. Cedric's not happy about it, but I tell him not to worry.' She threw her husband a complicated look of impatience and solicitude.

'Well, it would be a shame.' Thea offered the

23

remark more as a palliative to the unhappy Cedric than from any genuine feeling of her own. She was tempted to add something consoling about even if the worst happened it was a mere six acres out of hundreds, a mere ten new houses, in a region where there was still a lot of open space and greenery.

After the historical explanations, the Angells informed Thea that she could use anything she liked out of the freezer. 'Hope you like pheasant,' Cedric chuckled. 'I might be retired, but I still get my share of the bag.'

Babs threw up the lid of the stately white chest to reveal a jumble of meat in plastic bags almost to the top. Thea gasped in awe: there had to be easily fifty or sixty items to choose from. 'Venison, rabbit, bit of lamb down near the bottom, bones for the dogs – but mainly it's pheasant,' said Babs.

'Not many labels,' observed Thea.

Babs laughed scornfully and closed the lid.

It seemed that the closest neighbour was a surviving farm, boasting a thousand head of sheep. The buildings were clearly visible from the back of the Angells' house, two large modern barns and an older one stacked high with bright yellow straw in big circular bales. 'Don't let the dogs go over there,' Cedric warned. 'That Henry's very twitchy about dogs getting among his sheep.'

'But it isn't lambing time,' said Thea.

Cedric shook his head. 'Lambing's not a worry, with them all indoors. Dogs'll chase sheep any time of the year, if they get the mood on them.'

Thea looked at Hepzibah and smiled at the

image of the floppy-eared spaniel in pursuit of a large woolly prey.

'They seem pretty friendly,' she observed, eyeing Cedric's two dogs.

'They're good old boys,' Cedric agreed. 'Not much of a life, but Babs insisted we have them as guards. They've got each other, and the chains are good and long.'

'But presumably you untie them sometimes for exercise?' The thought that the animals remained perpetually tied up was untenable.

Cedric ducked his chin in a gesture of shame. 'Not as often as we ought,' he admitted.

'So – am I allowed to walk them? I can't bear to leave them tied up the whole time. It's just not in my nature.' She struggled not to sound accusing or critical.

'If you must. But make damned sure they don't get away from you, that's all. Best take them one at a time, maybe. That's the safest. Babs paid a pretty penny for that huntaway – she's not going to take it kindly if he comes to grief.'

'Huntaway?'

Cedric indicated the short-haired dog, with black and tan colouring. His feet were tan socks on black legs, which gave him a characterful appearance. 'They're a three way cross – alsatian, sheepdog and something else. I can never recall what the last one is. Very good with cattle, so they say.'

Various sketchy details were provided about dustbin day and the best place to buy milk and bread, and then detailed arrangements had been made for the Friday departure. Five days later,

Thea's father had died, and she had been on the brink of cancelling the whole commission. She phoned the Angells and told them what had happened. The horrified silence at the idea that she might not fulfil her promise was enough to persuade her she couldn't let them down. 'We're not sure when the funeral is, but if we have it in the church, it'll probably be the end of the week, which is quite quick these days.'

Babs Angell had coughed, rather than attempt a response to this.

'It gets very booked up at the crematorium,' Thea elaborated. 'People have to wait nearly three weeks sometimes.'

'That's a disgrace,' said Babs. 'Well, dear, I'm sorry for your loss. We only have one Dad, don't we?'

The kindness had made Thea cry, and she put down the phone after promising thickly to do her best to keep to the arrangement.

They had been gone several hours when Thea and Hepzibah arrived. The sun was casting low rays over the sheep farm at the back of the house, the earlier clouds having cleared in time for a few last moments of summer evening.

The romantically named Hawkhill Farm stood on comparatively level ground to the south-east of the village of Lower Slaughter, the Roman-straight A429 a few fields away. The road slashed diagonally from Cirencester to Stow, as much part of the area as the butter-coloured buildings and the tumbling hills and valleys. Well-rambled footpaths crisscrossed at this point, the

26

Slaughters one of the most popular attractions for tourists. Thea could see a marker post just beyond the corner of the Angells' garden, showing where one of the paths ran. She found herself debating the pros and cons of having people in stout boots and rucksacks on their backs passing within speaking distance. She could position a garden chair under that handsome cherry tree and wave to passing ramblers. It might add a welcome air of sociability to her stay.

Phil had known better than to offer to share this commission with her. Once she had convinced him that she was intent on continuing the house-sitting work, he had been forced to accept that he couldn't be with her every time. Still recovering from a severely slipped disc in his lower back, he had missed too much work to be able to take time off so soon, anyway. The proposed week in Greece could not have happened until the end of September at the earliest, he admitted.

And Jessica, her daughter, had made no suggestion of joining her, either. 'Seems we'll be on our own this time,' Thea said to the spaniel, trying not to think about the long solitary evenings ahead. It was her own choice, after all. If she minded that much, she could get a proper job in an office and stop messing about.

The livestock under her care seemed only mildly suspicious. The dogs had their own quarters in a stone-built shed set at right angles to the house, and were content to have their food provided by a new person. Feeding them was a simple matter of scooping dry complete nuggets from a metal bin into two large aluminium bowls, and presenting them to the animals. The huntaway was the more friendly, approaching her with a slow tail-wag, before politely consuming his supper. The other was black and white, with a long full coat and looped-over tail like a husky. Their names had not been disclosed, which Thea found made her feel more detached from them than she would otherwise have been.

Three tabby cats sat on a flight of slate steps running up the outside of the barn to a door at the top. They made a charming picture, and Thea wished she'd thought to bring her camera. The door at the head of the steps had once been a corn store, 'the granary' Babs had called it. Now it contained discarded furniture and had been taken over by the cats. A small square hole had been cut in the door for their convenience. Thea gave them their complete dry food, in three cream-coloured ceramic bowls, and swiped her hands together. 'Now there's just the parrot and the ferrets,' she said.

The ferrets occupied yet another part of the property – a wooden shed at the back, approached by a weed-strewn path around the side of the house, or through from the kitchen and scullery. They too had pre-packaged food, comprising pellets of various colours and shapes. Mr and Mrs Angell must have quite a job keeping up supplies, she realised, imagining the car coming back from a cash and carry loaded with all the different bags of animal feed, and the subsequent distribution to the various sheds and rooms.

The ferrets were restless, weaving their slender bodies round and round the cage, raising sharp pink snouts to sniff this strange hand that was feeding them. Thea had experience of ferrets – at the age of four, when visiting a small friend, she had poked a finger through the wire-fronted cage of the prize hob and had it savagely bitten. Not until Pauline's father had arrived and pinched the animal's tail had it released her. The screams had quickly become legendary. But Thea held no permanent grudge. She liked the streamlined creatures with their intelligent little faces. It came as no surprise that a former gamekeeper should keep them. They would still be used to start rabbits from their burrows, in places where rabbits were proving too much of a pest.

Ignatius held the privileged position of being the only creature allowed inside the house. He had a large cage in a corner of the front room, and a perch close to the window, where he was invited to sit when a change of scene seemed in order. A slender chain attached his leg to the bar, giving him perhaps twelve feet of scope for flight or exploration. Ignatius made Thea – and her dog – infinitely more nervous than all the other beasts put together. He sat hunched in the cage, his head cocked cynically as she approached and attempted to introduce herself. Like people always did with parrots, she tried to entice him to speak. 'What a pretty boy, then,' she prattled. 'Where's your Mummy and Daddy gone, then? Will you be good for me and Hepzie?'

The bird gave an inarticulate snort, and sank its head sadly into its chest.

The bedroom was the second door on the right at the top of the stairs. Carrying Hepzie's blanket, and followed by the dog, Thea went up soon after ten. She needed to process the day, the momentous event of her father's burial, the ongoing issues of Phil and the future and money.

She opened the door and suddenly the spaniel was yapping and leaping crazily at something inside the room. Switching on the light, bemused by the dog's behaviour, she was aware of something flittering erratically above her head.

A bat! Increasingly hysterical, Hepzie was straining every nerve to catch it, bounding in matching zigzags after the creature. Thea threw the door wide open, hoping the bat would leave and somehow find a way out of the house. Instead, it darted in swooping dives at the central light, seeming to be both attracted and repelled by it. Holding up the blanket, Thea strove to direct it out through the door, flapping encouragingly when it headed in the required direction. But it repeatedly returned to the light, and the irrationality of it began to seem oddly sinister. The dog's incessant yapping made everything worse.

After several futile minutes, she decided to try switching off the light in the room, and turning on the one on the landing, only to find that the now invisible bat darting around her head was intolerably alarming. It might catch in her hair, and cling there with its nasty little talons. Quickly she put the light on again, and renewed her efforts with the blanket. With Hepzie very slightly calmer, the strategy eventually worked and the flittering creature swooped out of the door and disappeared.

Shaking, Thea slammed the door after it, and threw herself on the bed, hugging the spaniel to her chest. Already she foresaw the whole episode repeated, night after night, as she tried to oust the bat from what it might well regard as its territory.

'Never mind,' she said to the dog. 'It's only a bat. Until now, I always thought I liked them.'

CHAPTER TWO

It had taken her a long time to get to sleep, and when she did, she dreamt her father was still alive, playing with Hepzie and laughing. But to her own shamed surprise, she woke with an urgent desire for the dream not to have been true. She had loved him, even rejoiced in him at times, and yet now he was dead, she wanted him to stay that way. The Lazarus story came to her mind, with the horror of that raised corpse stumbling through the streets, repelling everyone he encountered. The dead, she concluded, really ought to stay dead.

All of which led to a nagging feeling of guilt towards her mother. Not only had Thea abandoned her in her grief, but she had been infinitely relieved to have a good reason to do so. Despite the fact that she had experienced widowhood herself and might be expected to offer empathy and consolation in abundance, she knew her mother would adopt an entirely different pattern of mourning from her own. When Carl had been killed without warning in his early forties, Thea had been numb for weeks, and then so wracked with pain that she could scarcely function at all. Only her daughter and her father had been permitted anywhere near her, and they often proved to be intolerably irritating. Even a year afterwards, she had still preferred her own company, sinking into strategies that she had finally recognised as unwholesome – inventing ways to hurt herself in order to drown the emotional anguish. The distraction of the house-sitting had saved her, she believed now. She had met people with their own crises and losses, and slowly discovered in herself a hard-won wisdom that sometimes seemed to help.

Saturday morning dawned uncertainly, streaks of grey across the lower part of the sky suggesting a possible build-up of rain clouds later. Hepzie had clearly not forgotten the bat of the night before. She worked around the room, sniffing hard at skirting boards and glancing up at the ceiling every now and then.

The room was small, furnished with a single bed, chest of drawers and a round table covered with a cloth embroidered lavishly with honeysuckle and poppies. A hand-made rug was placed beside the bed, its pile pleasantly long and warm to bare feet. Thea had left her suitcase on the floor, still packed apart from pyjamas and spongebag. There was nowhere to hang clothes, and she wasn't tempted to use the chest of drawers. Living out of a suitcase was no great hardship.

Phil had managed, after several months, to persuade her to make much greater use of her mobile phone. A busy senior police detective, he would often fail to answer a call, which forced her to master the art of texting. Every time she did it, she felt she had stepped into a different world from the one she had expected to inhabit for the rest of her life. Part of her felt it was pure non-sense, sending a handful of words to a friend or relative or lover, simply to remind them that you existed and had not forgotten them. It was a typical British substitute for intimacy, which only served to emphasise to her that she was more than happy to maintain her independence and spells of isolation. But part of her had grown to enjoy the link it forged between them. She composed her messages carefully, using proper spellings and punctuation. He made no remark about this, for fear of deterring her from making contact, but he himself would use *u* for 'you' and even *l8* for 'late'.

So now she picked up the gadget from where it sat on the round table and thought about her mother, not Phil Hollis at all. She ought to phone and see how the new widow was feeling. Now, as never before, family unity was called for. But instead she found herself keying in her sister Emily's number. Safer, she thought, than intruding on a huddled hopeless mother who would not respond to bracing comments down a phone line.

Emily answered warily, sighing with relief when she recognised Thea's voice. 'Thank goodness,' she breathed. 'I thought you were Mum.'

'Why? What's she been doing?'

'Oh – you know. She wouldn't let me stay the night with her, and then spent about two hours crying down the phone at midnight. I told her to take a sleeping pill, but of course there aren't any in the house. I can see she's going to drive us all mad for the next twenty years.' Maureen Johnstone was seventy-two – another twenty years was entirely feasible.

'Bad luck,' said Thea, sincerely. It *was* bad luck for Emily that she was the default daughter that their mother chose to cry on. Jocelyn had escaped into her own teeming demanding family, and Thea had never been quite sympathetic enough for comfort. Her tendency to make logical comments highlighting the flaws in her mother's arguments or pleas for support seldom went down well. Perhaps, she thought, it was Emily's position in the family that had shaped her character, and really her essential nature wasn't so uptight and controlling after all. It was an idle thought, since there seemed little that could be done about it, but it helped give her patience. 'You ought to just take her at her word, and let her get on with it for a few days.'

'I'm going to, don't you worry. She has every right to be sad – but so do I. What about *my* grief?' The last words emerged on a sob that sent chills through Thea. She hadn't bargained for this. If she'd given it any thought at all, she'd concluded that Emily wouldn't especially miss her father; had never seemed as close to him as Thea had been, and often found him irritating. Emily kept emotion on a tight rein. Thea couldn't remember seeing her cry since she was thirteen.

'Oh dear,' she said feebly. 'I suppose this is how it usually goes. We all have to retreat into our burrows and deal with it in our own way.'

It was precisely the sort of sentiment that Emily could be relied on to agree with, in normal circumstances. But it seemed that a new normality was now in charge. 'I'd really like to talk to somebody about how I feel,' came the amazing reply.

'Oh. Well, I imagine Bruce is the person for that, then?' Emily's husband was in fact a most unlikely counsellor, a man who left the room at a brisk trot at the first hint of emotional revelations – but Thea was making no more assumptions.

'Of course not, you idiot. I want to come and talk to you.'

'When?'

'Well, sometime between now and Monday morning. I have to be at work then.'

'It isn't very salubrious here. There's a parrot...'

'Come on, Thea. Don't give me that. If it's good enough for you to live in for umpteen weeks, then I can cope with it for a weekend. The people need never know.'

'I'm here for two weeks,' Thea corrected her. 'Not umpteen.' The prospect of a visiting relative was far from unusual. People seemed to join her at most of her house-sitting commissions, for various reasons. They thought she would be lonely; they wanted to share the adventure; and in Phil's case, he saw it as a chance to enjoy a brief holiday with her. But Emily was the last person she had ever expected to suggest such a move.

'So?' her sister prompted. 'Did you say it was Upper Slaughter?'

'Lower. It isn't very far away. It'll take you just over an hour, at a guess.' Emily lived in Aylesbury, which Thea had always found faintly comic. 'There's a parrot,' she said again, as if this was a crucial detail.

'I don't mind parrots,' said Emily. 'Why do you keep saying that?'

'I don't know.' Suddenly Thea remembered that she too was in grief for her father. She, as much as her sister or mother, had cause to be in a strange state, irrational and forgetful. She felt as if something would break if there was any hint of overload. She wanted peace and simplicity. The parrot, perhaps, threatened to become complicated.

'Well, I'll come after lunch then,' said Emily as if it was all agreed. 'I'll bring an overnight bag, but I'm not sure I'll stay. It depends how it goes. Tell me how to find you. What's the postcode?'

'I have no idea. Why do you want that?'

'For the TomTom, of course.'

The thing in the car, Thea realised. The device that was supposed to stop anybody ever getting lost again. What price adventure and fairytales now? The children of the future wouldn't even understand the concept of not knowing precisely where you were at any given moment. 'Well, I haven't got the postcode. There are various ways to get here, but the easiest is probably to come to the middle of Lower Slaughter, turn left, up a narrow lane, and left again at the junction, round a bend and you'll see a stone farmhouse set back from the road.' She gave a few helpful landmarks, but said no words of welcome. She found that she quite badly did not want her sister to descend on her for a deep discussion of grief and loss. She had been quite pleased to have dodged all that, with the convenient timing of her latest commission.

'Why does it have such a nasty name?' Emily wanted to know.

'Slaughter, you mean? Oh, I know the answer to that. It has nothing to do with killing things. It's from "slough" which is a stretch of boggy ground. Like the Slough of Despond.'

'That's quite nasty as well,' said Emily, obviously determined to see the grey side of things.

Before her guest arrived, and after all the creatures were dealt with, Thea took the spaniel for an exploration of the village. As Babs had said, the farmhouse was less than half a mile outside the settlement, with the sold-off fields even closer. There was a lot more overt tourist activity in Lower Slaughter than in the other villages she had stayed in. Two stately hotels set the tone – claiming stars and crowns galore between them, to prove the luxurious quality of their beds and cuisine. There would be none of the quiet deserted mornings before the tourist coaches came through that Duntisbourne Abbots or Temple Guiting enjoyed. Hotel guests would tumble forth to savour the early sun on the little river Eye, and self-catering holidaymakers would saunter out for some local colour before breakfast. The characteristic restraint of the dozens of tucked-away villages in the area had been lost in the Slaughters. Recalling what Emily had said, Thea wondered whether it was the intriguing, slightly repellent, name that had singled them out for such relentless attention.

A well-behaved little river ran through the very centre of the village, with the road on one side, and a wide pavement on the other. This pavement could almost qualify as a promenade, inviting strollers along the waterside. At one end was a bridge just sturdy enough to take cars, and at the other, the path turned a sharp bend to the Mill, which had been converted into a shop clearly aimed at tourists. At right angles to it was a small museum, with old rural artifacts standing outside. A row of gorgeous old houses with colourful front gardens lined the footpath, conspicuous in their Cotswoldiness, and a narrow footbridge offered walkers a car-free way across the river. It all felt like being inside a picture postcard, or a fairytale. The air was still, the water merely flickering in its lazy progress.

Keeping Hepzie on the lead, she traversed the village from end to end, and met ten or twelve people in the course of fifteen minutes. Even in the comparatively large Blockley, there had not been so many pedestrians. It felt intimate, as if all these people should become one's friends, or at the least exchange something beyond a nod and a smile – an impression that Hepzie seemed to share. Three times she tried to jump up at a passing stranger, forcing Thea to rein her in tightly and make shame-faced apologies.

The tension between having definite tasks to perform on the one hand, and the irresistible sense of being on holiday on the other, had gradually become a familiar part of house-sitting. The fact that events had never unfolded as expected only added to this tension. There were many different motives for employing somebody to take care of one's house, she had discovered. The pets and livestock often turned out to be quite incidental to the real reason for importing a guardian. Simmering at the back of her mind were the comments made by the Angells about property development and the conflicts that were bound to ensue. Quite how any of that could possibly affect her, she wasn't sure. Probably it wouldn't. But now that she knew about it, she felt she ought to be on the alert.

It was impossible to know which of the people she encountered were on holiday, and which lived in Lower Slaughter permanently. She suspected the vast majority fell into the former category. Cotswold villages appeared to possess remarkably few permanent residents. Even those who did officially reside there were off down the motorway at seven in the morning, and didn't come back for a good twelve hours. To count them as 'residents' hardly seemed accurate.

But the one approaching her now was surely an exception. Not that he had straw in his hair or string tied round the knees of his trousers, but he certainly wasn't in the clean shirt and slacks of the typical tourist. He was wearing a khaki flannel garment that looked rather warm for August, crumpled at the collar and bunchily tucked into his jeans – which had a narrow tear across one knee, exposing pale-coloured threads. He met her eyes from a distance of several yards, his head slightly cocked in a friendly question. Why, she wondered later, had he singled her out for curiosity when she was surely indistinguishable from any other self-catering visitor? But during the encounter, the only thing she wondered was how anybody could have such a vivid shade of blue to their eyes. They were *gentian* blue, the colour glowing in a tanned face. As she held their gaze, the blueness seemed to outshine every other hue in their surroundings. There was red on the buildings, yellow and purple in the gardens and hanging baskets, green above and below – but the man's eyes were impossibly, inhumanly, blue.

He was about her own age, not particularly tall or slim or muscular. He smiled lightly, and nodded a greeting. 'Morning,' he said, as they passed. His voice was deep and rich.

'Hello,' she answered. Hepzie tugged at the lead, wanting to contribute to the exchange. The man took no notice of the dog.

It was over in seconds. Thea walked on slowly, blinking at the momentary dazzlement. So he had blue eyes – what of it? Phil Hollis had blue eyes as well, come to that. Phil would hold her gaze and bare his soul and invite her attention and love. There was no space in her life for sudden startling corneal intimacy with a scruffy stranger.

She increased her pace, letting the dog have more freedom on the extendable lead. The pretty river did its rivery thing, twinkling tidily between trim stone embankments and beneath charming little bridges. The slough after which the villages had been named was firmly channelled and drained and long forgotten. The essence of the Cotswolds was thriving here, everything safe and

41

predictable and lovely.

She bought an ice cream at the shop, wishing it sold wine and olives as well, and turned back to Schloss Angell, alias Hawkhill Farm. The first thing she did on arriving was to go to the utility area beyond the kitchen and open the chest freezer. Two plucked and prepared pheasants caught her eye. She would cook them for her sister. Somehow they seemed just right for the occasion.

CHAPTER THREE

Emily arrived at three, pausing in the gateway as if unsure that she'd come to the right place. Thea was on a rickety garden bench, which had small patches of lichen growing on it to give witness to its extreme age. She sat outside because it was August, and she wanted to watch out for Emily, but it was a chilly vigil, with clouds gathering in the west and a spiteful little breeze blowing.

Along with the Angells' bored dogs, she watched her sister park the shiny new car and emerge in a fluid elegant movement. Emily was superficially like Thea, but four inches taller. Jocelyn, the youngest, was much fairer and heavier, plucking her genes from the Johnstone grandmother, rather than Maureen's slighter, darker, father, Grandpa Foster, a man they barely remembered, but who was immortalised in Emily, who was said to look exactly like him.

'Don't sit here,' Thea warned. 'It won't take two. Every time I move it threatens to collapse.'

'Hmm,' said Emily. 'The place seems a bit ramshackle.'

'By local standards, it is – definitely,' Thea agreed. 'I quite like it.'

They went in through the front door and Thea instantly saw the house through Emily's eyes. It was dusty; the windows weren't very clean; the rugs and stair carpet had endured spillages and damage that left indelible marks. The curtains at the front window were ragged at the edges where the parrot had climbed up them countless times.

Ignatius was intently aware of a second intruder. 'Lock the doors, Daddy! Lock the doors!' it screeched, with impossible clarity. It was the first time Thea had heard him speak.

'My God!' said Emily faintly. 'I see what you mean. It's terrifying.'

'That's nothing,' said Thea with relish. 'There was a great big *bat* in my bedroom last night.'

'No!'

'I always thought I liked them until then. But it's all true what they say – you get a real horror that it'll tangle itself in your hair. I can't think why, when they absolutely never do that, at least according to Carl. They move so irrationally, darting and swooping, and you know they can't see you and don't know what you are.'

Emily shuddered. 'I would have run right out and driven home on the spot.'

'Well, I can't do that, can I? Whatever happens, I have to stay here for a fortnight.'

'Well, you're a lot braver than me, that's for sure. And braver than your dog, by the look of it.'

Hepzibah was circling the parrot's cage, eyes fixed on the bird, small squeaks emitting from her. 'Lock the doors,' said the parrot again, on a quieter note, sending the dog into further whining confusion. Distress was clear in every nerve.

Thea laughed. 'Come on, silly. It won't hurt you.' But Hepzie continued her patrol, thoroughly bewildered, but convinced she had some sort of protective role to play. Thea dragged her into the kitchen, where she made tea and engaged her sister in the conversation she had come to conduct. It wasn't long before they ventured onto the main topic – the death of their father and their mother's future. It ebbed and flowed, as they moved from kitchen to living room, and then outside to feed the dogs and ferrets. Thea spent half an hour in the kitchen, forbidding Emily from joining her as she set the pheasants simmering in a casserole, with carrots and onions and herbs. They were still slightly frozen, but she hoped that a couple of hours in a moderate oven would see them tender and toothsome. Emily called through from the main living room, every few minutes: 'Surely I can do something to help?' and 'I came to talk to you, not sit here twiddling my thumbs.' But hard experience had taught Thea that to invite Emily to share cooking was to consign yourself to a barrage of corrections and scathing comments about your technique. Nobody sliced carrots to Emily's satisfaction, and the idea of her discovering that the birds were not fully defrosted was too terrible to contemplate.

'I'll be right with you,' she promised. 'We can have an hour or more of quality time before I have to get some potatoes on.'

The conversation had already verged on the overwrought at times. Awkwardly, Emily had voiced her sense of disconnection after the funeral, only the day before. 'I've been trying to carry on as normal, especially with Grant going off to sixth form college in a couple of weeks. He needs all sorts of books and clothes, and I can

45

only do it at weekends. I should be sitting him down and making a proper list, not falling apart here.'

'You're not falling apart, don't be silly,' Thea argued. 'It wouldn't be very realistic to think you could just pretend nothing had happened. What sort of message would that give the boys? They'll be missing Dad as well.'

Waiting for the pheasants to cook, they doggedly forced themselves to stay with the painful subject of bereavement. Emily seemed determined to confront what she saw as an imperfect relationship with her father, dating back to her failure to adopt his values or interests. 'He always wanted me to make better use of my brain,' she said. 'To go into science and do some good in the world.' She sniffed. 'And I could never rid myself of the notion that most of the world's problems are rooted in science. I made him so *angry*.'

'You didn't do it on purpose.'

'Maybe not, but he thought I did. And then you married Carl, who was the embodiment of Dad's ideas. All that ecological stuff – it was wonderful for him. It left me even further out of the magic circle. My husband's a financial consultant, for heaven's sake.'

'Dad didn't mind,' Thea insisted. 'You're projecting too much onto him. He wasn't at all judgmental. He *liked* Bruce and he adored your boys.'

'Not as much as he liked Carl and Jessica. Oh, Thea – I feel so bloody *guilty*. I thought there'd be time to put it all straight and earn his approval. And now it's too late. It feels so *awful*.'

It made quite a lot of sense to Thea, as she meditated on the family history as she remembered it. 'You just have to go with it, I suppose,' she said vaguely. 'Wait for it all to settle down again.'

Emily twirled a strand of hair around a finger, like a fifteen-year-old. Outside, heavy rain had set in, thundering loudly on the tin roof of the barn. A glance at the clock told Thea it was high time she peeled some potatoes.

The meal was a modest success. 'Could have done with another hour on a slow heat,' said Emily. 'I'd have told you if you asked me. I did pheasant a few weeks ago for a dinner party. The flavour needs to come out with long slow cooking.'

'Thanks. I'll remember that for next time,' said Thea lightly. 'At least it's edible.'

'It's really quite nice,' said Emily graciously. 'Much better than I expected. Though it's a pity there's no wine.' She ate quickly, and in half an hour it was all over, including an apple and coffee.

'I think the Angells are teetotal,' said Thea. 'And it didn't occur to me to bring any booze with me.'

'Just as well, I suppose, since I've got to drive.'

'Look at that rain!' said Thea. 'You'd much better stay the night, instead of setting off into that. It's getting quite dark.'

'No, I'm not staying the night,' said Emily. 'I can't face the idea of that bat. I don't want to put

47

you off, but I don't like the atmosphere in this house. There's something *dingy* about it. Cobwebs and things going rusty and inches of fluff under the beds. It'll give me asthma if I try to sleep here.' She put a hand to her bronchial area. 'I can feel it already.'

'OK,' said Thea, trying to suppress the disappointment. It didn't seem very fair of her sister to invade like this and then abruptly leave again, with no thought for the effect she was having. Thea had not wanted family business to intrude on the Lower Slaughter job, especially so soon after getting there. Emily's feelings towards their father verged on the critical at times, which Thea found surprisingly upsetting. As far as she was concerned, he'd been perfect, and her sister had no right to jeopardise that comforting belief. After all, Emily herself had been a scratchy and even downright arrogant daughter at times. She'd always been a poor listener, disinclined to take the other person's feelings into account, argumentative and sometimes uncharitable. Thea suspected that if the conversation had lasted much longer, she might have been tempted to say some of this, with ghastly consequences.

So it was with more than a little relief mixed into the simmering resentment that she waved her sister out of sight, standing in the doorway only long enough to watch the car begin to move. The rain was bad enough to raise flickers of anxiety in the breast of anyone who had experienced floods over the past few years. This area, Thea remembered, had suffered severely. She wondered briefly whether the little river running through Lower

Slaughter ever misbehaved badly enough to threaten the houses alongside it. It might be interesting to go for a look in the morning. As far as Hawkhill was concerned, it appeared that any run-off water had been efficiently directed into ditches and channels well clear of the house. There was no sign of rivulets or even large puddles in what she could see of the yard.

So she closed the front door, went back into the living room, and tried to settle down on the sagging sofa. But she was soon up again, prowling around the room in search of diversion. The television's remote control didn't work, there was no DVD player, and the only light in the room was a rather dim energy-saving bulb, apparently bought when they first appeared and living up to its promise of lasting for fifty years. There were few books in the house, but she did find a stack of big jigsaws in one corner. Somehow Babs Angell had struck her as too busy for such fripperies, but when she examined them it was plain that they had all been used. Something about the afternoon she'd spent with Emily, the references to childhood and family life, made jigsaws seem entirely appropriate. She selected one depicting a small flock of sheep in the snow, with a lot of twisty bare tree branches, and resolved to try to finish it before it was time for her to leave Hawkhill.

The light was better in the kitchen, and a radio sat on the windowsill. The view was over the fields and farm buildings at the back. The table could be used for the jigsaw, with plenty of space left over for one person to sit and eat at one end.

There was a play on Radio Four, involving a Victorian governess and the younger son of the house, which kept her pleasantly diverted as she methodically sorted out all the edge pieces. Hours passed. Hepzie was curled on a muddy sheepskin in front of the Rayburn. The parrot was quiet and rain continued to thunder on the roofs outside. She made herself more coffee at one point, and wondered whether she should try phoning her daughter. It was Saturday night – Jessica ought to be out with friends, and Thea preferred not to know if the girl was alone in her flat, swotting for the next test in her police training. The absence of anything resembling a serious boyfriend was beginning to nag at Thea, however sternly she might reproach herself for it. At Jessica's age, Thea was firmly married and six months pregnant. So was Jocelyn, come to that. Early marriage and motherhood was a pattern in the Johnstone family, and while she had no conscious desire for her daughter to follow suit, there was a subliminal expectation that would not be shaken.

At half past ten, she went upstairs and checked that there was hot water available for a bath. The Aga evidently saw to it that this was never going to be a problem. So long as the thing was kept alight, all would be well. With a sigh of anticipation, she went into the bedroom to find her nightshirt and book, preparatory for a long indulgent soak.

The bat was there again! The moment the light went on, flittering wingbeats stirred the air around her head. This time, she was angry. She

50

shut Hepzie out, opened the window, and snatching up a towel, she flapped determinedly at it. It took five minutes to steer it outside, but it was accomplished eventually. Could bats cope with rain, she wondered briefly. Had she consigned it to a miserable death by drowning? Just at that moment, she didn't care if she had. She only knew she never wanted to see it again.

Hepzie scratched and whined at the door throughout the chase. Then, as Thea went to let her in, the whine turned to a yap, and the dogs outside started barking. Before Thea could go downstairs to investigate, there was a loud banging on the front door, which Thea had locked behind her sister.

Emily was standing there, pale and large-eyed, her mouth oddly tight. She was wearing peculiar shapeless clothes, and her wet hair was straggling around her face instead of neatly tied back as usual. 'Let me in,' she said.

'But – what?' Words failed her, her mind still on the battle with the bat.

'I've just witnessed a murder,' Emily shouted. 'I saw the whole thing. I've been at the police station. It was horrible. They took my clothes and my shoes. I can't face driving home now. Let me in.'

Thea had already let her in. Of course she had. But she found herself wishing that she didn't have to.

CHAPTER FOUR

The story took a long time to tell, mainly because Emily repeated everything three or four times, with little logical sequence. It seemed that following the arrival of the police after she'd dialled 999, she had been subjected to extensive questioning. That was clearly the part she found the most traumatic. She went over it obsessively.

Piecing the story together from the beginning, Thea understood that Emily had taken a wrong turning immediately after leaving Hawkhill and found herself in a maze of small roads beyond Upper Slaughter. Realising her mistake, she had tried to turn around in a gateway, managing to graze the rear bumper of the car in the process. 'It was only a little way from a big hotel – not out in the wilds or anything. I could see it only a few yards away. But there was nobody about. I switched the engine off, and got my torch out, and had a look at the map. I was doing all the sensible things,' she wailed, as if expecting blame for irresponsibility.

'Why didn't you use your Sat Nav thingy?'

'What?' Emily's eyes turned even wilder, if that was possible.

'You know – the thing that tells you where to go.'

'Oh. I didn't think I'd need to. I didn't think I was *really* lost.' She smiled weakly. 'But the truth is, I don't like it. It spooks me, that voice telling me what to do. Sounds daft, doesn't it.'

'A bit. I thought this would be the obvious situation where it was useful.' But this was Emily, she remembered. The big sister who could never abide to be told what to do.

She still hadn't got a coherent grasp of the story. 'What happened after that?'

'Then I got out to see what I'd done to the car, and how best to get back onto the road without any more damage. That's when I heard the shouting. A man yelling his head off. He sounded crazy – off his head with rage.'

'Scary,' Thea agreed faintly.

'So I crept along to see what was happening. They were in a layby. The shouting man was kicking and bashing at another man on the ground. I could hear the awful noise of his head cracking when the murderer *stamped* on it. He had a big stick or something. It was *frenzied*. So I yelled something, but he didn't hear me. I ran towards him, and finally he saw me, and with a kind a crazy yelp he just dashed off. I hadn't a hope of catching him.'

'No,' said Thea faintly.

'So then I did 999 on the mobile, and had a look at the poor chap on the ground.' At this point Emily choked and clutched her damp head in both hands, as if transforming herself into the injured man. 'It was so *horrible*. I knelt down beside him. There was mud everywhere, and puddles, the rain just *poured* down. He was lying in water. I got filthy. They had to find me these clothes. Look at them!' She swiped a disgusted hand down the baggy tracksuit. It was just about the last outfit Emily would ever have worn. Thea had to suppress a giggle at the incongruity of it.

'Weren't you scared the madman would come back?'

'What? Oh, a bit, I suppose. He ran away – why would he come back?'

It seemed the story had dried up for the moment. Emily sat on the sofa, hands clutched together, eyes on a far corner of the room. Her head tilted sideways, her ear almost touching her left shoulder. It was a strange childlike stance, oddly pitiful. Thea felt her own heart pounding at the ghastly story, the impossible thing her sister – already in an emotional state – had been witness to. 'You poor thing,' she said, reaching out to press Emily's arm.

'I should have stayed here,' her sister moaned. 'Why didn't I stay here?'

'You were scared of the bat,' said Thea. 'With good reason. It was back again just now.'

Emily's eyes lost all focus. 'It's all the fault of that bat, then. Isn't that ridiculous.'

'Well, the man would still be dead,' Thea pointed out.

Emily stared at her for a moment, and then seemed to sag. 'Yes. But I wouldn't have been involved, would I?'

It was typical, of course. So typical that Thea barely noticed the way her sister always put herself at the centre of every story. Now, she could hardly fail to see it. A man had been murdered, while Emily looked on. Which person warranted centre stage in that scenario? But she made no remark. What would be the use?

54

'The police were very kind,' Emily said, as if holding onto the single piece of light in a black story.

'That's good. They'll need you, of course, as the only witness. They'll want to look after you.'

'Yes,' Emily sighed.

Thea felt the unstable bog of despair under her feet. Why on earth did Emily have to get herself lost so stupidly? Why did it have to be raining so hard? Why could life never be easy and calm and *boring* for once? And why did she already have a dawning apprehension that she herself was going to attract some limelight over the coming days, because of her sister, and her relationship with DS Hollis?

A stillness came over them both, as the shock worked its way through their systems. Finally, Thea did her best to summarise, forcing herself to sound calm and businesslike. 'Well, as murders go, this doesn't sound a very difficult one to solve. It's obvious they knew each other, if the killer was so enraged. There must have been an argument or fight to get him into such a state.'

'Or it could have been somebody with mental problems, not taking his medication,' said Emily, valiantly adopting the same tone. 'He did seem completely mad.' She was shaking gently, her teeth chattering, despite the mug of sweet tea that Thea had made her.

'So – what did the police say would happen next? Where did you tell them you'd be?'

'Home. I gave them my address, obviously. I couldn't remember what this place was called, anyway.'

'Did you say anything about me?' Thea's relationship with the Detective Superintendent had raised her profile with the Gloucestershire police. And not only because of Phil: she had been involved in a number of murder investigations over the past year or so. The ramifications of this had escaped Emily, however. She stared at her sister in bewilderment.

'Why would I?'

'Because of Phil.'

'I thought he was still off work with his back.'

'It isn't as simple as that. For one thing, he is working as much as he can – desk stuff. The back's getting better.'

Emily wasn't interested in Thea's boyfriend. She had only met Hollis once, and they had not found much common ground. Phil's damaged back reminded the whole family of Rosie, wife of Uncle James, another Detective Superintendent. Over the years Rosie's invalid status had become a permanent part of the picture, something to be factored into every gathering or outing. Always the centre of attention, her pain a kind of force field impossible to ignore, she was nonetheless a lovely person, sweet and stoical. When Phil Hollis joined the same club there had been jokes and groans and advice to Thea to drop him immediately. Instead she had spent a fortnight in his Cirencester flat, nursing him through the most immobile stage of the injury.

'If you gave my name, there's a chance he'll pick up on it tomorrow. He knows I'm in Lower Slaughter – that alone is going to ring a bell with him.'

'I don't care. I just wish I'd never come here. This is the last thing I need. It feels as if there's no escape from death and dying.' This was more like the old Emily – cross at being thrown off course, resentful at the way the world could trip you up, however careful you were.

'It's not very nice for me, either,' muttered Thea. 'If you hadn't got involved, I could have gone through my stay here in blissful ignorance.'

'So why don't you? Stay out of it. I'll go home first thing in the morning, and you can feed your ferrets in peace.' Emily squared her shoulders as if some fresh decision had fortified her.

'Because it's not in my nature. Like it or not, I've quite a bit of experience of this sort of thing. Now there's Jessica as well – she's going to want to hear all about it. The best hope is that some blood-stained character will get himself caught before another day goes by. If he's a nutcase like you say, he's probably boasting about it to his mother as we speak.'

'And she might hose him down and burn his clothes and never say a word about it.' The brave words sat oddly on the white face and bloodless lips.

'That's true.' Thea forced a smile. In spite of herself, she was glad to have another person in the house, and Emily was certainly in no state to go driving off across Middle England at midnight. 'Have you phoned Bruce?' she asked.

'Oh, yes, ages ago. I played it down a bit, of course. Only told him the bare bones. He won't need to hear the worst of it.'

'Protecting him, as usual,' Thea commented.

'Don't start that.' The warning came as a low snarl that Thea found genuinely alarming.

'Sorry – but it's true, all the same.'

'So what if it is? You think I ought to describe a shattered head, with the brains and blood all seeping out into a muddy puddle to him and the boys, do you? I should tell the whole family and all my friends that I got covered in filthy slime and bits of bone when all I wanted was to get the car started and drive home? What bloody good would that do?'

Thea shook her head. All she could think was that if it had happened to her, she would have wanted everybody to know about it. But she was not Emily. She could even see some nobility in her sister's effort to keep it to herself. 'At least I agree with you about the boys,' she offered. 'It isn't something you'd want them imagining.'

Except, as far as she understood it, adolescent boys already spent most of their time fantasising about smashing skulls and disembowelling nameless enemies, and making cyber-vehicles crash endlessly into each other.

As for Bruce, he was what he was, and Emily seemed happy with him, which left little more to be said. When she had first elected to marry him, both her sisters had made cautious attempts to point out his limitations. Not, as their father had, to cast aspersions on his profession, but to query his ability to manifest an acceptable range of emotions. 'It doesn't matter,' Emily had insisted. 'He's funny and competent and highly intelligent. He'll be reliable and there won't ever be any rows. Don't worry, girls – he's going to be fine.' It had been a sign of her confidence that she hadn't been the least bit angry with them for their impudent suggestions.

It seemed she had been right. The marriage was entering its twentieth year with little or no sign of strain. The three children, after an unpleasant miscarriage in the first year, had been reared methodically, with old-fashioned discipline. Sent to a fee-paying school, they seemed to be finding life rather more agreeable than did many of their peers. If Thea could somehow never quite find the right things to say to them, then perhaps that was her failure and not theirs. And although she preferred the noisy chaos of Jocelyn's big family, she tried to keep quiet about it.

They went to bed suddenly, well after midnight. Or rather, Thea did, and Emily snuggled down on the accommodating sofa, with a pillow and a blanket from the airing cupboard. 'I still don't like this house,' she said, eyeing a dusty cobweb directly over her head. 'I just know there'll be mice and spiders running over me as soon as I go to sleep.'

'Of course there won't,' said Thea. 'But if you insist, I could change places with you. Then you've only got a bat to worry about.'

'Don't be silly. There'll be even more mice and spiders upstairs. There always are. Especially in the spare room – you're invading their territory.'

There was no sign of any return of the bat, much to Thea's relief. She and Hepzie quickly settled down and fell asleep for a pleasantly uninterrupted night.

CHAPTER FIVE

The mobile, which was dutifully attached to its charger on the bedside table, went off at seven fifteen. Blearily, Thea reached for it, only opening her eyes as an afterthought, to find sunlight streaming through the window.

'Hello?' she croaked. 'Who's that?'

'Thea? Are you awake?' It was her mother.

'No, of course not. What do you want?'

'I tried to phone Emily just now, and Bruce says she's with you.'

'You tried to phone her at seven in the morning? What on earth for?'

A whine entered the maternal voice. 'She *said* it would be all right to phone any time. I'm not managing this very well, Thea. One of you should be here with me. I've got four children, and they're all too busy to spare a few days for me. Daddy and I were married for forty-nine years. You can't imagine what it's like not having him here any more.'

I can, Mum, Thea wanted to shout.

'Emily says you told her you didn't want anybody staying with you.'

'Well, of course, I could see you all had better things to do. I didn't want to *impose*.'

'Right.' It seemed to Thea that her mother, having read or seen on TV scenes where the new widow berated her selfish children, was now

60

adopting the role for herself, in preference to taking on the task of discovering what she really felt and wanted.

'So, *why* is she there?'

'She came over yesterday, to talk about Daddy. And something happened last night, so she decided to stay.'

'Something happened? What?'

'Oh, nothing to worry about. She's perfectly all right.'

'Did you get drunk?' The tone was accusing, with the merest hint of envy.

'No, not at all. Listen, Mum, it's awfully early. You must have woken Bruce as well as me. Why don't you go back to bed with a mug of tea, and spoil yourself? Think about what you really want us to do. But it isn't fair to say you'd rather be on your own and then complain when we take you seriously. You don't want to turn into that sort of silly old nuisance, do you?' The phrase was a special one in the Johnstone family, with its roots in the generation before Thea's mother. It was used as a gentle joke, albeit with a warning note.

But Mrs Johnstone was in no state to take it as it was meant. She gave a protesting yelp. 'You know what I mean,' Thea went on quickly. 'Remember your Auntie Pamela.'

Auntie Pamela had been the original silly old nuisance, self-pitying and impossible. A figure of legend, she had lived to ninety-six. Thea remembered her mainly as an object of terror, although the appeal of hearing first hand memories from the 1890s had done much to overcome her reluctance to visit.

'Don't be so unkind,' her mother sniffed. 'It isn't like you.'

'I didn't mean to be,' Thea apologised. Where was her father when she needed him? He would have laid down his newspaper and come quietly into the room to say exactly the right thing. 'But you really can't expect us all to know what to do if you contradict yourself so much.'

There was a brief silence. 'You're right,' came a small voice, finally. 'Thank you, Thea. I can always rely on you to cut through the crap.'

This time Thea yelped. 'Mum! You don't have to go that far.'

Laughter converged on the airways, relief verging on hysteria, and Thea congratulated herself on averting a decade or two of self-pity and manipulation.

'So why is Emily *really* there?' came a suddenly acute question. 'Why didn't she go home again last night? Precisely what happened?'

'Well–' Thea heaved a sigh. After the bracingly honest way she'd just confronted her mother, she could hardly start telling lies now. 'She saw something horrible, on her way home, and came back here because she was upset.'

'What – like a dog being run over? Horrible like that?'

'A bit like that. She saw a man beating up another one, and he died. She was a witness to one man killing another man. She had to give a statement to the police.'

'You *are* in the Cotswolds, aren't you? Did I get it wrong? Are you house-sitting in the middle of Birmingham?'

'No, Lower Slaughter,' said Thea miserably.

'That's what I thought. I suppose your policeman will be called in to sort it all out.'

'I doubt it. He's only doing desk work at the moment, and from what Emily said, it won't be very difficult to catch the killer. It wasn't a very subtle attack.'

'Poor Em. She won't have liked that, will she?'

The phonecall tailed off, and Thea went down to see if her sister was awake.

Emily was curled awkwardly on the sofa, her head pushed into a corner and her feet angled against the arm at the other end. It looked about as comfortable as a seat on a longhaul flight. 'Are you awake?' Thea whispered.

'Not really. That was a *very* long night, let me tell you. I had quite nasty dreams, with Daddy covered in blood. I'm *traumatised*, you know. I'll have flashbacks for the rest of my life. There was all that vile *stuff* on me.'

Thea was struck by a sudden resemblance between this sister and the other one. Jocelyn, so different in appearance, could adopt the exact same voice and use the exact same words. 'You sound just like Joss,' she giggled.

'Oh, I might have known there'd be no sympathy from you. Did I hear you talking to somebody upstairs?'

'Our mother phoned. She wanted to know what you were doing here.'

'And I suppose you told her,' Emily groaned.

'Yup. She said it must have been horrible for you. That was after I told her to stop being a silly old nuisance.'

'Aunt Pamela,' Emily nodded. 'Did it work?'

'More or less.'

'Good.' Emily seemed to lose focus, staring as before into a corner of the room, and seeming to forget where she was.

'I'll go and make some tea, then.'

'Coffee,' Emily corrected, giving herself a shake. 'I've got to have coffee. And I'll need to borrow some of your clothes.'

Emily left soon after eight. They went out to the car together, and Thea inspected the small scratch on a rear wheel arch, which Emily said had been inflicted by her clumsy turn in the gateway. The car was very clean, otherwise, treated as it was to a weekly wash. 'That'll be easy enough to fix,' she said reassuringly, fingering the scratch.

'Maybe. They're usually worse than they look. It might need a whole new panel.'

'Surely not.'

Emily was scrutinising her car with close attention. 'Looks all right otherwise,' she said softly. 'Now I see it in daylight.'

'So – the police took you to Cirencester and back, did they?' Thea was still trying to flesh out the picture of what had happened. 'Or did they let you drive yourself there?'

Emily heaved a dramatic sigh. 'That was another thing – there was *endless* discussion about it. In the end they drove me, because I was "emotionally disturbed" – and covered in yuck. I didn't really want to get it all over my seats. They brought me back again later.'

'Did they keep your clothes?'

Emily nodded. 'They want to do tests on them.'

'You're their only witness,' Thea said, as if this fact had only just dawned on her. 'Whatever you tell them has to be vitally important. Especially your description of the killer.'

'Killer,' Emily echoed. 'Yes. Except I'm a lousy witness. I never even glimpsed his face.'

For the tenth time, Thea tried to visualise the precise details – the shouts and shadowy figures; the rain and mud and sense of unreality. 'It's like a nightmare,' she said.

'I know it is.' Emily was suddenly forceful. 'A total bloody nightmare.'

It was a signal to shut up, but Thea still had niggling questions. 'So tell me again,' she insisted, 'why you came back here, instead of going straight home?'

'I *told* you. It seemed too far to drive. I was so shaky and confused. And Bruce would have made such a *fuss*. Plus the boys would have woken up and demanded to know what was going on. Besides you needed to know everything that had happened, and it was much easier to tell you face to face.'

'Right.' It made good sense, and Thea felt vaguely flattered that she had been given such a prominent status by her big sister.

Emily had helped herself to a long-sleeved top and cotton trousers from Thea's meagre collection of clothes. 'Will you ever get yours back?' Thea wondered. 'And what about shoes? I haven't got any I can spare.'

Emily shuddered. 'I don't want them,' she said.

65

'But there's a pair of sandals in the car some- where, luckily. I drove in bare feet last night,' she added wonderingly. 'I've never done that before, but I didn't want to waste time looking for the sandals.'

'Well, it was only half a mile or so, as far as I can work it out.'

They found the sandals on the floor in the back, and Emily got into the driving seat. She was pale and frowning. 'Well, I'll be off then,' she said, making no move to start the engine. 'I'm really sorry about all this. If only I hadn't been such a fool, turning the wrong way like that. I wasn't really thinking, you see. Not about roads and stuff. And now look at the trouble I'm in.'

'You're not in trouble,' said Thea. 'You were just the innocent bystander.'

'Right. Yes. But all those questions ... they're not going to leave it alone, are they?'

'Obviously not. Until they catch him, of course.'

Emily sighed. 'Oh, well...' she shook her head with an effort.

'Take it easy,' Thea said kindly. 'It's been a ghastly shock for you. You must have actually seen him die.'

Emily shook her head more vigorously. 'So please don't go *on* about it. I don't know exactly what I saw. It was *dark*. And pouring with rain.' She looked more miserable than Thea ever remembered seeing her. 'I've got to go. Thank God it's Sunday. At least I don't have to get myself to work.'

'Take some days off,' Thea advised. 'Compas-

66

sionate leave – on two counts. Don't try to be brave and British about it.'

'And sit about at home obsessing instead? I don't think so.'

'OK. Well, they'll probably have it all sorted out in a day or two, anyway. Even without a description from you, this bloke's liable to give himself away. As we agreed last night, he's sure to be covered in blood and not behaving normally.'

'For heaven's sake, stop sounding like a detective,' Emily snapped.

'Sorry.' Thea felt a need to justify herself, leaning down to speak through the open car door. 'It's just – the cases that Phil and I have come across up to now have all been rather more, well – *civilised.*' She grimaced at the word. 'Sounds daft, I know. A killing's a killing, and you could argue there's less wickedness in a spur of the moment rage than something that's been planned. But this is so – shattering. The violence of it.'

'Right,' said Emily shakily. 'And now I want to go home, if that's all right with you.'

It was past nine when Phil phoned, as Thea had known he would. Even without Emily's murder, he would have called to check how she was getting on at Hawkhill. It wasn't instantly apparent whether or not he knew about the connection between Thea and the killing.

'What's it like?' he asked. 'Does the parrot like you? Has it eaten Hepzie?'

'The parrot seems to be keen on security. The only thing it's said so far is "Lock the doors, Daddy" which is rather funny in a way.'

'What else is there – I can't remember?'

'Ferrets, cats and dogs. All quite amenable and easy. A bat which won't leave me alone. You haven't heard, have you?' she added.

'Pardon? Heard what?'

'Last night. A violent incident where a man died? Somewhere quite near here, apparently.'

'I did see something,' he said warily. 'But you're quietly minding your own business, aren't you, and not encouraging any mysterious or unlawful activity?'

'I am, yes. But Emily isn't. Emily – my sister, that is – is the only witness and she saw the whole thing.'

He went quiet, and she heard a keyboard tapping. 'Mrs Emily Peterson. That's your sister?' His voice had gone faint, as if there was hardly any breath behind it. It was an unfortunate co-incidence that Thea's sister had the same name as Phil's dead daughter, a fact which ought not to have made any difference to anything, but which caused Thea to mention Emily less than she might otherwise have done. Now she felt as if this delicacy was rebounding on her.

'I'm sorry,' Thea said. 'I really am. But yes, she was trying to turn round in a gateway, and heard shouts and went to see – and there was a murder happening before her very eyes.'

'Could happen to anyone,' said Phil, utterly failing to sound amused. 'Did he see her seeing him?'

'Very much so, I'm afraid. She frightened him off.'

'Well, we'll do all we can to keep her identity

confidential. But her name's here on the file – open for anyone here to read. It could easily get out. Where does she live?' He didn't wait for a reply, but supplied the answer himself. 'Aylesbury. Far enough away, I should think.'

'Phil, stop talking to yourself and explain. Do you know who the victim was?'

'Not confirmed yet, as far as I can see. I'll have to get Jeremy in to brief me. It won't be my case. At least, I'm assuming it won't.'

'Hang on – it's Sunday. Are you at the station?'

'No, no. I'm on the laptop at home – but I checked in first thing, to keep up with what's been happening. All done by remote control. All I need is a password and I can see everything that's been put on file. Saves a lot of time.'

'And you don't even have to get out of bed.' She was thinking how flimsy the barrier of a single password was, and how a clever criminal or dodgy police officer could be accessing Emily's details as they spoke.

'Excuse me. I was up before eight, doing my exercises.'

'Is it better?'

'Every day and in every way. I can actually twist sideways now. I'd forgotten that such a thing was possible.'

'Good.'

'So where's Emily now?'

'She's gone home already. I was hoping I could settle down with my jigsaw and forget there was ever an incident last night. You'd like that, wouldn't you?'

'Definitely. But I don't believe you.'

69

'Believe me, Phil. I'm not even interested. One man bashes another to death and runs away – not a very fascinating story. Plus, I've had enough of death this past week or two. I want to smell the flowers and read PG Wodehouse and pretend everything's all right.'

'That's my girl,' he approved. 'Be nice to yourself for a bit.' For no reason at all, an image of the man with the vivid blue eyes floated across her vision. The nicest thing she could imagine, just then, was a chance to get to know him better. The stab of shameful horror at this blatant piece of infidelity made her gasp.

Phil mistook it for a huff of laughter, and gave an echoing chuckle. 'I mean it,' he said.

'Right. Are you going to come and see me one day? Take me out to lunch?' Since his back was hurt, there had been no proper sex between them, a deprivation that Thea was beginning to find oppressive. That, she told herself, was the root of her outrageous thoughts about the blue-eyed stranger. Not a very worthy explanation, but the best she could find.

'I'll try,' Phil Hollis promised.

Thea did her best to put the whole thing out of her head, but it was a losing battle. Questions kept arising unbidden, as her unruly imagination attempted to construct a full picture of what had occurred. She still had no precise idea as to where the killing had taken place, hoping it was further from Hawkhill than Emily believed. Then it occurred to her that Emily must have had a location to report to the police when she phoned

70

them – how could they ever have found her otherwise? There were details she had not included in her account to Thea, and who could blame her? The police questioning must have been wearying at best. But the gaps in the story provoked an unwelcome curiosity in her mind, which she knew would be hard to quell.

Stop it, she adjured herself. Hadn't Emily already told her off for thinking like a detective? Too many murders over the past year had warped her brain and made her search for subtleties that did not exist. This was a sad and messy fight between two young men, a fight that had gone too far, fuelled by drink or drugs and maybe a girl in the story somewhere. The aggressor would be suffering agonies of remorse and fear this morning, unable to believe what he'd done, knowing his only avenue was to present himself to the authorities and submit to his rightful punishment.

Then Phil phoned again. Thea was outside with a mug of coffee, the spaniel at her feet. For once she had kept the mobile close at hand, consciously training herself to make proper use of it.

'Now, listen, love,' he began cautiously. 'This is turning out to be a bit more complicated than we thought.'

Before her mind could engage, her body had reacted. Her heart was suddenly filling her entire chest and something fuzzy had lodged in her throat. 'Oh?' she said.

'The dead man. He's a university lecturer – an Oxford don, apparently. His brother's a vicar,

71

standing in for a few months in the Slaughters. He – the victim – was staying at one of the big hotels in Lower Slaughter. It's astronomically expensive and very select.'

'So what's complicated?'

'Come on, Thea. You don't get that sort of bloke brawling in a dark field, for a start. He wasn't drunk or drugged.'

'No, but he could easily have been mugged. I don't see why you're sounding so doomy about it.'

'Muggers don't hang about in Cotswold fields. They don't lose their rag and kick people to death with massive blows to the head.'

'So there wasn't a weapon? No knife or anything?'

'No knife. Your sister said something about a stick, but she couldn't have seen it clearly.'

'That's right. I'm surprised she could even see as much as that.'

'There's more. Brace yourself.'

Thea made a wordless sound of invitation to reveal the worst.

'We're not happy with your sister's story. It doesn't hang together. Thea – there must be something important that she isn't telling us.'

CHAPTER SIX

Phil refused to give away any details, merely repeating that as it stood, Emily's story raised some puzzling questions. Thea would not allow herself to be thrown by something she felt sure was a failure on the part of the police to think clearly.

'So?' she challenged robustly. 'It would hardly be surprising if she forgot something, or made a mistake. You're always saying how witnesses only provide fragments of the whole picture. And they fill the gaps with their own imagination, without knowing they're doing it.'

'Yes, yes, all that's true. This is different. There's something you don't know – or I assume you don't. I oughtn't to be telling you, of course. Your loyalties are very likely to lie with your sister. But–'

'Wait a minute.' She had jumped ahead of him. 'You're right. If you're going to present me with a choice between my sister and the forces of the law, I might well choose the former.'

He said nothing, silently letting the dilemma stand. Thea's throat felt strange again.

'Phil, she's never been here before, she doesn't know anybody in these villages. She can't possibly have been involved in that killing in any significant way. You're going to tell me she's protecting the killer, or there's the blood of a third party on her clothes, or – I don't know.'

'No, I'm not going to tell you either of those things. But I am going to tell you that the injuries on the body don't match with what she told us. The body wasn't curled defensively. No damage to the hands. This wasn't a fight of any kind. The man was attacked suddenly from behind, blows rained on his head and neck. One vertebra is shattered.'

She clung to her initial position. 'I can't see how that contradicts what Emily said. She admits it was dark, and by the time she got to the scene, the killer – or killers – had run away. What's the big deal?'

'You might be right,' he conceded. 'But everyone's coming up with all kinds of questions. This all happened only yards away from a big hotel, and dozens of people. Why didn't your sister go there immediately and call for help? Why stay out there in the dark with a dead body? Wouldn't she be scared?'

'She was probably too shocked to think straight – and she didn't *know* it was a hotel. She might not even have realised it was there at all. She was totally lost.'

'That's another thing. How is it possible to get lost between Lower Slaughter and the main road? It's barely a mile.'

'She must have turned the wrong way out of my gate – I wasn't watching and didn't think to give her directions again. If she did that, she'd have gone towards Upper Slaughter, then around in a big loop somehow. *I* don't know – I haven't worked out the lanes myself yet.'

'Well, it's difficult to make sense of it – why she chose to turn round in that little gateway, for example.'

'Oh, this is ridiculous!' Thea flared. 'You've no cause to be suspicious of her at all. I know what it's like getting lost in these little lanes. I've done it myself. The signs don't make any sense unless you know how the places relate to each other. She knew she'd come out on a road she recognised eventually.'

'That still doesn't explain why she turned round where she did.'

'Phil, stop it. What are you implying, anyway? What do you want me to do?'

'I don't want you to *do* anything. I want you to be aware of what the evidence suggests.'

'And what's that?'

'That your sister hasn't told us the whole story. I won't say any more than that.'

Another silence as Thea's head filled with swooping dipping thoughts, like a room full of bats. 'Well, that's not saying much, is it?' Then she remembered what Phil had said about the victim. 'Um – hang on a minute,' she added, thinking he was about to curtail the call. 'You said the victim was an Oxford don. What was his name?'

She heard him tapping the keyboard briefly, before replying, 'Dr Samuel Webster, MA, D.Phil.'

'Oh my God,' said Thea faintly.

Phil's tone altered dramatically. 'What do you mean?' he snapped.

Sam Webster, as Thea reluctantly told Phil, had

been a close friend of Bruce Peterson since college days. He was unmarried, geeky, clever, dedicated to his academic career, and Thea had met him only a month or so ago at Emily's house. 'I remember him quite clearly – they put me next to him at a dinner party, because we were the only singletons. He was nice – very old fashioned and gentlemanly. I remember thinking how much his students must love him, if he treated them with the same respect and politeness. He was that sort of rumpled bachelor that girls especially take to.'

'Did your sister like him?'

'She did, I think. She talked about him a lot, and read his books. She was proud of having such a distinguished friend.'

'Were they...? Was she...? I mean – did you detect any – um – undercurrents?'

Too late, Thea saw where this was leading. She laughed scornfully. 'Between him and Em? No, no, of course not. Don't be stupid. He was a geek. She said that lots of times. Fine for an evening's conversation about German cinema or melting ice caps, but not for anything emotional. Besides, why would she, when she's got Bruce? The two men are cut from the same length of cloth. If Emily ever has an affair it'll be with some earthy Spaniard, or leather-clad biker.'

Phil persisted. 'But Webster might have made advances to her?'

'Not that I ever heard. No, it would be totally out of character. He was far too *polite* for anything like that.'

'But you guessed it was him, didn't you? When

76

I said he was an Oxford don.'

'Sort of,' she admitted. 'At least – I wanted to check that it *wasn't* him.'

'And here's an even bigger question: Why didn't she tell you who he was, right away? What in the world possessed her to keep it secret? She must have known you'd find out and connect him with her.'

'Precisely. Obviously she couldn't have realised it was him. That must be it – if his head was so badly damaged, she'd easily miss recognising him. I'm certain that if she'd known, she would have told me. Why bother to keep it from me? That makes no sense at all, when she'd know you'd identify him soon enough.'

'You could be right,' he said again. 'It's true his face was an awful mess. Not just covered in mud, but just about flattened. His nose was pushed right back into the cavity behind.'

Thea shuddered, holding her stomach as if afraid it would do something violent. 'They've done the post-mortem, then?' she asked, hoping for some sort of diversion.

He groaned. 'After a fashion. There's a locum at the mortuary, a doddering old fool who should have retired ten years ago. They wheel him in to cover for holidays. Bill Morgan's gone off to Florida for three weeks. The locum went through the motions, and reported that death was caused by severe crushing of the skull, consistent with heavy blows. Small traces of rubber were in the wound, which could have come from the sole of a boot. He did the necessary, I suppose. No surprises, except that the only damage was to his head. And neck.'

'Poor chap.'

'Indeed. But it was pretty quick, we think. We're still trying to figure out just how it was done. And now you tell me that your sister actually *knew* him – well, that's a pretty big coincidence, wouldn't you say?'

'Emily knows a lot of people,' said Thea, thinking suddenly of the forty-eight condolence cards she'd received. Had one of them been from Sam Webster?

'Could be she also knew the killer,' he said lightly, as if half hoping she wouldn't really hear the words. 'Could be, even, that she had some sort of assignation at that hotel from the start, which she didn't want you to know about.'

She wanted to feel rage and contempt for such outlandish ideas. She wanted to scream at him that he was living in a fantasy world and she would not hear anything so idiotic. But she remained calm. 'No, I don't think that can be right,' she said. 'I know my sister. She's not a good liar, and she is probably the last person to get involved in anything as messy and chaotic as this is. I don't blame you for exploring all the options, and letting suspicion fall on the only witness – but I hope that when I next see you, you'll have wiped it from your mind.'

She heard him swallow. Nobody spoke to Detective Superintendents like that. Even Thea had never been so icily uncompromising with him before. 'I mean it,' she added. 'There are some things that ought not to be spoken, and what you just said is one of them.'

'No, it isn't,' he countered. 'There can't be any no-go areas in a murder investigation. We have to go where evidence takes us. My mistake was to voice it to you. For that I apologise. I should have known better. I'll try to come over later this afternoon, if you'd like me to. We don't have to talk about this any more, if that's how you want it.'

There seemed to be nothing she could say. She felt wrong-footed and confused. 'All right,' she mumbled. 'That'll be nice.'

Thinking the conversation through again, she was appalled. She felt breathless with the implications and the divided loyalties. Breathless, too, with anger – not just at Phil, but also at her sister for bringing another murder enquiry into her life. *Damn, damn, damn,* she repeated to herself, *damn, damn, damn and DAMN.*

She did her best not to think about it as she checked the animals in her care and made herself a modest lunch. But the need to justify her sister and find a satisfactory account of what she had done and why, sent her to a large-scale Pathfinder map in her bag from which she tried to work out just where Emily had driven. As Phil had said, it made very little sense. She located Lower Slaughter Manor, which was indeed a hotel, just as Upper Slaughter Manor was, as well as The Lords of the Manor Hotel. Plenty of scope for confusion there, augmented by the existence of at least one Manor Farm and stretches of quiet country lane flying in every direction.

Her heart was less and less inclined to pursue the researches. The sun was high and bright outside, and the knowledge that September was only a week away made it a matter of urgency to exploit fine days while she could. The map had shown just how many footpaths connected the various villages; lovely walks away from traffic via disused quarries and something called the Wagborough Bush Tumulus. She found herself drifting into her favourite topic of local history – a subject that forced itself onto her attention every time she spent more than a few hours in this area. How many people immediately made the leap from the presence of the distinctive stone houses to the necessity of digging all that stone out from somewhere? The awareness that there were innumerable deep man-made holes carved into the landscape, many of them now full of water and pretending to be natural lakes, had to be included in any appreciation of the way the land now looked.

Cedric's dogs must be desperate for some freedom, too. It was cruel the way they were kept cooped in that shed on days like this. Almost as bad to tie them to long chains, giving them no chance to run. She longed to untie them and let them roam around in freedom. How big a risk could that be, for heaven's sake?

Too big, came the reply. But if she kept one of them on a lead at a time, as Cedric himself had indicated would be acceptable, that would guarantee that there'd be no mischief. Feeling like a rescuer, she found a grimy leather lead on the back of the scullery door and went to tell the animals the good news.

A problem arose immediately – neither dog was wearing a collar. There was nothing to which a lead could be attached. The chains that held them all day had their own built-in arrangement which looped off over the heads. Thea considered borrowing the collar from her own dog, but it was too small, and to leave Hepzie untetherable would be too worrying. With her usual determination, she went back to the scullery and rummaged amongst the old macs and donkey jackets hanging on a row of hooks in a vain search for a collar. But there was plenty of plastic bale string coiled untidily in the dogs' shed. That could be looped and knotted and fashioned into a restraint for a dog, and she acted accordingly.

Selecting the black and tan one, as being marginally smaller, she pulled her home-made collar over his head. The big ears had to be squashed flat and it seemed rather tight around his neck. The dog looked into her eyes trustingly, and she spent a few moments fondling his handsome head and murmuring sweet nothings to him. 'I wish I knew your name,' she said. 'Can I call you Basil, just for a little while? Would that be all right? Basil!' she chirruped. The dog wagged its tail tolerantly.

'And you can be Freddy,' she told the other one. 'And you have got to behave yourself, OK? If I let you run free, you have to stay where I can see you.'

Hoping that the plan would work, she set off with the three dogs. Hepzie ran loose, sniffing and zigzagging, pausing to grin at her mistress.

81

Freddy tried to follow her, but his method of covering the ground was so much more direct and quick that he soon gave up any attempt at companionship. For the first quarter of a mile, Basil walked calmly at her side. They were on a footpath, heading well away from the farm that Cedric had warned Thea to avoid. Then, with a flurry and a sudden loud yelping, Freddy must have raised a rabbit. Thea's spaniel joined the chase, and Basil, appalled at the prospect of being left behind, gave a powerful lunge and easily dragged the end of the lead out of Thea's hand. In seconds there was no sign of anything canine.

'Oh shit,' she said, before drawing a deep breath and shouting loudly for her own dog.

She knew it was futile. Hepzie gave the appearance of obedience only because her wishes generally coincided with what Thea wanted her to do. When these wishes diverged, the dog did exactly what it liked.

The hope – which she already knew was a faint one – was that the spaniel would eventually persuade the other dogs to give up the chase and return to quarters. There was no real worry that Hepzie would get lost, with her limited sense of adventure. Left to herself she would run round in a few circles, make noisy threats to the rabbit that its days were numbered, and then rejoin her mistress as if nothing had happened. Hepzie was not the worry.

What she had done was unforgivable. She had arrogantly assumed she knew best what was good for the dogs. She had directly disobeyed an instruction. She deserved to be blacklisted and never allowed to house-sit anywhere again.

Then common sense kicked in, and she told herself that the dogs would certainly come home again when they got hungry. They were relatively well-behaved and domesticated, despite their boring outdoor existence. Just so long as they committed no dreadful crimes while they were loose, everything was going to be all right.

A man was coming towards her, his eyes narrowed with some uncomfortable emotion that looked at first glance like anger. 'Were those your dogs that just dashed past?' he demanded, from some distance, his voice raised.

She smiled weakly. 'I'm afraid so,' she said. 'They flushed out a rabbit and decided to give chase.'

'You'd better catch them quick,' he advised. 'Not much tolerance for stray dogs around here.'

'They'll come back soon,' she said with feigned confidence.

'I could be wrong, but that huntaway looked to me like Cedric Angell's. Am I right?'

'That's right,' she admitted. 'I'm the house-sitter.'

'Did he tell you it was all right to release the dogs out here?' The anger had segued into disapproval and suspicion.

'Not exactly. I just thought a walk would do them good.'

'A *walk*,' he sneered. 'You think dogs like that expect a *walk*? They're workers; they know their job and do it well. Otherwise, they need to stay tied up.'

'OK,' she said, opting for submission, despite an argumentative inner voice insisting that Cedric Angell had no work for the dogs – that they were superfluous yard ornaments and nothing more. 'So how do you suggest I get them back?'

'Not my problem,' he said unpleasantly. 'I've got better things to do.'

Thea gave him a closer look, wondering how to react to this lack of courtliness. He seemed to be in his fifties, slight and weather-beaten. There were crinkle-lines around his eyes, as if he might do a lot of sailing. He did appear distracted, impatient, moving his feet on the spot as if mentally still walking.

'That's perfectly true,' she said calmly. 'I'm sure it'll all come right. Things usually do.'

A look of contempt and disbelief crossed his face. 'Do they? If that's your experience, then all I can say is that you've been very lucky. As I see it, the very opposite is true.'

She could feel him needling, wanting her to panic, infuriated by her persistent optimism. She smiled briefly. 'Well, don't let me keep you,' she said.

He remained stationary for a few more beats, and then set off briskly without another word, leaving Thea to insist to herself that the chances of anything seriously bad happening to the dogs were very slim. They'd dash about for a bit, as the freedom went to their heads, then turn back for home full of cheerful rabbit-chasing memories. Even if Cedric had been right about the gun-toting farmer, it would be the direst of bad luck for him to encounter the dogs while armed and angry. Besides, they were half a mile from his land and heading in the opposite direction.

Her instinct was to keep walking and calling, hoping for a glimpse of them. Basil would still have the string trailing from his neck; it might get caught in brambles or on a fence. Then what would he do – howl for rescue or sit quietly trusting that someone would know he was there? In spite of herself, she began to worry. It was a big wide world out there, with fields in every direction, not to mention disused quarries and roads and copses sacred to the pheasant and gamekeeper. A lot of booby traps for unwary dogs unused to having it all as their playground.

Another instinct was to approach all the houses she could find and report the missing animals, hoping for assistance and concern. But after the encounter with the unhelpful man, she could not rely on a positive reception. And her impression of Cotswold residents was that they were too busily involved with their computers and social clubs to perform anything as time-consuming as combing the landscape for lost dogs.

It was only a couple of hours before Phil was due to arrive. He was the fond owner of a pair of dogs himself, and could surely be relied on to make useful and sensible suggestions. He would also chastise her for such careless disobedience. With a sense of walls closing in, she understood that she really might be in trouble. There really might be cause to fear for Hepzie, too, if the delinquent influence of the others overwhelmed her already shaky response to her mistress's calls.

They knew the way home, that much was certain. They could retrace their own scent and that of Thea. She should go back and wait for them to give themselves up. If they still hadn't returned when Phil arrived, then the two of them could conduct a search. But it felt entirely wrong when she turned round and started back, empty-handed and ridiculously lonely.

CHAPTER SEVEN

Phil had other things to think about than missing dogs, and he listened irritably to the story, tutting to himself and shaking his head. 'I can't believe you were such a fool,' he said. 'I thought you *knew* about dogs.'

'I know about Hepzie. I'm sure she'll be back any minute now.'

'How long ago was this, did you say?'

'Nearly three hours,' she admitted.

'Well, I'm sorry, but I've no intention of traipsing over hill and dale in the faint hope of finding them. When I was a boy, our dogs could be gone for twenty-four hours at this time of year. Even in those days, it was a worry – you never knew what they'd get up to. Nowadays, they stand a real risk of getting themselves shot. Luckily for you, there don't seem to be any sheep farms left around this area.'

'There's one – just over there.' She pointed towards the back of the house. 'Mr Angell warned me about it.'

Phil sighed and tutted again, and Thea fought against the image of herself as an irresponsible teenager. She looked at him closely, analysing him as if for the first time. There was nothing especially remarkable about him; his skin was good, lightly tanned and smooth. The brown hair had a narrow fringe of silver over the ears and temples. His eyes were set deep, blue and thoughtful. Even before the onset of political correctness he would have considered the effects of his words before he spoke. But inevitably he had lost some of the natural human bounce he must once have possessed, thanks to the deadening influence of the police force. He had seen too much, suffered too many traumas and crises and attacks to maintain the kind of smiling resilience that Carl had had. The damage to his back a few months earlier had further weighed him down. Now he thought twice before making any sudden movement. It had added to his air of caution, and made him a more frustrating companion in Thea's eyes.

The murder of the previous evening had quickly been transformed from a simple piece of one-on-one aggression to something much more complicated. Phil plainly had a lot he wanted to say about it, but was inhibited by her words on the phone. The diversion of the errant dogs was as annoying to Phil as it was a relief to Thea. She found herself more and more resistant to the thought of discussing Emily and the suspicions that the police were apparently entertaining.

'I'm sorry to ask you this,' he began stiffly, once the subject of the missing dogs had been brushed aside. 'But you can't evade it entirely. Did your sister tell you she'd got lost almost as soon as she left here?' he asked.

'More or less, yes.'

'But did you know she had a SatNav in the car?'

'Is that the thing she calls a TomTom?'

He kinked a reproachful eyebrow. 'You know it is,' he said.

'Oh, well, it's all a mystery to me. As it happens, though, I did ask her about it, and how come she'd got lost in spite of it. She said she didn't like it giving her orders. That's typical Emily, by the way. It might be that she didn't know how to work it properly, either. I had to give her directions for getting here.' A thought struck her. 'Aha!' she chirped, holding up a finger to suggest a sudden enlightenment. 'I know why she turned right when she left here. I directed her that way when she was coming here – I told her to come through the middle of Lower Slaughter, because I wasn't sure she'd find this road from the south. So naturally she tried to retrace her steps. Then she must have missed the next right turn into the village, and headed straight for Upper Slaughter. It all makes perfect sense,' she concluded, with satisfaction.

Phil had listened closely to this verbal map, one eye closed in concentration. 'I think I get it,' he said slowly.

'I can draw it for you if it helps,' she patronised. 'It just makes me all the more certain there are perfectly reasonable explanations for everything she said – or didn't say. She obviously wasn't hiding anything when she came back last night – she told me the whole story and it all rang quite true.'

'She didn't tell you she knew the victim,' he reminded her.

'Because she had no idea it was him,' Thea flashed back. 'I'm in absolutely no doubt about that.'

'OK,' he nodded. 'You've just about convinced me. Now – how about coming for a little walk with me. It's not such a bad evening, compared to last night.'

'I will, once we've done something about those bloody dogs. I can't just leave them out there all night. I'm getting really worried about Hepzie. She's never been off for this long. They must be leading her into wicked ways.'

Phil paused, his brow wrinkled. 'I'm surprised you're not frantic by now. Are you sure she could find her way home in a strange area?'

'I don't know,' she admitted. 'Do you think we could go back along the same path and call her? I can't just wait and hope. It feels much too irresponsible. But dogs always *do* come back in the end – don't they?'

'Nearly always,' he said.

He went with her the half-mile to the point where the dog pack had eluded her. The sun was still high, but there was an evening feel to the light, and a gentle breeze had sprung up. Unself-consciously, Thea called her dog, lifting her voice as if throwing it across the fields. Then she would stop and listen intently. Phil went into gateways and scanned the landscape, one hand shielding his eyes from the sun. Then, very faintly, Thea heard a distant yelp, repeated three or four times.

'That's her!' she cried. 'I can hear her. She's over there.' She pointed to a patch of woodland away to the right, on the crest of a gradual slope. Heedlessly, she scrambled over a gate and began to trot towards the sound, calling the dog's name every few yards.

'Do you want me to come?' Phil called from the path. 'I doubt if I'd be much use.' He had a precautionary hand to his back, anxiously eyeing the uneven ground.

'Up to you,' she panted, already breathless. The woods were not looking any closer, and there were two thick hedges across her path with no sign of an opening. As she called and listened, the direction of the dog's cries seemed to change, until she could almost convince herself they were coming from a different patch of trees entirely. But they did grow gradually louder as she kept to her original trajectory, and she pressed on.

It took ten minutes to get to the wood, and even then the quest was not over. Hepzie's yelps went infuriatingly silent as the spaniel assumed it was about to be rescued, and quite possibly chastised. 'Where are you?' Thea shouted, peering amongst the trees. It was a fairly narrow band of woodland, with a footpath sign pointing through the middle, and rough patches of bramble on either side. The road to Lower Swell ran close by.

In the end she stumbled upon the dog when least expecting to. A squeal alerted her, and she found Hepzie curled awkwardly at the foot of a large tree. 'For goodness sake, you bad dog. What do you think you're playing at?'

Large miserable eyes met hers, and a convulsive movement showed that something was very wrong. 'What happened to you?' Thea demanded.

Bending down, she found that a length of barbed wire had wound itself around the dog's lower body, digging tightly into her soft belly,

91

drawing blood in places. 'Oh, Hepzie!' Thea moaned. 'That must really hurt.'

Knowing the wire could only be removed with great care, but desperate to be clear of it, Thea made little progress at first. Where the hell was Phil, she wondered? Had he been fool enough to take her at her word and leave her to deal with this on her own? Apparently so. Well, bugger him – she'd manage well enough.

Eventually she found an end of the wire, and by methodically unwinding and pulling, she got it free – though not without several punctures to her own hands and wrists. As if alive, the stuff would whip round and attack bare skin as it was being manipulated. At one stage, a barb narrowly missed one of Hepzie's eyes. The other end of the wire was firmly attached to a post alongside the tree, remnants of a fence no longer functioning.

'Poor baby,' Thea crooned as she worked. 'Nearly got it now. Soon be home. What an awful thing to happen.' The dog kept still, only squeaking when a tuft of hair came away with part of the wire. She was thick with mud from ear to tail, which didn't help.

Finally she was free and Thea set her down to assess the damage. 'Can you walk?' she asked.

With a slow wag of the plumy tail, Hepzie tested herself. All four legs seemed to be working. 'Good!' encouraged Thea. 'Come on then.' She chivvied the animal back towards the footpath, ready to carry her if necessary, but hoping fervently that it wouldn't come to that. Not only because of the mud, but there was blood mixed in, and Hepzie had always been an awkward armful at the best of times. Picking up the pace across the fields, they made the journey back to their temporary home.

Phil had gone back to Hawkhill, and was waiting impatiently. He obviously had not planned for such a long stay, and had been stewing about it in her absence. *He ought to have come with me*, Thea thought crossly. *How unchivalrous he can be sometimes.* Since hurting his back he had avoided physical risk as far as possible. Now it was well on the way to recovery, he was braver, but the memory of the pain and disablement was still too fresh for comfort.

'No sign of the others, then?' he asked as she crossed the yard to where he sat on the lichened seat by the door.

She gave him an unsmiling look before answering, 'No. I hoped they'd have come back here in the meantime.'

'How's Hepzie?'

'I won't know till I've washed her. She was tangled in barbed wire. It was wrapped round her about three times. She's got a lot of cuts, but she can walk all right. It would have been nice to have some help.' It had to be said, so she uttered it straight, loud and clear.

'I'm sorry, Thea, but there are four or five very good reasons why I opted to leave you to it. It made no sense for me to get filthy dirty and probably torn on brambles. I could see you for most of the time, and it was obvious you didn't need me.'

She looked down at herself, streaked and splashed with mud, punctured by the barbed wire, and sighed. 'At least she's home,' she said.

'When does she get her beating?'

The joke fell flat, girlfriend and spaniel both giving him the same humourless look. He laughed anyway, more at their faces than his own jocularity. 'I can only stay another hour at most,' he said.

'It's Sunday,' she reminded him. 'Can't you have the evening off?'

'I can, actually. But I said I'd take the boys to Painswick. Linda is having them this week, and she likes to settle them in by about nine.'

'Gosh – what time is it now, then?'

'Nearly seven.'

'No wonder I'm so hungry. I had no idea it was as late as that. Do you want some soup or cheese or something?'

'If there's anything handy, that would be nice. But you should get on and bathe your dog – and do something about the missing two. Linda will have something waiting for me.' Linda was his sister, who shared the care of his corgi and Gordon setter, taking them when he was working long hours, giving them a break from the confinement of his Cirencester flat.

Thea took a deep breath and did her best to concentrate. 'Well, it doesn't look as if we're much use to each other at the moment, does it? You with the dogs and me with your murder. I feel exhausted, to be honest. Don't forget that my father died only a week ago. You need to bear that in mind with Emily as well. That's why she came here, you know – to talk about Daddy. She was in quite a state about it, feeling guilty and aban-

94

doned and a whole lot of other things.'

'She was oddly calm when she called the police.'

'Damn it, Phil – will you stop implying that she's done something wrong! Everything you say carries so much suspicion. It's horrible. She got covered in blood and gore, not to mention soaking wet and terrified. Give her a break, for heaven's sake. It's not like you to be so down on somebody.'

'I'm not down on her, as you put it. If you must know, I'm bending over backwards to give her the benefit of the doubt.'

Thea was searching for a reply to this when with a skittering scrambling noise, two filthy dogs came trotting towards them, heads and tails hanging low, tongues lolling out. With brief glances at the people, they made as one to a shallow trough of water standing outside their shed, and gulped great quantities of it for a full minute.

'Well, thank goodness for that,' said Thea. 'But look at the state of them!'

The fluffy coat of the one she called Freddy was matted and lumpen with rapidly drying mud. Basil, being short-haired, was less bedraggled, but still coated liberally with the same substance. 'Where did they find so much mud? Even after yesterday's rain, this is pretty excessive,' said Thea, retreating from the panting animals.

'In the river, I suppose,' said Phil. 'Or at least the edges of it. That's where the mud must be. At least there's no sign of any blood.'

Thea was to remind him of this remark in the

days to come. 'You said there was no blood. You're their witness. There wasn't *any* blood on them – was there?'

The trouble started less than half an hour later. The Angells' phone rang, and when Thea answered it, a furious male voice began yelling into her ear. 'Those dogs – I know they've been loose. They were seen. And I've got four prize tups dead and another five torn to bits and needing to be destroyed. The dogs have got to be shot, there's no two ways about it. I'm coming over now, so be sure to have them shut up and waiting for me. The law's on my side. They've been asking for it. They've got to be shot.'

At last he quietened down enough for Thea to make a shaky response. 'They're not guilty,' she said. 'They have been on the loose, but they haven't killed anything. There's no blood on them. You can't shoot them without proof.' Then she had the sense to add, 'There's a policeman here now. He'll tell you. You can't shoot the dogs without proof.'

CHAPTER EIGHT

'I don't know the exact law on this,' Phil said. 'And I need to be off. For God's sake, it's not my job to act as defence for a pair of wild dogs. I have a strong suspicion that he'd be within his rights–'

'Don't be stupid,' Thea expostulated. 'You can't go round shooting innocent dogs.'

'OK, wait a minute.' Phil ran his fingers through his hair. 'No, that's right. They have to be caught in the act. I remember now. Your neighbour probably knows that. I doubt if he'll turn up after all. Besides, not many men can just shoot a dog in cold blood – not even a furious farmer. His rage will have died down a bit by now, and he'll start to see sense.'

'Phil, you're not thinking of leaving me to deal with him by myself, are you?'

He glanced at his watch and ruffled his hair again. 'I suppose Linda can wait. I'll phone her.' He chewed his upper lip agitatedly. 'I'll give him until half past eight. It'll be nearly dark by then – I doubt if he'd leave it any later than that.'

He was proved right when a man with a shotgun under his arm appeared from behind the house as Thea was with the dogs, trying to get the worst of the mud off. She had fed them as usual, but they seemed uninterested in the food.

'Trying to hide the evidence, I see,' said the

97

man, standing in the doorway of the shed and blocking all the remaining light. His silhouette seemed huge to Thea. *Hagrid* flickered through her mind, making her feel foolishly optimistic. The feeling was strengthened by something in his voice – the standard English accent, and the barely audible thread of humour suggested a man who was capable of reason.

'Not at all,' she said robustly. 'There's nothing to hide. They came back muddy but not the least bit bloodstained.'

She approached him and he stood back, letting her out of the shed. 'You can't shoot them,' she said firmly. The man was in his forties, and really was big. His voice suggested a businessman more than a farmer. 'You have to prove them guilty first.'

'I know that,' he said with a nod. 'You're lucky it's me here and not my father. He'd have blown them away by now, no messing about.'

'So why are you here?'

'To warn you. To tell you this isn't done with, by a long way. I've told Cedric Angell that if these beasts get loose again, we'll go to law about it. There'll be an injunction this time.'

Phil made a slow appearance, standing at a distance, listening calmly. The man took a moment to notice him. 'Good evening,' Phil said.

'Oh – I thought she was bluffing when she said there was a copper here. That's you, then, is it?' He peered more closely at Phil's face. 'I know you. Hollis, isn't it? Bit senior for a sheep worrying case, aren't you?'

'I'm afraid you have the advantage,' said Phil.

98

'Henry Galton. We were in the sixth form together, a million years ago.'

'Good God – Giant Henry! So it is.' Phil extended a hand, which the farmer took, once he'd shifted his gun to the other armpit.

Much to her relief Thea found herself sidelined as the men assessed each other. The dogs, it seemed, had achieved a stay of execution, at least. Hepzie was firmly shut in the kitchen, in the hope that her very existence would remain unnoted. But Phil was inviting the man in, offering him a drink, suddenly in no rush to get to his sister's. 'I'll go and put the kettle on,' said Thea, hurrying into the house. The spaniel was still very dirty, although the scratches on her underside had been washed and disinfected. There would be bloodstains on her, visible to anyone looking closely. She really ought to be kept out of sight, for fear of inclusion in the threatened trouble.

But where to put her? She couldn't be allowed in a bedroom or on a sofa, the state she was in. That only left cupboards or the cold little scullery with its bare stone floor. 'Well, it serves you right,' said Thea, as she bundled the dog into this unwelcoming space. 'It won't be for long.'

To his credit, Phil did his best to defend Thea and the dogs. 'She's here for a fortnight,' he explained. 'By the end of that time, all this can be forgotten, can't it? If you get an injunction on the dogs, what's their owner going to say when he gets back? Besides, there wasn't a trace of blood on them.'

'Blood washes off,' Galton waved this away as

irrelevant. 'They're covered in mud and muck – that's all the proof I need.'

'It wasn't them,' insisted Thea.

'Well *something* killed my tups,' said Galton. 'If it wasn't these two – and I still think it's too much of a coincidence that they were loose just when it happened – then who was it? It's good enough evidence to convince a magistrate, and you know it.' His tone was level, letting the facts speak for themselves. Thea couldn't avoid an image of dead and dying rams, their terror and suffering impossible to deny.

'Has it happened before in this neighbour-hood?' asked Phil.

'A couple of years ago, aye. Lost a dozen ewes that time. You know what the buggers do, don't you? They tear great chunks of flesh from the back end, like wild animals. It's not funny, not at all.'

'Presumably it wasn't these dogs that time?'

'We never proved anything. The thing is, there's not much sheep farming round here any more. Makes me more vulnerable to it. When they get a mind to it, dogs'll travel two or three miles easily, often more. And they can be somebody's pet labrador or setter. It's not just huntaways and rottweilers. Jack Russells can do some damage, once the blood's up. It's the pack mentality. Get two bitches together, one moonlit night, and there's a massacre waiting to happen. Three or more, and you're really sunk.' He shook his head. 'It's a jungle out there, even these days. You'll have heard about that bloke having his head kicked in last night?' It didn't feel like a change of

100

subject – more of an obvious link.

'I'll have a word with the local chaps,' said Phil. 'As you say there's been a killing here, which is going to raise the police profile by a factor of a hundred or so. Bloodstained dogs won't go unnoticed over the next week or two, I can promise you that.'

'Huh,' grunted Galton. 'That'll be the day when the cops take sheep-worrying seriously. Still, not much I can do tonight.' He drained his coffee cup and got to his feet. He had to be six foot three, thought Thea, and had the weight to go with it. Not fat, but *big*. Must be a good eighteen stone, she calculated. And with the dissipation of his rage, he seemed irresistibly *cuddly*, she realised. My God, she thought – am I going to feel like this about every new man I come across? If Phil didn't get his back to a point where he could risk having sex again soon, she wasn't going to be responsible for who she found herself jumping on.

'And I must get my skates on,' Phil said, with an alarmed look at the kitchen clock. 'Linda's going to be in a right old mood at this rate.'

Galton cocked his head, sensing a situation. 'Linda?' he murmured.

'My sister. Three years older than me. You won't have known her. She looks after my dogs when I've got a big case.'

'And last night's incident's a big case, is it?'

Wow, thought Thea, *he's sharp, this chap. Doesn't miss much.*

'Could be,' said Phil tightly. He looked at Thea. 'You'll be all right now, then?' he said. 'Sorry it

101

turned into such an interrupted afternoon.'

'It wasn't your fault,' she said. 'I brought it all on myself.'

'Yes, you did,' he said. She searched for a palliative twinkle in vain. At some point in recent weeks, Phil had changed. He no longer delighted in her as he once had. He had become older, slower and sadder, and she suspected she was more of a duty than a pleasure to him now. She sighed.

'We'll need to talk to Emily again,' he said softly, on the doorstep. Galton was following them, oddly lethargic, and Thea found herself wondering whether Phil would wait to see the man completely off the premises.

It turned out that he did, because he had last minute instructions to issue. 'I realise it doesn't feel fair, but I'd be very grateful if you refrained from discussing my thoughts with your sister – OK?'

'I doubt if I'll be speaking to her during that time anyway,' she shrugged. She'd watched the bulky Galton depart the way he came, across one of his own fields, in near darkness. After all, he only lived next door, she reminded herself. Next door might be half a mile away, but there were protocols of neighbourliness that might be called upon in a crisis. Besides, he had already said they hadn't heard the last of the sheep-worrying business, even though it was clear that Phil had succeeded in obtaining a stay of execution.

'You'll be all right, will you?' he said, with an air of having said the same thing just a few too many times.

'Oh yes. I'm always all right,' she smiled, knowing this was not strictly true – that safety was never guaranteed. People could sometimes behave alarmingly badly.

As soon as he'd gone, she let Hepzie out of the scullery and stood her on the slate slab beside the sink, hoping to get more of the mud out of the long coat. She had never had her spaniel trimmed professionally, dealing with knots and lumps herself as they arose. Now the matted hair down the dog's chest and along both sides presented a daunting task. 'You've never been as bad as this before,' she complained. 'Where on earth did you go?'

'Buckets of blood, Cap'n, buckets of blood.' The voice came clear and penetrating from the living room. It took Thea several seconds to remember Ignatius, during which time she clasped the spaniel to herself and froze with fear.

'Oohhh,' she exhaled. 'The bloody thing. What have they been teaching him, for heaven's sake?'

'Get your gun and follow me,' continued the bird. 'We'll have that varmint.'

'Madness,' concluded Thea. 'This is madness. What was wrong with "Pretty Polly"?'

Hepzibah was plainly confused – the bird sounded like a human being, and yet clearly was nothing of the sort. Her mistress was talking to her, wasn't she – not that other creature? She shivered and yawned. It had been a long day.

Thea lifted her down, and went to confront the parrot. 'Who do you think you are?' she demanded. 'I suppose we'll be hearing about pieces

103

of eight next. I must say you've got a very violent repertoire.' She stared at the handsome plumage and pale flickering eye. There was definitely something unsettling about parrots, the way they would come out with utterances that fitted the occasion uncannily at times. She wondered about the teenaged Martin Angell, repeating such bizarre snippets of film and literature to the bird. How many times did you have to repeat a thing for the avian mind to retain it? And how much did they pick up from ordinary family life? Surely 'Lock the doors, Daddy' was something from real experience, and not deliberately taught? But was it Babs or Martin who had been so concerned with security?

This way lies madness, she concluded. It didn't matter, anyway. Let the parrot say what it liked, she'd be used to it in another day or so.

The nicely progressing jigsaw was still on the kitchen table, disturbed slightly by a Galton elbow as he drank his coffee. Neither he nor Phil had commented on it. With gritted teeth, Thea sat down to work on it a bit more. Whatever happened, she was going to finish it before she left.

But she made little progress. The strange events of the previous evening, the unreliability of her sister's story, the knowledge that there was far too much to come in the days ahead – it all crowded in on her. Phil had asked her how well she knew her sister, or words to that effect, and her instinct had been to protest that she knew her extremely well. But was that true? She and Emily had never shared many interests, beyond a united impatience of little sister Jocelyn, and worship of big brother Damien. Emily as an adult was almost a stranger. When Thea had become more and more committed to environmental matters, expressing horror at the sight of her sister throwing bottles into the dustbin and keeping her house far too hot, Emily had not even troubled to defend herself. 'We've gone our different ways,' she said. 'I don't see the world the same as you do.'

Their husbands had typified the differences, and although there was never any animosity, everybody knew that they found each other just a bit boring.

Still, she was certain that Emily would never get involved in covering up the identity of a killer, or directly lying to the police. She wouldn't have the *courage* for a start. And the shame and humiliation of public exposure would be enough to deter her from such behaviour. So Thea's original theory that the murdered man had been too disfigured for Emily to recognise must be the right one. Then a terrible thought occurred to her: what if *he* had recognised Emily? Had he been conscious in those final moments? Would he have tried to say something to her?

From one minute to the next, all too aware of what was happening, Thea was engaged. She had resisted and distracted herself, she had refrained from asking questions of Phil or Emily, she had devoted herself to the dogs and the Hawkhill responsibilities – all in vain. She had, after all, *met* Sam Webster. He had seemed a decent human being, clever and cheerful. He ought not to have been bashed to death as he had been. Nobody deserved that. And if Emily had any means of helping to catch and punish his killer, then she had a duty to use them. And her sister, Thea Osborne, was going to make sure she did.

CHAPTER NINE

Monday was overcast, with a serious threat of rain. Basil and Freddy were still subdued, but did finally eat the meal that Thea offered them again. Ignatius muttered, 'Frankly, my dear, I don't *give* a damn,' five times in a row, when she removed his night-time cover. The voice was so completely unlike Clark Gable's that it took Thea four of the repetitions before she got the reference. Then the bird cracked a lot of sunflower seeds and threw the shells onto the floor. The ferrets squirmed and frolicked and cheeped at her in a manner she took to be friendly.

'Everybody seems OK today, then,' said Thea. 'Except for you, that is,' addressing the spaniel, who had spent the night in the kitchen on an old blanket. The dog had yapped intermittently, in the hope that this was an oversight and she could sleep as usual on her mistress's bed. Thea had shouted at her from the spare room, until she quietened down. The resulting reproach over-flowed from the liquid eyes by the bucketful. Hepzie was not enjoying herself, that was obvious. The parrot continued to horrify her, and banishment to the kitchen just because of a bit of mud seemed the height of cruelty. Plus she had a lot of sore scratches from the barbed wire that needed intensive licking at regular intervals.

Freddy and Basil were still far from presentable, particularly Freddy, with his long hair. Thea took each head in turn and looked into the clear trusting eyes. 'Did you slaughter those sheep?' she asked each in turn. 'Are you really guilty of murder?' For reply she got two slowly wagging tails, two earnest gazes of friendship. 'Oh, God, I hope you didn't,' she groaned. 'You're such nice boys. It wouldn't really be your fault. I never should have let you go.' She had reattached their chains soon after they returned home, wondering whether it felt like much worse confinement after their hours of freedom.

'I suppose we could go for another walk,' Thea capitulated, having noticed Hepzie's gloom. 'On the lead, through the village, no nonsense – right?'

Even under grey skies, Lower Slaughter was gorgeous. The ancient stone alongside the little river, the quiet solid atmosphere, as if nothing could really matter after so many centuries of continuity – it all combined to create a picture of perfection. The buildings took precedence over everything. If a seam of pure gold were to be found underneath them, there would be no question of mining for it. There was no imaginable human need that could justify the destruction of these beautiful symbols of the Cotswolds. It was restful to know this, as if there were no need to make difficult decisions or worry overmuch about anything. There was a strong impression that even after humanity was long gone, these well-constructed houses would remain.

She walked slowly alongside the river, which

was only slightly deeper and faster than it had been on Saturday, despite all the rain, a breeze ruffling the water where it widened on the western side of the village. Now and then a car would pass by on the other side of the river, moving slowly, the driver giving her a good look. She felt considerably more self-conscious than she had on her previous stroll, before her sister had witnessed a murder and the dogs in her charge been accused of wholesale slaughter. Now she felt conspicuous in her delinquency, sure that people were whispering about her behind the curtained windows. Further attention must surely be drawn to the scruffy spaniel, still show-ing signs of yesterday's mud bath.

'Morning,' came a voice behind her. She turned, and met the vivid blue eyes of Saturday afternoon. Useless to deny to herself that this was exactly what she had hoped would happen.

But something had changed. The good-natured face, the startling eyes, were the same. But beneath them was the distinctive white collar of a clergyman. Her fantasy lover was a vicar. She almost laughed in his face.

But then she noticed another difference: the man was under some great strain. His blue eyes were sunken into skin that was a nasty shade of putty. Lines pulled his mouth into an inverted saucer, like a cartoon of a sad person.

'Hello,' she said, with a little frown. 'Can I help you?'

He shook his head with a grimace. 'That's normally *my* line,' he said. 'But, yes, you might be able to. I think we're connected, via our siblings.

109

That's if I'm right in assuming you're the house-sitter at Hawkhill. Your dog gives you away – I was told it was a lady with a cocker spaniel.'

'That's right,' she acknowledged. 'Thea Osborne. But I'm not with you about siblings.'

'Of course you're not,' he agreed. 'I'm still rather muddled myself. But as I understand it, the lady who saw my brother being murdered was – is – your sister. And – is this right? – they knew each other? Your sister's husband is Bruce Peterson, isn't he?' He smiled flickeringly, as if the muscles had to be coerced into action.

'Your brother!' She stared at him, unable to compute this sudden rush of apparent coincidence. Then she remembered that Phil had said Sam Webster had a brother who was a vicar. This must be the man. Even in her confusion and apprehension, she felt a flutter of excitement. Whatever happened, she was going to get to know him better. But – a vicar! That was still a most unwelcome shock.

'I was thinking I would probably bump into you. People find it hard to keep away from this spot if they're staying locally. The village acts as a kind of magnet. They all pause and stand just where you did, though most of them take photographs as well.'

She was finally mastering her thoughts and impressions. Wasn't he being unnaturally *calm*, given recent events? Where was the horrified grief and rage at what had happened to Sam? Even a vicar might be expected to show some strong emotion under the circumstances. But she could hardly ask him how he was feeling. Instead she looked around her. 'Are you living in one of these houses, then?' she asked. 'Is there a vicarage?' How did he come to have time to hang about on the offchance that she would stroll by?

He grimaced. 'No such luck. Can you imagine the poor old C of E affording one of these? Although I mustn't grumble. Not about that, anyway.'

'Oh?' The calm manner continued to puzzle her, until she noted the rigid jaw and the tremor in his hands. Hepzie was ignoring them both, sniffing idly at a patch of grass. Thea felt an urgent need for explanations, but forced herself to remain silent. Far better to let him reveal exactly where he stood, in his own words. There were, she was starting to realise, large areas of awkwardness where she ought not to venture.

He did not respond to her note of interrogation. Instead he shifted the focus to Emily. 'Your poor sister. It must have been awful for her,' he said.

'Yes. She was in quite a state on Saturday night. She was a bit better the next morning, though. But infinitely worse for *you*. I mean – I can't imagine losing *my* brother.' She devoted a few seconds to trying to envisage life without Damien, in vain.

The man nodded slowly, his face registering something closer to anguish. The story began to emerge jerkily from his lips. 'He'd come to see me. We'd had a meal at his hotel and I left him finishing off a brandy and planning to go to back to his room to read.'

'I'm awfully sorry. When did you first hear

111

about it?'

'Early yesterday. The worst part was having to conduct two Sunday services, having just been to identify Sam's body.'

'Good Lord! Surely you didn't! That must have been ghastly.'

'Well,' he smiled deprecatingly, 'actually it was quite a help, once I got going. I didn't think I'd be able to do it, but it felt right, in the end.'

'I suppose that's what God's there for,' said Thea tactlessly. 'I mean – my father's funeral was just last Friday. So, well–'

'Oh dear. Your *poor* sister!'

The sympathy for Emily was starting to feel slightly excessive, and Thea made a small brushing motion with her hand. 'She'll get over it,' she said, afraid she sounded callous, but concerned that the man was overlooking his own good reasons to be distraught. 'Were you very close?' she went on. 'To your brother, I mean?'

'Oh – you know. Brothers generally tend to drift apart once they're adults. I've been abroad for quite a long time, and since coming back I've seen him precisely twice. So, no, not exactly *close*. But that doesn't make it any easier – you find yourself going back to the early years, reliving all the childhood pranks and so forth. It hasn't quite dawned on me how much has gone with him. Memories that nobody else can share.' His face crumpled and he gazed fixedly at the river.

'No other brothers and sisters then?'

He shook his head. 'Our mother is still alive, but she's not very lucid these days. I'm not at all sure how I'm going to tell her the news.'

112

Hepzie had been waiting patiently for the conversation to finish. Normally inclined to jump and scrabble at people's legs, she was much more subdued than usual. Just as well, thought Thea. The man didn't look as if he would welcome such demonstrations.

'I'm sorry – I didn't tell you my name, did I? One gets into the shameful habit of assuming everybody knows it. It's Peter. Peter Clarke.'

Thea could not avert the blink of surprise, and the blurted, 'But I thought–'

'Oh, yes. Sam Webster. Same mother, different fathers. We grew up together, though. His Dad died when Sam was a year old. Mum wanted to change his name, but his grandfather wouldn't hear of it. Carrying on the family escutcheon and all that nonsense. My father came on the scene quite quickly, and they had me just before Sam's third birthday.'

'Right.' The story had emerged as a rehearsed speech, something he'd had to explain a hundred times before. Thea visualised the situation, how it might have been her own story if she had been younger when Carl died, and found somebody to sire another child. She briefly tried on the shoes of each person in the picture – the little boy who never knew his real father, the secure second child with the slightly anomalous big brother. 'I see,' she said.

'You do, don't you.' His tone carried surprise and a small breath of relief. 'You strike me as someone to whom things have happened.'

Powerful stuff! She met the jay-feather blue of his eyes, letting herself believe in a merging of

113

experience and emotion that would make long conversations with him a delight. But, oh blast, he was a *vicar*. And besides that, he was virtually certain to be married.

'Well, my husband died, about two years ago. That's all, really.' Not true, but how could she begin to tell him the things that had taken place since then – the adventures that a house-sitter finds herself heir to; the unpredictable course of her relationship with Phil Hollis; the daughter and the dog and the bleak prospects for her mother?

'It's getting to be quite a list, isn't it,' he said ruefully. 'All the people who've died. And we've not finished it yet. I had a wife in Zambia. She died of AIDS last year.'

Thea felt only the slightest inclination to recoil, to suddenly regard him as unclean, infected – a latter-day leper. Surely if his wife had had the virus, then he must have caught it too?

He read her mind. 'Don't worry – I managed to avoid it. We knew she had it when I married her.'

This time Thea could not in any way stand in his shoes. They had become strange distorted alien things that her feet could not come close to fitting. Was the man a saint, or a lunatic, or simply so desperately in love he would do such a thing merely to be with the adored woman? She stared at him in bewilderment. 'Gosh,' she said weakly.

Peter Clarke smiled, and the lines of misery disappeared. His expressive face plainly manifested that he was taken with her, found her appealing and easy to talk to. 'Gosh is about it,' he agreed. 'But I wouldn't have missed the experience. And I have a daughter to show for it.'

'So have I,' said Thea. 'Mine's twenty-two. There's nothing like a daughter, is there?'

He smiled again, and even emitted a quick laugh. 'Nothing at all,' he said. 'Mine's only seven.'

Thea was well aware that her official boyfriend would disapprove of this conversation on a number of levels. As an assistant to the police investigating Webster's death, she had failed completely. As a woman encountering a new man, she was behaving outrageously, at least in her secret recesses. She had moved beyond the amazing blue eyes to the personality behind them, and found it very attractive. She already liked him too much to risk upsetting him by asking any more about his brother. Besides, why in the world should she? She wasn't a detective and her sister was under a cloud of suspicion that dictated that Thea ought to tread carefully.

Even so, Peter Clarke's brother *had* been murdered, and he must be finding it hard to think about anything else.

Hepzie was getting restless, circling Thea's legs and entangling her in the lead. But Thea was thinking about the brothers. 'Why did he stay at a hotel?' she asked. 'And such an expensive one at that? Haven't you got a spare room?'

He blinked, and she realised such questions might sound intrusive. She made no attempt to retreat, however.

'He insisted. He wasn't too sure how things would go between us, and thought we might

115

need space. He'd read some review of that particular place and decided to give it a try.'

She nodded carelessly at this explanation. 'Well, I'd better get back,' she said. 'I'm in a bit of trouble, actually, with my house-sitting. I need to keep an eye on the resident dogs. They're under suspicion of murder, themselves.'

The flash of alarm in his eyes made her rush to explain. Could he really have thought she meant that Freddy and Basil had killed his brother? She quickly told the story of the slaughtered sheep. The vicar grimaced and shook his head.

'Nasty,' he said. 'Sounds a bit like *The Silence of the Lambs.*'

'No,' she told him seriously. 'That's different. But I suppose it's going on as well. If I've got it right, this is the time when most lambs do go to the butcher. I remember a lot of noise last week, where they were separating them from their mothers.'

'In Africa they just chop their heads off, in one quick swing. I came to the view that that was a lot more merciful than all this long-distance driving and waiting about in the abattoir that goes on here.'

'We're back to death again,' she pointed out. 'Isn't there any other subject we could talk about?'

'Not today,' he said regretfully. 'I've got work to do, policemen to talk to, letters to write.' He sighed and the droop came back to his mouth. 'And a mother to visit, God help me.'

'I expect he will,' said Thea, feeling entirely insincere.

She trailed back to Hawkhill, ignoring the lavish scenery, her insides swirling with self-dislike. What was it with women, she asked herself, that they were always leaping forward to a distant future? She had been unable to prevent her imagination from settling her as a rural vicar's wife, ministering to waifs and strays that Peter Clarke brought to her for solace. The daughter would accept her as a perfect stepmother, encouraged to remember all the details of her African childhood. All madness, she assured herself. Complete and utter fantasy, and I should be old enough to know better by now. An absolute lack of any religious faith firmly disqualified her from any such scenario, anyway. She'd never be able to attend his services or share the things that most urgently mattered to him.

'Best stick with Phil, then,' she muttered. 'He's not so bad, really. We're just going through a stale patch. Once his back's completely better, it'll be fine.'

The jigsaw on the kitchen table had an abandoned look, and Thea admitted inner doubts as to whether she'd ever go back to it. There were so many calls on her attention, requiring phone calls or visits, too much hanging over her that could at any moment descend with a crash. The Angells' dogs were a source of growing guilt, as she tried to imagine how their owners would react if the worst happened and they were summarily executed. They hadn't seemed unduly fond of the animals, but it wasn't safe to make such an assumption. Most people were viscerally attached to their dogs, whether it showed or not. In a way, their guilt or innocence was a secondary consideration. Thea had defied her clear instructions and let them loose. It was her fault, fair and square, and she deserved to be chastised. The Angells would be within their rights to withhold payment for the house-sitting, she realised. They might even sue her for negligence.

And there was Emily, behaving oddly and telling dubious stories to the police. Thea was steadfastly convinced that it was all a result of the death of their father and the terrible shock of coming across a violent killing only a few days later. Besides, as far as she could see, Emily's account of her experiences had made pretty good sense. The vivid details of the victim being assaulted so savagely remained clear in her mind. The shadowy attacker was easy enough to imagine, with his sturdy boots and vicious weapon. Her imagination recoiled from the moments of contact, the skull cracking, the face driven ruthlessly into the mud. It was too horrible, and little wonder if Emily too wanted to erase it from her mind.

But there were other things demanding her attention, too – all of them worrying. Her mother and Phil could be added to the list, that included Basil and Freddy. It all combined to make her far too restless to attempt any more of the jigsaw. It was all the worse, because she could see no obvious course of action on any issue, whether Emily, the dogs, Phil or her mother. Where exactly did she stand with the Galton man, for example? Had Phil pacified him enough for her to be able to forget him for the time being? It would have been an interesting distraction, that afternoon, to walk over to his house and have a look at his sheep, if circumstances had been different. Not the dead ones, but the flock in general. Although no expert, Thea had quite a liking for sheep, and had encountered many different aspects of them over the past year. Shearing, lambing, the use of their wool – even now the Cotswolds retained at least a faint shadow of the creatures which had originally endowed the whole area with its prosperity. She had learnt about the old Cotswold breed, now officially 'rare', but featuring in documents going back over a thousand years. Sheep in England were not quite as sacred as cows in India, but they had earned a place in people's respect here in Gloucestershire. You didn't let your dogs tear them to bits anywhere, but least of all *here*.

And neither did you permit men to bash each other's brains out. Underlying all the other concerns was the murder. It was unarguable that the killer must be caught. And like it or not, Thea once again found herself on the spot, an observant stranger with every excuse to ask pertinent questions and get to know some of the characters involved. Regardless of Detective Superintendent Phil Hollis, she would want to do her bit. And after this morning, she wanted to regain her own self-respect. She was not a silly moony adolescent with hormones out of control. She was forty-three, for heaven's sake. Most women had finished with sex and romance and all such nonsense by that age. In many societies she'd be a grandmother by now. Even in Britain it was very far from unusual. If the hormones were misbehaving, it was because they were drying up and marking the end of her fertile years. Which meant she should be giving much more scope to her experience of life, her knowledge of people, her own sharp wits.

'Right, then,' she said.

'Lock the doors, Daddy!' cackled the parrot. 'Lock the doors!'

CHAPTER TEN

Emily phoned late that afternoon. The mobile was sitting on one of the worktops in the kitchen, its charger connected. 'How are you?' Thea asked. 'Did you go to work today?'

'Yes I did. I'm all right I suppose.'

'You don't sound all right.'

'It's catching up with me, I think. Thea – the police came here yesterday, and told me who the dead man was. It didn't really sink in at the time. I was concentrating on being OK for work, and getting Mark organised. But now – well–' her voice disintegrated into gasps, which to Thea sounded worse than normal crying.

'It's all right,' said Thea awkwardly. 'Take a deep breath.'

It was half a minute before Emily found her voice again. 'What on earth was he *doing* there? It never *occurred* to me it could be someone I knew. It makes it so much worse. I can't *bear* it. I'll have to – I mean – I can't stop thinking about him.'

Thea kept silent with difficulty, merely making an encouraging grunt. Words were now tumbling out at the other end of the line. 'You remember him, don't you? He was an Oxford don. Bruce was *devoted* to him. He went all silent when they came to tell us. I've never seen him like that. Oh, God – what am I going to do?'

'You don't have to do anything,' Thea told her

121

gently. 'What do you mean?'

'I have to get through all this.'

'Yes. And you will.' But Thea had her doubts. She was still wrestling with the coincidence of the identity of the murder victim, and the insidious effects of Phil's suspicions.

As if reading her thoughts, Emily said, 'The police weren't very nice about it. They don't seem to believe that I didn't recognise Sam.'

'Well–'

'For heaven's sake, don't tell me you agree with them! Why can't anybody understand what it was *like?*'

'Calm down, Em. I believe you, of course I do. It was wet and dark and he was face down. Of *course* you couldn't see who it was.' She was speaking warmly, urgently wanting to console her suffering sister. In an effort to move things on, she added, 'I met his brother this morning, as it happens. The vicar. Peter Clarke.' She wanted to kick herself hard for the little thrill that saying his name brought about.

'What? How could you possibly–?' Emily's voice rose. 'Have you been talking about it to everybody you meet? I bet you have, you little blabbermouth. Oh, Christ – this is a nightmare. I still can't believe it was Sam, and now you've produced a brother. Oh – it's all getting much *much* worse. I never thought...'

'Calm down,' said Thea again, trying to overlook the blabbermouth remark. 'It was a horrible shock, that's all. It was just terribly bad luck that you were there at the time.'

'It was, wasn't it?' Emily's tone turned to a

sudden eagerness. 'The whole thing was just a terrible piece of bad luck. Even more unlucky that it was Sam.' A squeak on the final word suggested that tears were imminent. 'At least he wasn't married,' she added. 'I was so worried that it was somebody who had a wife and six children.'

'That's right,' Thea murmured agreement.

'The police seemed to think I could have recognised the killer as well,' continued Emily bitterly. 'They went on and on about it. Trying to make me say if he was fat or thin, tall or short. And how I could be so sure he was white, if it was so dark.'

'Well, you *are* the only witness. You're the only person they *can* ask.'

'Yeah,' groaned Emily. 'It's all such a bloody mess. And now it's got even worse. I'm never going to be able to sleep tonight, with all this going round in my head.'

'I met Sam Webster, don't forget,' Thea said. 'He seemed a really nice man.'

'Yes, he was nice enough.' Emily sounded reluctant. 'I never liked him as much as Bruce did.' Then the note of hysteria returned, more evident than before. 'We'll have to go to the *funeral*. I'll have that ghastly picture of him in my mind, while everybody's singing "Abide With Me". Oh, shit, I never thought last week that there'd be another dead man to worry about.'

Emily never used bad language. Her mild expletive shocked Thea more than anything else. 'I know,' she soothed, adding the line that women so often use to reassure each other: 'But it wasn't your fault.'

123

'No,' Emily agreed, with a hollow tone. 'That's right. It wasn't my fault. That's what I keep telling myself. It doesn't make me feel any better.'

'We all having lurking guilt, I suppose. It gets activated all too easily.'

'Oh, shut up,' said Emily wearily. 'I can hear Bruce's car. I'll have to go. He's probably had just as bad a day as I have. God knows how we'll ever manage to do it again tomorrow.'

'Good luck, then,' said Thea.

There were two hours or so of daylight left, and Thea felt she ought to be outside. Freddy and Basil needed further grooming, to get more of the tangles out of their coats. She had attached them to their chains in the morning, but they had spent all day slumped under the big dogwood bush at the edge of the front lawn. It still seemed unreasonable to expect them to live such constrained lives, and she found herself wondering whether she might dare to take them singly for short walks along the footpath and back, as Cedric had plainly sanctioned. Again she asked herself just how much affection the Angells had for them. Very little had been betrayed during her visit for instructions. If anything, the ferrets seemed to have a higher value, at least for Cedric.

The cats were virtually invisible. They took the food she put down for them, and slunk through the shadows of the outhouses, low to the ground. Their role seemed to be to keep vermin levels down and nothing more than that.

Ignatius, however, was a whole different matter. Special in a number of ways, he dominated the house. His voice was chilling, like a ventriloquist's dummy – human and yet horribly *in*human. He had obviously learnt that anything he said would earn a gratifying reaction, from laughter to screams of alarm. His repertoire ranged from low muttering to loud shouts, and by this, her third full day, Thea was only just getting used to the suddenness of his remarks. There would be no warning, and usually her back was turned at the time. 'Tell him he's a fool,' was the latest offering. It was tantalising, wondering where he had learnt the things he said. Probably not the TV, since it was in a different room, a small back sitting room containing two very ancient armchairs and a glass-fronted cabinet full of dusty china. There was no computer, no music system, no sign of handicrafts or other hobbies. It was tempting to think the couple simply slumped in the back room and watched telly for much of the time, leaving Ignatius to rule supreme in the main room.

A glance at the papers on the bureau flap revealed letters from the Council Planning Office, leaflets about planning law and stacks of hand-written notes on lined A4 paper. Thea had forgotten the burning issue of the proposed new houses, until now. Thinking about it, she found it impossible to believe that such a preciously conserved area could ever contemplate much development. Admittedly, the outskirts of Bourton-on-the-Water, as seen from the A429, had become a densely packed estate of new houses, but if anything that must add weight to the opposition to the Hawkhill proposal. It surely made sense to confine it all to the Bourton side of the road, leaving the Slaughters and the Swells in peace?

Funny, she reflected, how alarm bells had rung when Cedric had first told her of the controversy. New houses in lovely rural parts of England were always going to arouse furious feelings. But it certainly had nothing whatever to do with the death of Sam Webster, Oxford Don and brother to a vicar, and she opted to shelve the whole subject as needing no further consideration.

She felt a distinct need to talk everything through with someone, only to discover that there were aspects to the story that had to be concealed from anyone she spoke to. One aspect especially was too shameful to reveal – her idiotic yearnings for the Reverend Peter Clarke. Which was, of course, precisely the thing she most wanted to talk about. The only person who she could discuss him with was the man himself, which was daft.

As she wrestled with this jumble, she brushed at Freddy's long coat, yanking lumps of mud away and making him yelp now and then. 'Good dog,' she murmured, 'there's a good dog.' And he *was* a good dog. Some animals in his position would have snarled and snapped when a strange woman started painfully attacking his coat. All he did was stand there and make token protests. One or twice he licked her hand, as if to say, *isn't that enough?*

'Hiding more of the evidence, I see,' came a loud voice behind her. As if the intervening twenty-four hours had never happened, Henry

Galton stood bulkily between her and the setting sun once again, eyeing her treatment of Cedric Angell's dogs with a frown. The words might have been jokey, but his expression was severe.

'Oh, hello,' she said, standing up. 'It's you again.'

'It is,' he agreed. 'No police boyfriend here now, then?'

Perhaps without the low growl from the dog, she would never have detected the underlying threat in his voice. Perhaps without the growl, Galton would have relaxed and changed his manner. As it was, his frown deepened and he took a step towards her and the dog, legs slightly apart as if poised for action.

Thea gave herself an urgent pep talk. There couldn't be any actual danger from this man. What was the worst he could do? *Something quite bad*, came a nervous inner reply. 'You're alarming him,' she said, as Freddy bared his teeth. 'Don't come any closer.'

'Why should I care whether or not he's alarmed? He should be dead by now – I'd have shot him yesterday if Phil Hollis, of all people, hadn't been here. Him and the other dogs.'

'Dogs!' The plural raised her fear levels considerably. Nobody had mentioned shooting Hepzie – Thea had assumed the farmer knew nothing of her existence. 'What do you mean?'

'I'm reliably informed that you let *three* of them loose on my land, not just these two. Three dogs is officially a pack, and a lot more likely to do the damage than two.' His gaze fell on the spaniel, who had approached him interestedly when he

127

first arrived, but had not greeted him as she would most newcomers. 'Spaniels are notorious for chasing sheep, let me tell you.'

'Not this spaniel. The idea's ridiculous. She's as soft as a lamb.'

It was an unfortunate choice of simile, as the man's curled lip demonstrated. But Thea was gaining in courage as they stood facing each other. 'I really am very sorry about your rams. It's an awful thing to happen. But the evidence against these dogs isn't really very strong. They didn't have a drop of blood on them when they came back. They were so muddy, they can only have been in the river and along its banks. I'm assuming your sheep weren't anywhere near there?'

'So you think it's nothing more than a coincidence that the worrying happened just as this pack was roaming freely across the countryside, do you?'

Something about the age-old use of the word 'worrying' made her reassess the man and his complaints. Sheep-worrying was a problem that occurred in Victorian novels by people like Thomas Hardy, not in the barely rural reaches of modern Gloucestershire. And yet it did still matter, and the law still recognised the rights of the farmer as paramount.

She squared her shoulders, wishing as so often before that she was taller. 'That's the only explanation I can suggest, yes. Some other dog or dogs must have been on the loose. I don't suppose it's all that unusual, is it?' Suddenly she remembered the man she had met on the path;

128

the man who had issued his apocryphal warnings about what was going to happen. 'It must have been the man I met who told you these dogs were loose,' she said. 'Nobody else knew about it.'

'People have eyes, don't they?' he snapped back. 'Anybody could have seen them and known they came from here. *I* don't know what man you're talking about, do I?'

'Quite small, not much hair, early fifties, wearing a blue sweatshirt kind of thing. Talked with a westcountry accent. I'd say he must be local. He seemed to know all about you.'

'Sounds like Mike Lister,' said Galton indifferently. 'And so what if it was him who alerted me?'

'Does he have an axe to grind with Cedric Angell?' Thea asked slowly, beginning to glimpse a possible pattern behind the previous day's events.

A sudden glint in his eye alerted her. A flash of surprise, quickly covered up. He gave no direct reply to the question, saying instead, 'Seems to me he was being neighbourly in telling me what was going on. He couldn't have known he'd be too late.'

She was sorely tempted to cross-examine him as to the precise time and place of the attack, as well as exactly when the Lister man had spoken to him. From what she'd heard so far, it all sounded suspiciously neat. But despite his revealing reaction, she refrained from pursuing the notion of a convoluted conspiracy to bring pain to the absent Angells on the part of Mr Lister.

'At least you didn't bring your gun this time,'

she said lightly, fighting the continuing fluttering in her chest. If this man chose to execute the dogs, there was very little she could do to stop him.

'I came to tell you it's not over. Keep them chained up, and don't think you can hide what you did from Cedric. He's going to have to know about it. If I was him, I'd feel perfectly justified in docking your pay for disobeying instructions.' As on the previous day, she detected an underlying reasonableness in his voice, as if the effort to maintain the aggression was too great to sustain for long. He cared about his mangled sheep – of course he did. But he perhaps wished as much as she did that the whole business could be dropped.

'I suppose that's between him and me,' she said stiffly. 'I don't feel I have very much to reproach myself with. He did say I could walk them, so long as they were on leads.'

'Except they weren't on leads, were they? They were running wild all over the countryside. *Three* of them,' he added, with a pointed look at the spaniel.

'Goodbye, Mr Galton,' she said tiredly. 'I don't think there's anything more we can say to each other.'

CHAPTER ELEVEN

Tuesday stretched bleakly ahead, as Thea woke at seven to the sound of more rain dashing against her bedroom window. She had no expectations of enjoyable social exchanges, apart from a flickering hope that Peter Clarke might pay a visit. Phil was likely to phone and she tried to rehearse what she would say to him. From her own selfish standpoint, the issue of the dogs was more urgent than that of the dead don, although she understood that this would probably change once she gave the murder more thought. Phil might well decide not to include her in the investigations anyway. He had never been comfortable with her getting close to a murder enquiry, and there was ample opportunity to exclude her this time.

She dealt with all the animals, braced for whatever Ignatius might try to startle her with, only for the bird to remain stubbornly silent. She spent some minutes standing in front of his cage, trying to meet his eye and get some grasp of how he functioned. She was familiar with stories of parrots saving people in burning houses, or making incredibly pertinent remarks as part of the household proceedings. Owners of parrots insisted that their pet knew exactly what was going on, and understood most of the conversation. This one was perhaps disturbed by the presence of a stranger and the disappearance of

131

his known people. That might account for some of his more alarming utterances; even the Rhett Butler line hinted at marital strife.

He met her eye with his head cocked, dancing gently on the perch, the great talons curled loosely around the wooden pole. Once or twice he opened his beak to reveal a thick grey tongue that looked completely wrong for speech. If a parrot could talk so well, why couldn't an ape? Did parrots in the rain forest converse lucidly together in their own language? She reflected idly that she might activate her laptop one day and do some research into the whole parrot kingdom.

Freddy and Basil seemed restored to normal, running to the extremity of their chains and then circling frustratedly, gaining almost no opportunity for real exercise. The rain seemed irrelevant to them, although they pushed further under the dogwood than previously when they finally lay down. A tabby cat ventured into the open, staring up at her warily, poised for flight. The ferrets twined and twisted and squeaked in apparent contentment.

The silence was finally broken by the mobile playing its diddly-pop tune. 'Thea? How are you?'

'Hello, Mum. I'm perfectly all right, thanks. How are you?'

'Damien's here. He wants to go through Daddy's papers and books.'

'Oh.' She tried to establish how she felt about that, remembering the way her grandmother had cleared out all her husband's possessions barely a week after his death. Everything had gone –

clothes, tools, hairbrush, toothbrush, cigarette card collection. Was her mother going to behave in the same way?

'I'll keep some of the novels, but all that historical stuff can go. And the bound magazines. Damien says there's quite a good market for them. He's got *Punch* and *The New Statesman* going back to the forties.'

'Yes, I know.' She had loved the carefully arranged collections, dipping into old copies of *Punch* in her teen years, with delight. 'It seems a shame to dispose of them.'

'Do you want them then? You've never said.'

'Well, I haven't really got room.'

'That's what I thought. It's no use being senti-mental about it. I know *I'll* never look at them, so what's the sense in hanging on to them?'

This, then, was what normal people did, was it? When their spouse died, they discarded all his effects. She hadn't done it with Carl. She was still in the same cottage in Witney, the one they had bought when Jessica was a year old, and which had no mortgage on it now. Carl's books and music and wellingtons and socks were all still there. Only a few of his clothes had been given away. Their lives had been sufficiently enmeshed for the things that were Carl's to be more or less Thea's as well. They had liked the same things, bought pictures and furniture together, received joint gifts of kitchenware and china. 'Mmm,' she said to her mother, noticing belatedly how much better she was sounding. 'It's completely up to you, of course. I'm glad you feel up to it already. That's really good.'

133

'Oh, I'm tougher than you think,' her mother asserted, with a little laugh. 'And it has to be done sometime. It's not as if he really had very much. Men don't, as a rule. They're not so inclined to hoard things as women. The papers are just business letters, work stuff, nothing very interesting.'

Thea thought of Sam Webster. Unmarried, as far as she knew, and liable to have a study somewhere stuffed with books and lecture notes and jottings for his own writings. He must have left everything as if returning to it imminently. And who more likely to be dealing with it all than his brother? Would some parish woman offer to help – or might Thea be justified in suggesting it? Would that seem very strange, on such a slender acquaintanceship?

'Have you heard from Emily?' she asked her mother.

'Not a word. I realise there's something you two aren't telling me. That attack she's supposed to have seen on Saturday, I suppose.' She spoke resentfully, a tone Thea had heard many times before. Keeping things from Mother had become habit from childhood, for no very good reason. She seldom over-reacted or issued stringent punishments, but somehow it has always seemed easier not to tell her too much.

'It really was horrible. I expect she'll tell you all about it any day now.' She felt awkward, knowing it was not her story, but Emily's. She was almost at the point of telling her mother she was asking the wrong daughter, when Mrs Johnstone took an audible breath and said, 'Well, I think I'd

134

rather not know, actually.'

'Very wise,' Thea approved. 'It's lovely to hear you sounding so together, Mum, honestly. Not that I ever really doubted you. As soon as I've finished here, I'll come and see you.'

'You do that, darling. And bring Jess, if she's free.'

The call left Thea feeling that all would be well with her mother – a small oasis of relief in a world full of worries. Clouds of suspicion hung over everything else – the death of Webster, the savaged sheep, the way the police apparently regarded Emily. There seemed to be nowhere she could safely repose her trust, and worse than that, she felt that she herself had become untrustworthy. She had let those dogs escape through sheer incompetence. She might well find herself betraying Phil, at least in thought, if she saw much more of Peter Clarke. She was letting her father down by thinking about him much less than she expected to. What would Peter advise – that she pray for Dad's soul, and bathe his memory in love and gratitude, probably. She *wanted* to do all that, to grieve gently, without letting the emotions become too raw and painful. But it all felt blocked and diverted by events at Hawkhill. And those were all either her own reckless fault, or her sister's awfully bad luck.

The rain slowly abated, until by eleven it was a thin drizzle. *Rain before seven, Fine by eleven,* Thea repeated to herself. It had been a favourite saying of her father's, and was generally reliable, although Carl had been very sceptical, even to the extent of drawing meteorological maps for

135

her to show how it couldn't possibly work.

An image was lodged in her mind, prompted by Peter Clarke's remark about the growing list of dead relatives: an untidy pile of bodies, like the prey of a cat left alone for a week. It would frantically slaughter anything it could find in the hope that the stack of delectable bodies would lure the beloved owner home again. Not really what Thea was imagining, but the same random collection of victims, their presence intruding into everything. The remembered disagreement about rain between her father and Carl, felt bizarre now they were both dead. Would they be out there in some unimaginable heaven, still debating the matter?

Had her father ever met Sam Webster, she wondered? Was this another peculiar connection that ought to be taken into consideration? It seemed important to know, all of a sudden. Important, too, to learn more about Webster, as the police must surely be doing as part of their investigations. Was it permissable for her to wander over to the mysterious hotel where he had been staying? Could she come up with a reasonable excuse for such a move? Much easier if she had somebody to go with, of course. Then they could be dropping in for a coffee in the lounge, and get chatting to a member of staff who'd be full of gossip about the murdered man. That, at least, was the way it *should* happen. And of course she *did* know a few people in the area. Cold Aston was less than three miles away, and in Cold Aston there was Ariadne, long-time friend of Phil Hollis and recent acquaintance of Thea.

Ariadne was a real character, prickly and argumentative, but with a good heart. She devoted herself to various old ladies, quietly ensuring they could remain in their own homes by handling the chores that had got beyond them. She ran classes in spinning, and sold flamboyant hand-knitted garments at local fairs. It would be good to see her again.

The next big question was whether to walk or to drive. There was a footpath almost the whole way, but the journey there and back was a good five miles, and Thea wasn't sure she could face quite so much walking. Besides, Ariadne disliked dogs, and if she took Hepzie, she'd have to be invited in, and then taken into account for the rest of the visit. It would be much easier if she could just be left in the car. Besides, if Ariadne could be persuaded to have a drink – or even lunch – at the hotel, they'd need to drive there.

She hadn't used her car since she arrived, and she got a whiff of warm dog when she got in, the August heat having worked on the molecules deposited by Hepzie, especially on the passenger seat where she habitually sat during their drives together. 'Could be worse,' said Thea cheerfully.

The village of Cold Aston straggled along a single street, with a small triangle outside the pub that might at a stretch be termed a village green. Ariadne owned a cottage at the northern end, not far from the school. She might well be out, of course. Thea did not have her phone number, and would have been reluctant to call ahead, anyway. She wanted her visit to be a surprise, a spur of the moment thing. That way, she could more easily assess the other woman's mood, and the general trend of her life over the past nine months.

There was no response to her knock on the door, but she could hear a radio playing at the back of the cottage. Walking around the side, she found her friend picking blackcurrants from a well laden bush, the radio sitting on a little table on a tiny paved area. She was able to observe Ariadne for a moment before announcing herself. Ariadne was tall, with broad shoulders and a thick creamy neck. Her hair had been dyed in dreadful stripes the previous year, but was now a more acceptable copper colour. The radio was playing "I Get a Kick Out of You" and Ariadne was singing quietly along with it.

The words warbled high and clear, and Thea understood that the mood was good. In fact it was better than she could have imagined.

'You sound happy,' she said.

Ariadne spun round, her face well tanned and relaxed. 'Hey!' she cried. 'Fancy seeing you.' She sounded much less surprised than the words suggested. It was as if she had half expected the visit, and Thea remembered that she was also a pagan, immersed in country lore and the secret ways of nature. Perhaps she'd foreseen this encounter in a crystal ball.

Calmly, Ariadne fetched elderflower cordial, home-made almond biscuits and the latest piece of knitting, sitting Thea down next to the radio, which she switched off. 'I heard you were in the area again,' she began, deflating Thea's romantic notions of second sight. More than likely, of course, that village gossip would have passed on the information.

'So what's new?' Thea asked.

The other woman flushed and fiddled with a flake of wood on the table top. 'Something I never expected in a thousand years,' she smiled.

'Let me guess,' said Thea. 'From the look of you, it must be a man?'

'Is it that obvious? I feel such a fool. It can't possibly go on – I know it'll all end in heartbreak. But just now it's amazing.'

'Why shouldn't it last? What's the problem?'

'Oh, it's not that he's married or anything. But we're so *different*. He's bound to go off me sooner or later. And he's *smaller* than me. I thought of you a few days ago, wishing I was five foot nothing like you.'

'Five foot *one*, if you please,' laughed Thea. 'So – who is he?'

'He hasn't been here for long. We met at a church jumble sale, would you believe? I just caught his eye, and something – well – we sort of *clicked*. It was the most incredible thing.'

Afterwards Thea marvelled at how slow she'd been. 'It does happen,' she said, feeling mildly envious. 'Though not very often, and not to everybody.' Hadn't it happened to her, when she'd be so drawn to Phil Hollis at Frampton Mansell? With hindsight, it felt like something much less than Ariadne was describing. 'Lucky you.'

'I know. And he keeps saying he's the lucky one. He's so *sweet*. And he's got the most fabulous

139

blue eyes. But the really insane part is that he's a vicar – a fully paid-up Church of England vicar. Isn't that hilarious!'

Thea felt sick. She could feel bile rising up her gullet. 'Peter Clarke,' she whispered. 'You're talking about Peter Clarke.'

'Right! You know him, do you? I suppose that's not surprising. Everybody knows the vicar.' She was innocently prattling on, pleased that her beloved was known to Thea. 'Where exactly are you staying? I gather it's another house-sit?'

'Lower Slaughter.' Her mind was in meltdown. That man – had all that intimate confiding smiling act been nothing more than the look he turned on for everybody he met? If so, what had he done extra to make Ariadne so confident of his devotion? Had she, in her admitted naiveté, got it wrong – had she mistaken his normal manner for something exclusive to herself? Were they sleeping together? Were vicars *allowed* to have sex outside marriage?

'Did you walk here?'

'No, I came in the car. I thought you might not want Hepzie in the house. And it's a bit far to walk both ways.'

'What's the matter?' Ariadne belatedly noticed the sudden change. Her eyes narrowed. 'Is it something to do with Peter? Lower Slaughter is one of his parishes.' A frown hovered. 'And how come you know him, when you're not really from around here?'

Thea forced a smile. 'We met when I was walking Hepzie. Nothing's the matter. I'm just getting used to the idea of you and him. You're not the

140

most likely of couples, are you?'

'That's what I *said*. It's going to be the joke of the Cotswolds when people get to know about it. But he's only here on a temporary contract. He wants to get a much busier parish, preferably in a city.'

'And you'd go with him, would you?'

'If he wanted me to, of course I would. Thea – nothing like this has ever happened to me before. I'd swim the Atlantic to be with him, I'd walk barefoot from here to China, I'd–'

'Yes, I get the idea,' said Thea, with a forced laugh. 'How do you get on with the daughter?'

'Daisy? I haven't met her yet.' A certain vagueness had come into Ariadne's eyes. 'But I'm knitting this for her.' She held up the work – a patterned rectangle that looked rather small to Thea's inexpert eye. 'It's a waistcoat. This is the back.'

'She's seven, isn't she? Have you got her size right?'

Ariadne gazed at the knitting. 'I did have to guess, but Peter says she's quite small for her age.'

'I'm sure she'll love it. The colours are wonderful.' There was a rich chestnut brown, combined with a natural white and a shade of yellow reminiscent of Cotswold stone.

'She's not his, you know. I mean – her father was an African. She's not mixed race.'

'Oh?' Thea struggled to remember the exact words with which Peter had disclosed the child's existence. She had certainly assumed she was biologically his. 'Sounds a bit complicated.'

141

Ariadne chuckled. 'What isn't complicated where families are concerned?'

'So you haven't heard about his brother?' Thea found herself almost hoping she had this modest, if unpleasant, advantage on her friend. It would be a small recompense for the shocked disappointment she was feeling.

'What – you mean the one that got himself killed on Saturday? Of course I've heard. Peter's dreadfully upset about it. The police have been all over him, wanting to know everything about their history.' She paused, and Thea watched her friend remember the events of the previous November. 'You must be feeling a bit sick about that – another murder, I mean,' she said sympathetically. 'I know I am. After what happened last year, I never thought I'd have to go through anything like this again.'

'Neither of us is directly involved this time, though, are we?'

'The ripples spread wide,' said Ariadne, sounding as if she was quoting. 'I gather Phil's leading the investigation?'

'Not exactly. He's still not entirely fit.'

'Why? What's wrong with him?'

'He slipped a disc a few months ago, and hasn't been working full time since then.'

'Poor old man. I bet he hates that.'

'He's not happy.' Thea felt trapped in a multitude of betrayals. She had unholy feelings towards Ariadne's new lover, which meant she was not playing fair by Phil – who had once been the object of Ariadne's adoration. *Maybe we can just swop men,* she thought wildly.

'So – how's life with you?' Ariadne asked. The question was posed with a slight rise of the eyebrows and tilt of the head, encouraging, whilst aware that the answer might be painful.

'For a start, there's my father: he died last week. We had the funeral on Friday. Everybody else is OK. Jessica's still doing her probationary training. Phil and I had a week or so in Temple Guiting in June. That's where he hurt his back.'

'And unearthed a human skeleton. Yes, I heard about that.'

'I expect you did,' Thea sighed.

'So where next – assuming you're still going to do this house-sitting stuff.'

'I am. I'm in the middle of Stow in September for a week, then Hampnett in January for nearly a month. I can't say I'm looking forward to that.'

'Blimey! I hope they're paying well. You could be snowed in. You'll go mad.'

'Well, you'll just have to come and visit me, won't you? I'm hoping I can find one or two people to stay with me, at least for a bit.'

'I'll come if I'm still around,' Ariadne promised. 'But I'm not making any firm plans. Peter's time here finishes at the end of the year.'

'Oh.'

Thea glanced at her watch, mindful of the dog in the warm car, and lunchtime almost upon them. 'Listen – I had the idea of going for a look at the hotel where Peter's brother was staying. I suppose they do lunches for non-residents, don't they?'

Ariadne pulled a dubious face and looked down at her skimpy clothes. 'It's terribly posh. I

143

couldn't go like this. Besides, they're sure to want you to book in advance. And the *price!* It's the last place I'd think of going, to be honest. Plus, isn't it a bit *ghoulish* to want to go there.' She sucked her lower lip for a moment. 'You want to get involved, don't you? Helping the police with their enquiries takes on a whole new meaning with you, Thea Osborne. You missed your vocation, didn't you.' There was a sting behind the words that Thea couldn't fail to detect.

She nodded carelessly. 'I suppose you're right.' With the other woman's gaze still on her, she forced a laugh. 'I mean, right about the hotel. I'm not sure about the rest of it.'

'I'm right about everything. You have no reason to concern yourself with a dead professor, even if you are staying close to where he was killed. Just butt out, for once. Do yourself a favour.'

'I wish I could,' she sighed. Then, 'Did you ever meet him?'

Ariadne shook her head. 'Peter hardly knew him, really. They'd barely seen each other at all over the past ten years.'

'Yes, that's what he told me,' Thea said carelessly.

Ariadne gave her a sharp look. 'Did he? Have you been talking to him about it, then?'

Thea took a deep breath. 'I might as well tell you, I suppose. It was my sister, Emily, who called the police. She was there when he died. She heard the fight that killed him.'

Ariadne's expression revealed the complicated processes that arose from this disclosure. Bewilderment, disbelief, suspicion and finally

144

fury. 'Damn you, Thea Osborne,' she hissed. 'Why do you have to spoil it all by telling me that?'

'Well–' Thea stammered, thoroughly shaken, 'I–'

'Shut up,' Ariadne snapped. 'Shut up and go away.'

CHAPTER TWELVE

When she thought about it more calmly, in the car, Thea could understand something of Ariadne's reaction. Anything that might rock her new love affair would be regarded with a defensive rage. But it had still been unexpected and peculiar. Shouldn't Ariadne have been curious, at least? Perhaps even concerned for Emily and ruefully amused at Thea's apparent inability to stay clear of violent crime, even by association. Instead, she had thrust her visitor away from her, almost physically, a powerful instinct controlling her. There had been alarm just below the surface and something almost like *disgust*.

A wave of loneliness swept through her, at the thought that Ariadne might never speak to her again. She had forgotten how appealing the woman was, how insightful and gentle. Seeing her in the throes of a passionate affair had been a delightful surprise, in the few moments before she knew who the other person was. But now it had all turned sour, and she had no idea where to turn next.

She drove back along the A429, turning off to the left along the first of the roads leading to the Slaughters. A right fork took her along the quiet lane that passed Hawkhill and then on to Upper Slaughter. What, she wondered again, had Emily done exactly on Saturday? The distances were all so short, missing a turn that took her north to Upper Slaughter instead of south to the main road would become apparent within a few minutes.

Emily's account of the time span of her adventure had been hazy. Thea had not questioned her about it, not regarding it as a very important element in the story, but wouldn't her sister have made a bigger point if it had all happened within five minutes of leaving Hawkhill? Had she really driven round in disorientating circles for half an hour, until almost back where she began?

In an attempt to check the probability of this, Thea herself started to take random turnings, starting with a right that led straight through the middle of Upper Slaughter. Trying to envisage Emily's efforts to get back to the main road to the south, she waited for another right turn, which took her directly into Lower Slaughter less than a mile away. This in itself was potentially confusing, with the road veering sharply to the left and then right, with a junction where it was just possible that Emily would have gone the wrong way, taking a curving lane back to the small road which Thea had been on ten minutes previously, instead of heading back to the A429.

In the dark, all this would be difficult, even mildly alarming. Not far from the final junction, she passed the gates of the extremely grand Manor Hotel, which stood imposingly at the end of a broad drive. How could she ever have contemplated turning up here in search of lunch? The idea was lunatic. The place was so select and

147

self-confident that there was virtually nothing to indicate its identity. The gates were closed, and it struck her that there might be another entrance from a different road. But there was no mistaking the fact that this was the hotel where the murdered man had been staying. And that meant the site of the slaughter was somewhere between here and the junction – a deduction confirmed by a stretch of yellow police tape across the mouth of a small layby, a few yards from a gateway where Emily must have been trying to turn her car. It was just about a mile from Hawkhill – closer than Thea had expected, or hoped.

But she had the car navigator thing – the TomTom! a voice insisted. Even if she disliked it, wouldn't Emily have made use of it in the circumstances? If she had, then it would have told her she was going the wrong way. Wouldn't it? If it knew where she was, and where she wanted to go, what scope could there be for such meanderings in a ragged circle around the two villages?

Perhaps it was the unpleasantness with Ariadne that caused her to reconsider everything that Emily had told her. A nasty hostile little alter ego that whispered doubts about coincidence and odd timings, and made her wonder about her own sister, began to blossom inside her. And if Emily's story was threaded with evasions and lies, then that suggested she might have been planning to meet Sam Webster all along. She might have been well aware from the start that the dead man was him. Was it remotely thinkable that she had been having an affair with him? Or that there had been some incomprehensible business between them that led to his being murdered by somebody known to her sister? She permitted herself to give these outrageous notions some consideration, only to hit a brick wall at every turn. Emily was too much of a conformist, too obsessed with her status and image, for any such scenario to be worth a moment's serious attention. And Thea would stake her own status and credibility on the sure and certain knowledge that Emily had not known the dead man was Sam Webster. Her tone during Monday's phone conversation convinced her of that much at least. Whatever else she might have fibbed about, that single fact was rock solid in Thea's mind.

She had missed lunch without even noticing, hunger finally sending her into Stow for some hasty food shopping. It was well past two when she got back to Hawkhill and let the dog out of the car for some much needed exercise. Before she had taken a step away from her car, another vehicle followed her into the yard.

It was Phil, peering at her from under the lowered sun visor, his face serious. She was aware of a need to rally herself, to assemble her thoughts and guard her emotions. Her boyfriend suddenly seemed threatening, a source of anxiety and shame. *How sad*, she thought, forcing herself to smile.

'Where've you been?' he demanded. 'I was waiting for you.'

'Were you?' She frowned. 'But you've only just got here.'

'No, I haven't. I was parked across the road, where I could keep an eye on things. You came from the other direction,' he added accusingly.

'So?'

'So I suspect you've been trying to do a bit of detecting for yourself. Where have you been?'

She tried to review her route since leaving the main road. 'Shopping, actually. I passed this spot twenty minutes ago. You weren't here then. I'd have noticed.'

He shrugged. 'Never mind that now.' He seemed to be making some sort of effort. 'It's nice to see you,' he offered.

'And you.'

They were like two particularly wooden actors, trying to present themselves as lovers. It wouldn't have convinced anybody. Even Hepzie seemed to be eyeing them with a degree of scepticism.

'So what's been happening?' he asked her.

'Well, the Galton man came back last night, very heavy and intimidating. If you hadn't been here on Sunday he'd have shot the dogs, you know. He said as much. He still wants them destroyed.'

Phil was a lot less alarmed by this than she would have liked. 'He does have a point. Have you ever seen a sheep after dogs have been at it? It's sickening. Plus they were his rams – worth hundreds of quid each, probably. It could delay next year's lambing, and lose him thousands. You can't blame him for being angry.'

'No, but he doesn't have to take it out on innocent animals. Do you know a man called Lister, by the way?'

He paused and then shook his head. 'Who is he?'

'Apparently it was him who dobbed us in it. I met him a few minutes after the dogs escaped, and he must have gone straight over to Galton and told him. Nasty little man – I didn't like him, even at the time.'

'And the other little matter? Where a man was kicked to death less than a mile away? Have you thought any more about that?'

'Oh yes. For a start, you never told me how close to this place it was. I'd imagined something miles away. That hotel is this side of Upper Slaughter, and I see the scene of the crime is even closer.'

'That's right. Practically within shouting distance, you might say.'

She shuddered. 'Well, I didn't hear any shouting. I was in the house with the curtains drawn, minding my own business.'

'Quite right,' he approved, his expression slightly warmer.

'Oh, and guess who I saw this morning.' Here was safer ground at last, she thought. Knowing he wouldn't even try to guess, she went on, 'Ariadne. Your boyhood chum from Cold Aston.' And then she realised it wasn't really safer ground at all.

'She wasn't my chum when I was a boy. I was nearly twenty when I first met her.'

'Really? I thought it was younger. Whatever – she's doing all right for herself these days.'

'Has she still got those terrible stripes in her hair?'

'Not at all. It's completely different now.' She found she did not want to say any more, the subject of the Reverend Peter Clarke to be avoided at all costs.

'And was she pleased to see you?'

'At first, yes. But then – well, we don't really have anything in common, after all. I didn't stay very long.'

'Thea,' he sighed. 'You're being very strange today. I know, of course, that Mary – Ariadne – is seeing Peter Clarke. He's the murder victim's brother. We've been delving into his life from every angle since Sunday morning. Obviously, he's a suspect. Apart from anything else, he's next of kin and stands to inherit a very nice house in Oxford and a healthy bank account.'

She felt cornered, and reacted with all the defensiveness of an irate rat. 'I didn't know whether to believe her. It seems such an unlikely relationship. Him a vicar and her a practising pagan. Besides, she's bigger than him.'

'You've met him?' The astonishment in his eyes was almost funny.

'Twice, actually.'

'Well, I have to admit you work quickly. Does he know about you and Emily being sisters?'

'Yes.'

'I suppose it all seems nice and symmetrical to you. I suppose he was all blue-eyed charm and wounded brotherly feelings.'

The scorn in his tone startled her. 'What do you mean?'

'The man's a disgrace to his cloth. Ten years ago he was within inches of being defrocked, or whatever they call it, and managed to wangle a stay of execution on condition he buggered off to Africa. The trouble is, the Anglican Church is every bit as rigorous and righteous in Zambia as it is here – more so, if anything. His smarmy ways finally got on their nerves as well, and he was sent packing at the end of last year.'

'You can't fire somebody for being smarmy,' she objected.

'He's worse than that. He's a liar and a cheat. He got involved in a very dodgy adoption agency, finding homes for AIDS orphans, with a lot of money changing hands.'

Thea reran her exchange with Peter, his obvious suffering, his natural friendly manner. It failed totally to gel with what Phil was telling her. 'No,' she said. 'You must have got it wrong. What about his little girl, and his dead wife?'

'Oh yes, there's a dead wife all right. The child isn't his, though. Do you know where she is now?'

Thea shook her head.

'At boarding school in Cheltenham. At seven years old, in a strange country. Paid for by the long-suffering C of E.'

'But it's summer. She can't be at school now.'

'Right. But is she with her devoted Daddy? Not a bit of it. She's parked with his very ancient mother, who probably doesn't know what's hit her.'

'But his mother's senile! And the child *is* legally his. He adopted her when he married her mother, who is now dead of AIDS.'

His eyes widened. 'My God, you did have a

153

long talk with him, didn't you? You've got the whole story out of him. In fact, the mother's not senile at all, just old. We found her and the child playing a nifty game of ping-pong in the garden when we went to see her.'

Of course, Thea realised, the police would have to speak to Webster's mother. Peter Clarke's prevarications about informing her what had happened had been groundless. The falsities in what he had told her were emerging too quickly for her to assimilate. One factor stood above the others. 'Poor Ariadne!' she gasped. 'He's stringing her along, then? It's all some sort of horrible act?'

Phil raised his shoulders helplessly. 'Who can say? She's a handsome girl, with a good heart. Maybe he really has fallen for her.'

'And you think he killed his brother?'

'I'd love to think so – it would make my life very smooth. But unfortunately he seems to have a very convincing alibi.'

'Oh?'

'Yes, on Saturday evening, he was dining with the rector of St John the Baptist Church in Cirencester. He arrived at nine, perfectly calm and clean, ready for a rather formal encounter with some Diocesan bigwigs.'

'Oh,' said Thea.

Phil stayed just over an hour, sharing a pot of tea and some quickly prepared sandwiches which served as a combination of lunch and afternoon tea for both of them. They did not discuss the murder investigation any further, despite Thea's continuing concern over her sister's role in the matter. Instead, Phil asked after her mother, and how she was dealing with her new situation.

'She'll be all right,' Thea assured him. 'She's of a generation that doesn't like to make a fuss. Mind you, she lost it a bit over the weekend. I had to speak sternly to her.'

He laughed at that. 'What – told her to pull herself together, did you?'

'Yes, more or less. It wasn't as bad as it sounds. She understands me pretty well. I was just giving her some friendly advice. After all, there's nothing worse than self-pity.'

'I can think of plenty of worse things, but I know what you mean. It's very unattractive.'

They both remembered that Phil himself had indulged in this regrettable emotion quite a lot when his back was first damaged. Thea had told him to pull himself together, as well.

'So you think the dogs will be all right, do you?' Her worry about them was never far from her mind. 'I wouldn't trust that Galton man not to sneak over here when I'm out and shoot them.'

'My guess is he'd have done it by now if he was going to. The first white-hot rage will have died down after the first few hours. But he won't hesitate if he sees them loose again. I've been remembering more about him from college. He always had a quick temper, but being so big, he had to learn to keep it in check. It was a hard lesson–' he stopped, plainly censoring himself.

'Oh? That sounds as if there's a story.'

'Nothing much.' He eyed her thoughtfully. 'He hit another boy, a lot harder than he intended,

155

and broke his nose. There was quite a bit of trouble over it, but it calmed down in the end. I doubt very much if he's ever done it again. He's very decent at heart.'

'I feel sorry for big men. They're like big dogs, aren't they? Always having to stop and think before they do anything, in case they cause some damage. It must be awful.'

'I guess it's a matter of training in both cases.'

The reference to dogs returned them to their contemplation of Freddy and Basil. Thea sighed. 'It's not much of a life for the poor things, is it? I mean – why keep them if they have to be chained up the whole time? It's cruel.'

'It's also very common. I'd guess half the dogs in the country never get to have a proper run in their lives. They certainly don't have a chance to chase anything out in the countryside. They've come a long way since their wolf ancestors roamed the land.'

'Cats have done better, on the whole, haven't they. They take what they want from people, while making very few compromises.'

He made an effort to engage fully in the conversation, pointing out that a lot of cats were confined within four walls much as dogs were – especially in towns and cities. 'But I guess their survival instincts are in better shape than dogs', all the same,' he concluded.

After a pause, he began on a new topic. 'So there's no prospect of anybody coming to join you, then? You've got to get along on your own for a change.'

She snorted. 'You make it sound as if I'll find

that difficult. I'll be perfectly all right.'

'I hope so. If I remember rightly, this is the first time for over a year that you'll have gone without somebody to share at least part of the stay with you.'

'You're here,' she said lightly. 'I'm assuming you'll drop in like this, from time to time.'

'Are you?'

His voice was low, and he was looking at the floor, one hand holding the mug of tea. How could there be so much to scare her in those two small syllables? Something flexed and swelled inside her, and she stared hard at him. Her heart thundered and the air turned cold.

'Phil? What are you trying to say?'

He looked cold, too. 'Only that I don't feel sure of a welcome. You didn't kiss me when I arrived. You've hardly smiled at me. You weren't going to tell me about Ariadne and the vicar. What's going on, Thea? I'm not stupid, you know. I can read the signs of indifference as well as anybody.'

She desperately did not want to have this conversation. It was one thing to fantasise about another man, and to feel guilty about it, quite another to be confronted with the apparent end of a relationship which meant a lot to her. The chill wind of abandonment blew round her, and she reached out like a child whose hand has been dropped by its mother.

'No,' she said. 'Don't say that. I'm sorry. I didn't mean – I'm not *indifferent*. Not at all.' She stopped herself from employing the excuse of her dead father, because not only would that be playing dirty, it would carry little weight, since

157

they both knew the problem went back much further than that.

'You haven't felt the same about me since Temple Guiting,' he said flatly. 'I don't blame you. I know it was annoying having me laid up with my back. But I couldn't help it, Thea. Accidents happen to people – you can't blame them for getting hurt.'

She had always regarded herself as unusually mature and understanding. She, Thea Osborne, had interceded with people in a calm collected way, seeing through to the core of things, pointing out the bullshit that people employed to hide their real feelings. Now she felt like a child, a selfish blinkered child, letting her own frustrations wound a perfectly good man.

'I'm sorry,' she said again. 'I've behaved very badly.'

'No,' he sighed heavily. 'No, you haven't. I've asked too much of you. You gave up those weeks to stay with me in Cirencester and nurse me. You've never said a word about the sex – not having any, I mean. But you have been pushing me away more and more, whether you realise it or not. Every time I try to get near you, you go all chilly and withdrawn. So how much more of it can we take? Either of us, I mean. It's not exactly a barrel of laughs these days, is it?'

'If we were being grown up about it, we'd accept that there are bound to be down times.'

'That's true. But I'm wondering how solid a foundation there is to cope with down times. I mean – won't we both be asking ourselves what the point is, if we're not having fun any more?'

She looked him full in the face. 'It is all my fault,' she insisted. 'You wouldn't be saying any of this if I hadn't gone chilly on you.'

'I don't think blame comes into it. We never made any rules or promises.' He scratched his head uncomfortably. 'I want to say some things that will sound accusing and unkind. I don't mean them that way.'

'Go on,' she invited, feeling intense resistance to whatever he might be planning to say, but knowing she had to let him say it.

'Well – I think that for you the sex was the main thing. Neither of us realised it until my back put a stop to it. And I know we weren't at it five times a week–'

'Far from it,' she interrupted.

'Yes, I know. But it was something to look forward to, something we got a lot of pleasure from. And I'm not saying I wouldn't miss it terribly if it stopped altogether. But without it I'm not sure what else we've got.'

'We've had a whole string of murders to pre-occupy us. You've been very generous in letting me share in the investigations–'

'I'm not sure I could have stopped you,' he said with a wry smile. 'Besides, you were darn useful most of the time.'

'Yes, and a bloody nuisance at other times. I know. Which is why I don't know where I stand with this one. It's more personal to me than any of the others, and yet I feel very much detached from it.'

'My problem is,' he scratched his head again, 'you always seem so *vulnerable*. My instincts are

159

to protect you. And then I find out you can take perfectly good care of yourself, and it's just as likely to be me that ends up getting hurt.'

'Which we both know is no good basis for a serious relationship,' she summarised sadly. 'But I hate to think of it finishing. I'd be bereft.'

'We don't have to do anything drastic – I hope we're adult enough to disengage in a civilised manner. It's just – well, you don't have to feel I have exclusive rights.' He smiled into her eyes, suddenly fatherly and understanding. 'I wouldn't throw too violent a fit if you slept with someone else, for example.' It should have been what she wanted to hear, and yet it felt like rejection. He no longer felt she was his special partner. The pill was all the more bitter because she couldn't pretend to herself that he had some other sexual partner waiting in the wings. With his malfunctioning back, he could hardly be plotting to introduce another woman into his bed the moment he'd squared it with Thea. It was all much worse than that: he was being unbearably generous, releasing her to find what satisfaction she might with somebody other than him.

A tear escaped from the corner of her eye. 'Stop being so nice about it,' she sniffed.

'Oh, Thea,' he groaned, and took her to himself for a tight hug. 'What are we going to do with you?'

He could not have said anything more effective in giving her strength. She nuzzled briefly into his chest, and then pulled away. 'I'll be fine,' she said. 'You're absolutely right about everything. I've got to sort myself out and decide what I really want. In spite of how it might seem, I do like this house-sitting work. I like the different animals and the villages and the sense of adventure. The money's not brilliant, but it keeps me afloat. And surprising as it might seem, I'm in quite big demand.'

This time they both laughed. The growing number of crises during Thea's various commissions might be expected to ruin her for future work. Instead, she seemed to have a reputation for holding the fort, keeping her nerve and bringing order out of chaos. Nobody blamed her for the awful things that had happened, and each time she seemed to have emerged with an enhanced image.

'It's no laughing matter,' came a stern voice from the next room. Thea and Phil both froze for a moment, until she remembered Ignatius.

'It's the parrot,' she said. 'I don't think I'll ever get used to him. He says the most amazing things.'

'It all works by association,' said Phil knowledgeably. 'If he hears laughing, he'll remember what somebody once said about it not being a laughing matter. It's not as clever as it seems.'

'Hmm,' said Thea.

Phil left at about five, and Thea did the rounds of the animals, talking quietly to them, watching the ferrets for a few minutes. She was trying hard to persuade herself that this was all she needed right at this moment. If she had lost Phil, and been shown that she could not have Peter Clarke, then so be it. She had a big family, several friends, plenty of interests. She had her health and her looks and enough money. Where was the problem?

The immediate problem mainly lay, not with Det Supt Phil Hollis, but with Ariadne Fletcher and the Reverend Peter Clarke. It had been painful and shocking to be ordered out of the house by Ariadne because of a perceived challenge to her relationship with the vicar. Not since the fourth year at school had she contested with another girl for a man. It was undignified and embarrassing. It demeaned the man, too, by implying he could be taken by the triumphant female, regardless of his own actual preference. Besides, she knew perfectly well that she was one of those women who would choose to maintain a loyal friendship with someone of her own sex rather than make an enemy in order to get a man.

But her friendships had also proved less robust than she might have expected, since Carl died. Those closely bonded sisterhoods of the late teens and early twenties had worn thin under the weight of marriages and children and work and relocations. There was nobody she could readily phone for a heart-to-heart at that precise moment, and this struck her as a serious piece of carelessness on her part. 'I've got lots of friends,' she had often said and believed. The truth was, she knew a number of people, but very few of them would set other claims aside in order to be available to Thea Osborne, that pretty girl from school who'd lost her husband so young.

Which left sisters. Jocelyn and Emily. Both of them very much taken up with their own demanding lives, but the careless intimacy of siblings ensured that they could be leant on in times of need. And vice versa, of course. Just now, Emily was the needy one, and Thea ought to brace up to this reality. She felt a renewed surge of determination to help find Sam Webster's killer. She would have liked to summon her sister back and make her explain the holes in her story that Phil had pointed out. But Lower Slaughter was going to have gruesome associations for Emily for the rest of her life, and she was highly unlikely to voluntarily show her face again in the village. There was, if Phil could be believed, even an element of risk attached to doing so. If the killer had learnt who the sole witness to the murder was, then he might be tempted to silence her. A man capable of such a vicious and sustained attack was a man to be feared, despite Thea's tendency to dismiss warnings of danger.

An hour or two passed with mundane chores, eating a scrappy supper and assembling a healthy section of the jigsaw, which included the off-white sheep in the snow, and a broken old gate. Then two car doors slammed outside, and two pairs of feet walked to the front door.

CHAPTER THIRTEEN

It was Ariadne and Peter, she the taller by a good two inches, but he the more vivid presence by some margin. He spoke first. 'I understand you two know each other,' he began. 'And there's been a bit of a falling out. It seems to me that we can't let that situation persist, so we've come to bury the hatchet.'

All the damning things that Phil had told her came urgently to mind. He was 'smarmy' and deceitful. He had been dismissed from at least two posts in the Church and was here on sufferance because there was nobody else. She met the blue eyes, the frank smile, and could do little else but believe the evidence of her own senses. He was a lovely man.

'Come in,' she invited quickly. 'It's great to see you both.' She looked then at Ariadne, who seemed young and vulnerable, her emotions so naked and needy. She was also rather sheepish, after the way she'd spoken to Thea that morning. Thea herself felt relieved to the point of weakness that things seemed to have come right again between them so quickly.

She found them some olives and white wine that had been in the box of provisions she'd bought in Stow. The grubby living room with its poor lighting served as a surprisingly cosy venue for the intimate exchanges that followed. It was as if some layers of reticence had been shed at the door, leaving no necessity for caution. After all, she and Ariadne had shared some visceral moments less than a year before, and if Peter had such a convincing alibi for Saturday, there was no need to regard him with any suspicion over his brother's murder.

'Hey – a parrot!' cried Ariadne, spotting Ignatius. 'Does it talk?'

'Oh yes,' Thea assured her. 'He talks all right. But he doesn't seem to be in the mood just now.' Ignatius was hunched morosely on his perch, eyes almost closed, ignoring the activity in the room.

They wasted no more time in small talk. 'We want to tell you about Sam,' said Peter. 'Given that it was your sister who witnessed his final moments, it seems as if we owe you a bit of an explanation.'

'I'm sure you don't, but I'm happy to listen,' Thea said. 'You'll know about my involvement with Detective Superintendent Phil Hollis, of course?'

'Oh yeah – everybody knows everybody,' said Ariadne with a sigh. 'That's the trouble.'

'Well, we don't know who the monster was who smashed Sam's head in,' said Peter. 'I'm not at all confident that he'll ever be caught.'

'Oh, he will,' said Thea, surprising herself at the confident tone. 'If he's as crazy and out of control as it sounds, then he'll give himself away. Probably sooner rather than later.'

'You mean because he'll do it again?' Ariadne sounded scared.

'No, no,' Thea said quickly. 'He can't be *that* crazy.'

Peter took over from her, his voice was thick, and his hand went to his mouth. 'His body was such a mess. I've never seen anything like that before. They cleaned him up as well as they could, but with his skull so shattered – well, I honestly couldn't say for sure that it was him. Not from his face. It was his hands that clinched it. He had very long fingers and a slightly odd joint at the base of his thumb. He broke the scaphoid bone when he was ten and it was missed, so it mended crooked.' Thea recognised the outpouring of irrelevant detail as a reaction to trauma.

'Phil said his hands weren't hurt at all,' she said, without stopping to think.

'That's right. I assume that means it was all over before he had a chance to defend himself.' He was restless, fiddling with a spoon and kicking one foot against a table leg. 'Poor old Sam.'

Ariadne reached out a hand to him, while looking at Thea. 'Do we have to talk about it?' she asked. 'It's not very easy to take, you know.'

Did she mean for herself or Peter, Thea wondered? The reproach was no less real for being so gentle.

'Sorry,' she said.

'No, no, it's all right. We have to talk about it,' said Peter, giving Ariadne's hand a warm squeeze. 'I think our stomachs can take it.'

There were questions breeding more questions in the air between them. What was Peter Clarke really like? How did he really feel about Ariadne?

166

How much did he care about his brother's death? And why had Thea assumed that it was jealousy that had motivated Ariadne's angry ejection of her earlier in the day? Was it not arrogant of her, Thea, to make such an assumption, with virtually nothing to support it? It had been the reference to Emily that had done the damage, she remembered – and how could that connect to Peter?

'Can I say something about my sister first?' she asked, looking at Ariadne. At a nod, she went on, 'It's the fact that she was there that somehow made you angry, and I don't understand why.'

'Nor do I, now I've calmed down,' admitted the woman. 'It seemed to give you some special claim, I suppose. It meant you had a place in the inner circle, and I didn't. I just flipped. When I told Peter, he couldn't understand it, either.' She gave a giggle, which sat uneasily on her statuesque frame. 'Can we just say I've been in a funny sort of mood for a while now? I never quite know how I'm going to react.'

Peter patted her hand and smiled indulgently at her. Thea began to wonder how much of such mush she could take. The word *smarmy* came to mind again. But why in the world should he pretend to be in love with Ariadne if he wasn't? She had no great riches or influence, she could be awkward and inclined to utter outspoken remarks that made people uncomfortable. And she *was* genuinely lovable, as Thea had discovered for herself. She could do no other than believe him, just as Ariadne so obviously did.

'And the coincidence seemed all wrong, somehow,' Ariadne continued. 'Peter's brother and

167

your sister, out of all the people in Gloucester-shire, involved in such a bizarre incident right here on a wild wet night. It's just so *unlikely*.'

'It *was* wet, wasn't it,' she said deliberately. 'It was really pouring when Emily left here. That's why I didn't watch her go, and didn't give her proper directions for getting back to the main road.'

'The layby was very muddy,' agreed Peter. 'It washed away most of the tyre marks.'

Thea frowned. 'What tyre marks?'

'Oh – none directly concerned with his death. But cars use laybys, don't they? Especially all the tourists in the summer, stopping to look at their maps. And the view's not bad from there, either. There was a dirty great puddle. He was more or less lying in it.'

'The police told you that, did they?' She tried to keep the question light, while inwardly tense with this unexpected revelation that had not been lost in the little rush of verbiage that Peter came up with. How did he know what the layby was like?

'That's right,' he said, just as lightly. 'They had to explain why Sam was so muddy.'

That could make sense, she assured herself. They'd have wanted the body identified before the post-mortem – although she wasn't clear about the precise sequence of events on Sunday. She resisted the urge to ask him, not wanting to make any more of his slip – if it was a slip. Catching Ariadne's eye, she did her best to mask the suspicions that were rumbling just below the surface.

'So the murderer would have been all muddy as well as covered with blood,' she said.

'Right,' said Peter with a firm glance at his beloved.

Thea's thoughts turned unbidden to the mud on the dogs, Freddy and Basil, when they finally returned from their escapade. Could it be that it indicated their guilt, after all, just as it would on the mysterious human murderer?

And of course Peter Clarke could not have been covered in mud when he turned up at the Diocese Meeting or whatever it was, by nine that evening. He had to have been crisp and clean and calm, or somebody would have noticed and told the police when the alibi was checked.

Emily's description of the attack had been brutally clear. Phil had not given any further detail, but neither had he said anything to contradict the basic story. Emily had still been shaking and white-faced some hours later, repeating herself and muddling the chronology. 'The man who did it – do they think he had a car, then?' Thea asked.

'Presumably he must have done. I don't remember anybody saying anything about it, though.'

'No,' said Thea slowly. 'Emily didn't mention it, either. She just said he ran away when she yelled at him.' She had an image of the sudden cessation of the kicks and blows, the aggressor fleeing jerkily into the wet night. It was almost as if she had witnessed it herself. 'It must have been terrifying,' she added. 'Thinking he might come back, as she knelt by your brother.'

'She acted quite sensibly, calling 999 and not moving anything,' Peter said. 'After all, you never know how you'll behave in a crisis as horrible as that.'

There was a nausea developing somewhere in her middle, and she wanted quite badly to change the subject. Ironic, when she'd been the one to insist on gory detail. Much of her initial trust and confidence in Peter Clarke had been restored. Whatever Phil might have told her about the trouble he'd been in with the church, she could not believe he was a conman when it came to emotional matters. She believed what he'd said about his wife and the little girl, the brief glimpses of his childhood. But then she remembered the discrepancy over his mother. That had certainly been a deviation from the truth.

'Your daughter,' she blurted abruptly. 'Where is she?'

'Daisy? Oh, she's with my mother. They're great friends.'

'Your mother can cope then, can she? I thought you said she was almost incapable when we talked yesterday.'

'I said nothing of the sort. What do you mean?'

'You were dreading telling her about Sam. Of course, the police would have told her by then, anyway.'

'I had no idea of that. It never occurred to me.'

'Thea!' Ariadne remonstrated. 'Why the third degree, all of a sudden? Why does it matter what Peter said about his *mother?*'

It was a good question, if slightly odd in its

170

emphasis. 'Sorry,' she smiled. 'I just wanted to get the picture straight in my mind.'

'It was Phil, I suppose, seeing the dark side as usual. What's he been telling you?'

'It doesn't matter.'

The other woman was onto her in a flash, simply from the way she said those words. 'Hey! Something's gone wrong between you two, has it? And there was me thinking you'd be making an announcement any day now.'

Thea grimaced. 'What – you thought I was going to marry him?'

'Maybe not that, but moving in with him. You seemed so *together*, last year. What went wrong?'

'He slipped a disc,' said Thea sourly.

'Oh, yes, you told me.' Ariadne stifled a giggle and looked to Peter for rescue. The vicar was clearly not keeping up. 'Phil?' he queried. 'That's the police chap, is it?'

'Hollis,' Ariadne confirmed. 'Detective Superintendent. I told you – I've known him since I was a kid.'

'Small world,' said Peter. 'I feel as if I've walked into a very tight little community here.'

Thea felt suddenly weak. She wanted to hear more about Webster, while leaving Emily out of the conversation. She wanted to understand the jumble of feelings aroused by Peter Clarke. And she wanted to hang on to Ariadne as a friend and confidante. But it all felt out of reach. One or both of the others were in control of this conversation, effortlessly diverting it away from anything important and the struggle to guide it back was proving exhausting.

But at least she seemed to have her friend back. 'It was very nice of you to come,' she said, sounding pathetic in her own ears. 'I was upset to think I'd made you cross.'

Ariadne waved a dismissive hand. 'We've sorted all that,' she said, 'Don't say another word about it. I was a cow, and that's all there is to it.'

Thea watched Peter's reaction to this. It was very much as she'd expected. 'Hey, don't do yourself down,' he reproached his girlfriend. 'You've explained what you were thinking, and it makes perfect sense to me.'

Smarmy, thought Thea. *Definitely*. It gave her a small sense of relief to know that this man she might have thrown herself at was actually less desirable than she'd first thought.

'We'd better go,' said Ariadne. 'I hope you're going to be all right?' she asked Thea. 'I mean – does this place have everything you need?'

It was an odd question, especially from a woman who lived in a cottage to which the concept of modernisation was entirely alien. It was always intriguing to discover what people thought about house-sitting: precisely who was doing who the favour, and what was the deal regarding food and facilities.

'It's comfortable enough,' she replied, looking round the dusty streaky walls and threadbare rugs. 'It reminds me of my granny's house, when I was very young. She had a rug just like that one.' She indicated a handmade rug, with tufts hooked through canvas. In some places the canvas had frayed, leaving holes, and the colours had faded. 'It's a bit of a time warp.'

'And you just love to be surrounded by dogs,' Ariadne teased.

Thea groaned. 'Not this time. Those dogs have got me into some pretty deep trouble already.'

'Explain,' Ariadne ordered, settling back into the chair she'd been about to leave. Thea did as instructed, with gratifyingly serious results. 'My God, Thea – you don't want to mess with Henry Galton. He's practically the Squire of Lower Slaughter.'

'Too late,' said Thea. 'The damage is done – except I still maintain that Freddy and Basil are innocent.'

'Freddy and Basil – is that their names?'

'No, not really. I don't know their real names, so I rechristened them.'

'You're mad.'

'Aren't we all?' grinned Thea unrepentantly. 'Anyway, I don't think the Galton man is as bad as he'd like me to think. He calmed down eventually, when it got past the point where he might have shot them out of hand.'

Ariadne made a sceptical face, which did nothing for Thea's peace of mind. Peter Clarke, listening quietly, finally made a contribution. 'They'd have been shot on sight in Africa,' he said.

'They would have been here as well, if Galton had been able to catch them,' Ariadne assured him. 'It happens all the time – the law's on the side of the sheep farmer even these days. And – well, Thea, I hate to say this, but it does sound bad. I mean, it all points to them having done the worrying, doesn't it? I don't want to alarm you,

173

but I think you'll find you haven't heard the last of it.'

It was an unsettling note to end on, but nobody appeared able to think of a new topic. The visitors got up to leave, and Thea resigned herself to a quiet evening with the spaniel and parrot for company.

'Lock the doors, Daddy! Lock the doors!' cried Ignatius, suddenly waking up and noticing that something was going on.

'Good God!' gasped Peter. 'That's extraordinary. I've never heard a parrot say a whole sentence like that.'

'Didn't you have parrots in Africa?' Ariadne asked him.

'Of course not. They're in South America and Australia, not Africa.' He didn't quite add *you idiot*, but the scorn hung unmistakably behind his words.

'What about the African Grey, then?' Thea asked. 'Where does that come from?'

'Doh – silly me,' he said, easily. 'But I've never seen one.'

She watched them go without regret. They'd given her more than enough to think about for one evening.

CHAPTER FOURTEEN

When Wednesday morning dawned almost as wet as the previous one, Thea's spirits sank. What was a person supposed to do in a rainy Lower Slaughter? Abandon it, she concluded, for somewhere that had more indoor facilities to offer. A library or a museum or even, in a real emergency, a cinema. There were numerous attractive pubs in every direction, but she had never seen any appeal in sitting alone in a bar, whether it be crowded or deserted.

The 'fine by eleven' rule worked at least to the extent that the rain turned to a very English mizzle, but not enough to persuade Freddy and Basil to emerge from their dogwood shelter. Poor things, Thea thought for the fiftieth time. What a rotten life they lead.

Her mobile chirruped at her at half past eleven. A man's voice said 'Thea?'

She knew she knew him, a familiar voice that she just couldn't name for a moment. Damien? Uncle James? 'Bruce!' she finally managed. 'What a surprise!'

Her sister's husband was phoning her on a mobile number she couldn't believe he knew. 'How did you get my number?'

'It's on our pad by the phone,' he said, as if this was obvious. 'Listen – I want to talk to you. Can you get away for lunch?' He spoke hurriedly, his voice low, as if expecting to be caught at any moment.

'Today?'

'Absolutely today. There's a pub in Lower Oddington. The Fox, it's called. It's got virginia creeper all over it and flowers. Do you think you could get there for – say – twelve fifteen?'

'I suppose so, except I've never been there.'

'It's east of you, on the A436. Go to Stow and turn right. It's easy enough. If you get to Adelstrop, you've gone too far. But be aware that there are three Oddingtons, and you want the third one. Turn right at the sign for Lower Oddington, and the pub's a little way along there on the right.'

'This is very cloak and dagger, Bruce. Is there a password I have to say at the door?'

His sigh caused a slight turbulence in her ear. 'Sorry,' she said. 'I can tell it's something important. I'll set off in ten minutes – will that get me there in time?'

'Easily, if you don't get lost.'

She didn't get lost, and found Bruce sitting in his distinctive black 1978 Jaguar in the street outside the self-consciously traditional Cotswold pub. 'You'll never make a spy if you insist on driving that thing,' she said, once they were within speaking distance. 'It must stand out a mile on the CCTV and satellite surveillance systems.'

'It doesn't matter,' he said shortly. 'I haven't got anything to hide.'

She refrained from launching into her customary diatribe to the effect that there wasn't a person alive who could honestly say that. And

176

even if there was, why did that make it all right for Big Brother to track his every move?

Leaving Hepzie yet again in the car, they settled down in the fox-obsessed bar, having ordered beer and baguettes, and Bruce wasted no time in getting to the point. 'I need your help with Emily. She isn't sleeping and looks like death. I have no idea what to do for the best.'

'How should *I* know?' she flashed. 'I'd have thought a husband trumped a sister when it came to that sort of thing.' Bruce had always been essentially useless in a crisis, she remembered. When Emily miscarried their first baby, Bruce had become a neurotic mess, leaving others to support his wife through her misery. Over the years, the habit of shielding Bruce from anything unpleasant had spread through the family, despite mutterings about how over-protective they were being. His vulnerability had a dreadful power, which none of them was strong enough to resist.

Now he gathered his dignity, raising his chin and meeting her eye. 'Not at all. If it's grief over your father that's affecting her so badly, then you're in a much better position to understand than I am. After all, isn't that why she drove over to see you on Saturday?'

She had almost forgotten about her father, she realised to her shame. 'But what if it isn't about Dad?' she said. 'What if it's about your friend Sam Webster?'

The idea seemed to surprise him. 'Sam? But Emily has no reason to care particularly about him.'

177

Thea blinked. Was it possible that Bruce knew nothing of what had happened? 'Um – Bruce – you do know he was killed on Saturday evening, don't you? Emily *did* tell you what happened?'

'Of course she did. Damned bad luck, in one sense. But she did the right thing, scaring the chap away by blaring her car horn at him. For all we know he might have decided to have a go at her as well.'

Thea tilted her head thoughtfully. Had she heard the bit about the car horn? If not, did it matter? 'I thought she yelled at him and that's what sent him off into the dark.'

'Bit of both, probably,' he said carelessly.

'But – she'd left the car in the gateway. How could she have sounded the horn?'

'Thea – I don't know. She didn't want to go over it all again. I had trouble enough getting the basic story. You know how much she hates anything unpleasant.'

A classic piece of transference, Thea noted complacently.

She left the matter of the car horn, assuring herself that there was scope for both versions to be true, as Bruce had claimed.

'So how well did you know him – Sam, I mean? Emily seems to think he was more your friend than hers.'

'That's perfectly true. We were at college together. He was always a clever clogs, but we both liked old cars and Alice Cooper and we were in a bit of a group together for a while. I always thought he'd end up working for MI5, with his brains. He would invent codes just for the fun of it.'

She realised she'd assumed that Webster's subject was something like History or European Literature. 'Was he a mathematician, then?'

'Didn't you know? I thought you met him that time at one of our dinner parties?'

'Yes, I knew he was a don. But I don't remember asking him what his subject was. He talked about Proust mostly, if I've remembered right.' She paused to assemble her thoughts. 'Are you sure he didn't? Work for MI5, I mean. Maybe the Oxford thing was just a cover. He must have had plenty of money, to afford to stay at that Manor Hotel place. You should see it – it's like a castle!'

Bruce laughed. 'I'm fairly sure he wasn't with MI5, yes. Why – do you think he was murdered because he was working for a secret organisation? The way I see it, it was some drug-crazed psycho, choosing a victim at random, assuming anybody at that hotel must be carrying a wallet full of cash.'

'Was anything stolen?' Oughtn't she have asked Phil that question, she rebuked herself. Nobody had said anything about robbery, which now seemed rather strange.

'I have no idea.' Bruce had a small old-fashioned moustache, which he would nibble absently, catching at individual hairs and making his eyes water. Then he'd rub the sore spot with a finger. It was very distracting. 'To be honest, Thea, I agree with Emily – the less that's said, the quicker it'll all fade. The man's dead – that's all I need to know. I'll miss him, but we weren't exactly best buddies. I only saw him five or six times a year.'

'OK, but the fact remains that it was Emily who saw the whole thing, and it seems to me that it must have been pretty traumatic for her. And if I've got it right, you wanted to see me today precisely to talk about how upset she is. It might be about Dad, as you think, but it might just as easily be about Sam. Actually, I suppose it's a combination of the two. She's overloaded.'

'I probably haven't made myself clear. It's worse than just being upset. She's *ill*. She's like somebody having a breakdown. I don't know what to do about it.' He caught another moustache hair and trapped it against his lip in a complicated process that must have hurt.

'So call a doctor.'

Bruce closed his eyes in a give-me-patience sort of way. 'And what's a doctor going to say? Take some anti-depressants or sleeping pills and give yourself space to grieve. Why waste NHS money?'

For such a conventional man, Bruce could be surprisingly cynical, as Thea had discovered years before. He mistrusted institutions even more than she did herself, and the NHS had seldom earned a positive word from him, ever since his teenaged brother had died on a trolley from some obscure sort of blood poisoning. He didn't like the police very much, either, presumably because they carried such unpleasant associations with violence and lack of control and other dangerous aspects of human society.

'OK,' she tried again. 'From what Emily said on Saturday, it seems she feels guilty about Dad,

180

that she never said the things she meant to and now it's too late. She had a bit of a cry, and beat herself up for a bit, and then she seemed much better. It was all fairly normal stuff, as far as I could tell. She did have a more difficult relationship with him than the rest of us. He never seemed to approve of her quite as much – although I think she's exaggerated it tremendously, the way people do in families. It's turned into a myth in her own mind. If she'd ever managed to confront him about it, he'd have been mortified. I tried to tell her that.'

Bruce nodded dubiously. 'Good,' he murmured vaguely. 'Well, perhaps you're right that it was what happened next that sent her off the rails. Because she *is* off the rails, you see.' He looked forlorn and out of his depth, and oddly scared. Thea began to experience some reciprocal anxiety.

'Well, she didn't seem too bad on Sunday when she left. And then I spoke to her on the phone and she sounded all right. She went back to work, didn't she, on Monday?'

'I can't work it out. The police came on Sunday to tell us it was Sam, and that was obviously a big shock to both of us.' The moustache suffered a further attack, which presumably explained the tears in his eyes. 'But things were more or less normal on Monday morning. Then when I got home, she was weepy and distracted. Didn't make any proper supper and took no notice when Grant said he wanted to get his nipple pierced.'

'Gosh!' Thea murmured, with a wince of

physical pain in her own nipples at the very thought. 'That sounds bad.'

'Then she tossed and turned all night, and when she did fall asleep she woke us both up with a dream that had her shouting out loud.'

'It must have just hit her a bit belatedly. Delayed reaction.'

'Possibly,' he nodded. 'That's not really the point, though, is it? The point is what I am supposed to *do* about it?'

'Hold on. What's been happening between Monday night and now?'

'Well, Tuesday – yesterday – she said she couldn't face going to work. She would try and catch up with some sleep, and just stay quiet all day. I went off as usual, and when I got back last night, about half past six, she still wasn't dressed, and looked as if she'd done nothing but cry all day.'

'That's still fairly normal,' said Thea. 'All hitting her at once. It was a bit like that with me when Carl died. You have to get it out of your system.'

'And how long is it meant to take?'

'Is she still crying today?'

'No, she's trying to act normally, which is almost worse. All glittery smiles and jerky sentences. But she's so white and jumpy.'

'Well it sounds to me like plain old post-traumatic stress. After all, it's still terribly recent. She ought to talk to somebody professional, who can help her debrief. I wouldn't worry too much, Bruce. It'll all come right in the end.' A thought occurred to her. 'Although I suppose she might be scared that the killer will come and get her, in case she might be able to identify him. Did she say anything about that?'

'Not exactly, although that might explain the jumpiness. Any loud noise has her acting like a shell-shocked soldier.'

They'd talked right through their lunch, hardly noticing the food. The bar was well patronised, but most people were eating on a terrace outside, shielded from the damp day by an awning. It was the first time they'd been together, just the two of them, and Thea found him to be better company than she'd previously thought. There was something kind and solid about him; it was evident that he cared deeply for his suffering wife and was seeking advice on how best to help her.

'Encourage her to talk about it,' she offered. 'Not bottle it up.'

He looked doubtful again. 'Hasn't all that rather gone out of fashion? Don't we think now that bottling up has its uses? She obviously doesn't *want* to dredge it all up again.'

'Well, you won't be able to force her. Just let her know that you'll listen quietly if she wants to dump anything.' And it was a rare man who could manage to do that, she thought, with a twinge of envy at the knowledge that Bruce just might be one of them.

He sighed and nodded. 'I'll do my best. But honestly, Thea, she's in a real mess.'

'Poor old Em. She's always needed to be in control and have things predictable. She's the worst person I can think of to have this sort of thing happen.'

'And yet she coped magnificently. I told her that. She's got nothing to reproach herself for. She couldn't possibly have done anything else for poor old Sam. Everybody's going to think she acted heroically.'

'She ought to like that.'

He cocked his head at the hint of sarcasm. 'Well she doesn't like anything about it. She's utterly miserable.'

Misery was catching, and Thea found herself feeling pretty gloomy herself as she kissed Bruce goodbye and got back into her car.

The drive home passed in a blur as she mulled over everything Bruce had said. He had to be seriously worried to take an extra long lunch break and summon her as he'd done. Between Monday afternoon and Wednesday morning, Emily had apparently lost all composure, behaving alarmingly like a stereotypical madwoman. The speed of her collapse gave Thea an irrational hope that she would just as quickly recover. A momentary response to emotional overload, intimations of mortality, shock at the dreadful things that could happen – all had combined to send her reeling into a maelstrom of fear and guilt, but surely she'd come out of it again just as rapidly?

Poor old Em, she thought. And a tiny nasty voice muttered, *and about time too.* Emily had always been the one who pointed out other people's failings and weaknesses, how they brought trouble onto themselves, and everything could be traced back to some character defect.

Where Thea herself could be cavalier about trivial anxieties and excessive attention to danger, she hoped she was essentially kind enough to show sympathy for anyone in trouble. Jocelyn, however, the spoilt complacent youngest, who whined and complained at the unfairness of life, had nonetheless reared her five children in an atmosphere of good-natured affection. All three had had their share of setbacks and accidents – Thea outclassed the others by losing her husband to a speeding lorry, but Jocelyn had problems with her husband and Emily had suffered a miscarriage which came completely out of the blue, and which had left her and Bruce both very shaken.

They were all over forty, and might be considered grown up. The death of their father was a source of sadness, a good man gone forever, but they had rich memories of him and when a man in his seventies died, there was no great convulsion to the natural order of things. The sadness was a gentle sensation, not so much a source of pain as a reminder of the essential human condition. The conveyor belt of life moved inexorably and everyone sooner or later was tipped over the edge into the abyss. Emily's self-flagellation on Saturday had quickly passed. Thea had not seen it as a cause for concern. Her distress now could only be due to the death of Sam Webster – of that she was increasingly convinced.

She was pleased with the advice she'd given Bruce, confident that it was all that would be needed to set Emily right again, after a few more days. If the police managed to catch Sam

185

Webster's killer, that alone might be enough to calm her down – although the probable need for her to give testimony against him could be stressful.

Perhaps it was this thought that got her stomach roiling again. Small stabs of discomfort were occurring as she went over once more the account of how Webster had died. There was something unsettling about it, beyond the fact of the extreme violence employed. The filmic sequence in her mind only really acquired conviction at the point where the killer panicked and ran off into the darkness. That bit she could clearly visualise. The rest was still obscure – the kicking and shouting, the blood and brains and 999 call. The car parked in the gateway, the hooting horn and dauntless shouts – somehow that was harder to absorb. But it had to be true – Emily's car did have a scratch on it, as Thea had witnessed on Sunday morning, but it had not been muddy. Presumably the rain had washed everything off.

And then she was back on the small road to Lower Slaughter, choosing the one which took her through the village, and then off to the left for Hawkhill. Already it was familiar and easy, with no need to watch for landmarks or pause indecisively at junctions. She swept through the farm gates with an idea of taking Hepzie for a walk down a path labelled 'Warden's Way' on the map, well clear of Galton's sheep, and didn't notice for some minutes that there was something important missing.

CHAPTER FIFTEEN

The dogs had gone. Freddy and Basil were not on their chains, there were no welcoming barks, no friendly faces peering from their shed. Fighting to remain calm, Thea went all round the yard looking into the various sheds and logpiles, then did a circuit of the house, calling 'Dogs! Dogs!' across the weedy jungle that was the back garden.

They were not there. Their absence was tangible. Without even having to think about it, Thea piled herself and Hepzie back into the car and drove into the road, and quickly off again, down the track leading to Henry Galton's sheep farm. Quite how she knew the way, she could not explain, except that she had stared anxiously across the fields to the lambing sheds and hay barns several times over the past few days, until the geography was familiar. The track was bumpy with potholes and ruts, and longer than expected. It dived down into a hollow and then climbed up a final incline to the farmstead tucked into the lee of a gentle hill, facing south and sheltered on the other three sides. Even in her rage and panic, Thea had time to appreciate the clever siting, and the impressive age of the farm. The house was quite possibly Elizabethan, a modestly sized manor that had not been extended or modernised since its creation. By contrast, the farm buildings were considerably more recent and of poor quality. There were sheep on all sides, occupying many of the visible fields.

As she got out of the car, she caught her spaniel's eye. Sitting cheerfully on the passenger seat, Hepzie was entirely oblivious to the danger she was in. If Galton had kidnapped the other dogs and taken them into a barn to be shot, he might well decide to finish the job and grab the third marauder as well. Shakily, Thea removed the key from the ignition and locked the car. 'Stay there,' she mouthed at her dog. What if Hepzie had been left behind at Hawkhill when Thea went to Lower Oddington to meet Bruce? Would she now be a stiffening corpse in the corner of a dark shed as well?

But perhaps she'd arrived in time. Perhaps Galton was hesitating before he performed the execution. Perhaps he would, after all, abide by lawful procedure and wait until there was hard evidence against Freddy and Basil. And what would that evidence be? Matching toothmarks in the flesh of the sheep? DNA from the rams on the jaws of the dogs?

She marched determinedly to the front of the house and banged the brass door knocker loudly. Ten seconds later the door opened, and Galton stood there in socks, his hair tousled. 'What do you want?' he said with a puzzled frown. 'I've just been having a nap. Your car woke me. What time is it?'

'I don't know,' she said impatiently. 'Where are the dogs? What have you done with the dogs?'

He rubbed his face with a big hand. 'What

188

dogs? Wait a minute, I'm still half asleep. I've been all the way up to Shrewsbury and back today. Left at five, and got back just before two.' He turned and peered back into the house, where Thea could see a handsome grandfather clock in the hall. 'That was an hour ago, look. I haven't even had any lunch yet.'

She would not allow herself to doubt her own convictions. 'The dogs have gone,' she insisted. 'Who else would take them but you? Have you shot them yet?'

Galton seemed immensely more human than the last time she'd seen him. No longer intimidating, but genuinely bemused by her accusations, his story of the long drive might qualify as an alibi if Thea could accept it as true. 'Listen,' he said, 'you'd better come in and sit down and tell me what you think I've done.'

She followed him into the house, keeping her shoulders very square and her jaw tight. She was not going to take any nonsense from him, she promised herself. What he'd done put him completely in the wrong, and he should understand that. At the same time, concern for the dogs and the inevitable reactions from the Angells was undermining her resolve quite badly.

He led her into a big tidy kitchen, with a monumental Welsh dresser taking up one wall and a matchingly enormous old pine table in the middle. The floor and the worktops were slate. Did this man have a wife, she wondered for the first time? On the dresser the chunky china looked clean and expensively collectable. 'I need some tea,' said Galton. 'Wait while I make a pot.'

She had no idea what to say. Her accusations had been made, and it was for him to confess or deny his crime. Much too late, she wished she'd phoned Phil and told him what had happened. But what would he have said? That a search for lost dogs was slightly below his remit? That she ought to have realised this could happen and just be thankful Hepzie hadn't gone as well? For the first time, she felt the loss of him as somebody she could make unreasonable claims on. Now he was just a policeman, interested in anything connected with his murder investigation, but definitely no longer at her beck and call.

Galton set a large mug of tea before her, and laid a plate of chocolate biscuits where they could both reach it. Then he sat at right angles to her and looked at her fixedly for a moment. 'You are a very lovely woman,' he said as if only just noticing. 'I'm sorry if that sounds impertinent, but you are.'

And he was quite a handsome man, she conceded, with his big square head and thick springy hair. Though nothing like as attractive as Peter Clarke, of course. This man's eyes were a muddy mix of brown and green, not the vivid blue of the vicar's. She smiled carelessly, and flipped a hand at the compliment. 'So where are the dogs?' she said.

'You're going to have to believe me when I say I have no idea. I have not taken them, nor shot them. I've been too busy even to think about them. Those dead tups have to be replaced by the end of this month or my lambing schedule is shot to buggery. That's why I had to go to Shrewsbury and sort out a new lot. Luckily, it's all a done deal and they'll be here at the end of the week.'

'And are the dead ones insured?'

He nodded, with a grimace. 'After I've filled in about fifty different forms and persuaded the loss adjuster they were the best in the flock. And then the premium's going to rise and I lose my no claims. It's a bit different from claiming for a broken telly, I can tell you.'

'So where are the dogs?' She was beginning to sound repetitive, even to herself.

'I have absolutely no idea. Are we going to have to have this same exchange all day, because if so I warn you I'll get sick of it quite soon.'

'But – they've gone. I was out for two hours, two and a half maybe, and when I got back just now there was no sign of them. Somebody's undone their chains and taken them away.'

'Well it wasn't me.'

'Who else would do it? There's nobody else. It *must* have been you. Or somebody working for you.' She stared at him suspiciously. 'You must have people who work for you, farm hands. You'll have told one of them to do it.'

'No, I didn't. Sorry – but I don't know your name,' he said, suddenly. 'You never told me your name.'

'Thea Osborne.'

'And I'm Henry Galton.'

'Yes, I know.'

'And it's *Mrs* Osborne, is it?' He looked at the wedding ring she wore.

'Yes,' she said.

'Right. So now we've got that sorted, I'm not

191

sure there's any more to say. I can see I might owe you some sort of apology for shouting at you the other night. But in the circumstances I think I was justified. Even if I haven't stolen the dogs, I still think they're the ones who killed my tups. Could be the police agree with me, and they've taken them away. Unlikely, I grant you, but possible. Otherwise, I can't suggest any other explanation. People do steal dogs, of course. That'd be funny, if they were nicked for some fool who thinks they'd make good workers. That huntaway is a good-looking beast, once the mud's cleaned off him. Huntaways are worth a bit these days.'

'I'm surprised anybody's even heard of them – I hadn't until a week or two ago, when Mr Angell explained about them.'

'Well, my dear, you're not exactly part of the farming community, are you?'

The old familiar Galton was back, showing his nasty side, patronising and arrogant. She pushed her mug away and got up. 'I don't know what to do now,' she said quietly, almost to herself. 'Where do I start?'

'You believe me then?' Again he scrutinised her closely.

'I suppose I've got to, though I don't know why I should. You said you'd shoot them, you've got a gun – and now they've disappeared. It's all too much of a coincidence. And yet–'

'And yet it wasn't me. I might be a loud-mouthed bully, but I don't tell lies. Even my ex-wife would tell you that.'

She wasn't interested in his marital status, she discovered. He did nothing for her, not a flicker

192

of attraction could be discerned, as she met his eyes. He was a puzzle, affluent and yet an obvious manual worker; nicely spoken and yet unsophisticated. Was he the latest generation in a long line of lords of the manor, accustomed to respect and forgiveness from the locals, however outrageous his behaviour? He ought to have a gang of teenage sons at his heels, a wife fielding the phonecalls and pursuing some part-time career of her own. Instead it seemed he lived in the house alone, somehow keeping it clean and tidy while also running his vast flock of sheep. Across the yard was a huge barn, piled to the roof with massive bales of hay, each one a good three metres long and one wide. A tractor with a contraption at the front boasting long metal prongs stood close to the barn.

There must be a hundred places where two dead dogs could be hidden. There was even a JCB on a bank some distance away, apparently halfway through digging a new ditch. It would take less than a minute to dig a grave for Freddy and Basil, if necessary. And yet she found herself believing him, if only because he would want to proclaim the execution of the dogs, if it had indeed been carried out. He would be defiant and self-confident about it.

'OK,' she said. 'Well – could you let me know if you see them? Or hear anything about them?'

'If I see them loose on my land, I *will* shoot them,' he said calmly. 'Now I ought to get myself some food. And I suppose you'll have to contact Cedric and Babs and tell them what's happened.'

It hadn't even occurred to her. She stared at

him in horror. 'No – I can't do that.'

'Why not? They must have left you a number where you can reach them.'

'Yes – their son's in Hong Kong. But what would I *say?* It would only spoil their holiday for no good reason. I always think bad news can wait,' she added quietly.

'Well, it's not my business.' He turned away from her as if losing interest.

She forgot she'd locked the car and spent a few seconds wrenching in vain at the handle. Then she felt foolish, and hoped Galton wasn't watching.

'So what now?' she asked Hepzie.

She drove back, her mind almost blank. How did you begin to search for stolen dogs? Already they could be in the middle of Birmingham, confined in a cellar before being shipped to some sadistic buyer who might want them for dog fighting or vivisection. What possible course of action was open to her?

Just before she turned down the drive for Hawkhill, she saw in the road ahead a man with two large dogs on short leashes. For a crazy second, she persuaded herself they were Freddy and Basil, until she looked again and realised they were bigger and of a totally different hue.

The man was familiar, but she couldn't place him. Perhaps it was only that he had the animals, which were more or less what she had been hoping to find, that drew her attention to him. In any case, she braked and waited for him to come closer. He did not change his pace, walking with stiff legs, his arms out in front of him as he controlled the large beasts. They were fawn-coloured, short-haired and their shoulders were level with the man's hips.

Thea wound down her window, and restrained her own dog, which was eagerly trying to jump out for a frolic with these potential new friends. 'Hello,' she said. 'Haven't I seen you before?' Before she'd finished the question, she remembered. This was the man she had met on the footpath on Sunday afternoon, just after her charges had escaped. The man who told her they were highly likely to be shot. Somebody had mentioned his name to her – Lister! This was Lister, who turned out to be a dog-owner himself.

'You remember me, I'm sure,' he said, watching her dawning recognition with a brief smile. 'I heard what happened when you let those dogs go. Told you, didn't I?'

He was not a pleasant person, Thea concluded, as she had on the previous occasion. He took pleasure in other people's misfortune and in having his own dire predictions come true. His dogs danced impatiently at the end of their leather leads, until he jerked them viciously and swore at them to keep still.

'Rhodesian ridgebacks, aren't they? My uncle had one, when I was little. I was always quite scared of it.'

He smiled again, with a secret satisfaction. 'Most people are,' he agreed. 'It's the ridge that does it. They look as if their hackles are up.'

'But really they're quite docile,' she supplied, expecting him to say something to this effect.

'Strong,' he amended.

'I can see they're a handful. They look as if they're not really used to walking on a lead.'

'They've got their own compound at home, big enough for a good run. But now and then I take them out like this. Teaches them who's boss.' Again he jerked at the lead in his left hand, making the dog yelp.

'A girl and a boy,' Thea observed. 'Brother and sister?'

'Nope. A breeding pair. Worth a bit, I can tell you. The pups go for close to a grand, if they're good specimens. We've had two litters already.'

'Very nice,' said Thea, unable to repress a shudder at the idea of keeping dogs for purely commercial reasons. The man showed no signs of affection or even pride in his handsome beasts.

'So – did you find the runaways?' A glitter in his eye suggested that he knew exactly what had happened since their last meeting and was merely playing with her.

'They came home,' she said shortly. Some instinct kept her from splurging her latest trouble. After all, he had been a lot less than helpful the last time. To admit that they'd gone again seemed to be inviting scorn.

But he wasn't going to be brushed off. 'And they've behaved since then, have they? Henry Galton let them off, did he? Thanks to that police bloke, is the way I heard it. You were lucky there.'

It was like being poked in the ribs with a bony finger, over and over again. He was trying to get a response from her that she had no intention of giving. What was it with this man, anyway?

'Can't stop any longer,' she said, engaging the car's gears. 'Sorry.'

The Rhodesian ridgebacks had ignored her throughout. Although they pulled restlessly at their leads, they had a cowed manner that suggested lives passed in unhappy conditions, without play or treats. It was wrong to keep animals like that – just as the Angells were wrong to make theirs spend all day attached to chains. Was there a brotherhood of unkindness to dogs around here, she wondered, giving Hepzie a quick close hug as she drove one-handed down to Hawkhill.

Any lingering hope she might have that Freddy and Basil would have miraculously returned was dashed. The yard was as silent as before. 'What do we do now?' she asked the spaniel, glumly. 'Call the police,' was the only answer that occurred to her own question.

CHAPTER SIXTEEN

From habit, and a feeling that this would be the least embarrassing of a range of unappealing options, she called Phil's mobile. He did not answer it, so she left an incoherent message, trying to inject urgency without panic and probably failing utterly.

It was not yet four o'clock – too early to start the rounds of animal feeding, and a reasonably good time to take Hepzie for the walk she'd planned that morning. But she was not in the mood. The rain had stopped hours ago, but it was still a grey uninviting day, with an uncomfortable wind blowing. She went into the house, to be greeted by a sarcastic, 'How many eggs make five – huh? Five fours are twenty. See if I care.'

'Shut up, Ignatius,' she grumbled, while unable to resist a grin at this new piece of showing off. *See if I care* was rather good, in its way. She thought she could detect Cedric Angell's intonation coming through in the mimicry. If not him, then his son Martin with the bizarre sense of humour sounded very like his dad. By the end of her stay, she suspected she'd be able to make a good stab at understanding whichever member of the Angell family had taught the parrot its repertoire. A film buff, given to issuing orders, it seemed. But where did the bit about eggs fit in?

This way lies madness, Thea told herself with a shake. Perhaps that was the plan all along. Ignatius's tutor had merely wanted to drive everybody in Hawkhill mad. Just the thing, in fact, that a clever teenage boy would enjoy.

So she made herself more tea, and sat down in the living room for a think. It had been an eventful day, by any standards, leaving her with plenty to worry about. Her sister's decline into hysteria demanded some attention, and the missing dogs even more so. The latter emerged as clear favourite, if only because she was being paid to take care of them and her conspicuous failure was impossible to evade. Emily's condition was too far beyond her power to address. There was nothing she could do about it, other than perhaps make a supportive phonecall.

But the dogs! What on earth could have happened to them? Could she believe in the innocence of Galton, the blindingly obvious suspect in their abduction? If so, who had taken them?

She tried to trace a logical path through everything that had happened since Basil and Freddy ran off on Sunday. That man Lister had come into view less than five minutes later. She recalled his purposeful walk, his eyes on her face, narrowed in thought. She had supposed him to be wondering who she was, but on reflection he had seemed more as if concentrating on a plan. He had been pleased to see her – and almost gleeful in his prognostications as to what would happen to the runaways.

Now she knew he owned two large dogs, her

view of him had changed. And cogs began to turn, meshing together with the smooth inevitability of a water tight theory. If Freddy and Basil had not killed the sheep, then something else had. Something big and fierce and canine. A pair of semi-trained Rhodesian ridgebacks, for example.

It made unnervingly good sense. Perhaps Lister's dogs had somehow broken out, and he was anxiously searching for them when three other loose dogs surged past him after a rabbit. Knowing the terrible possibilities of sheep worrying and the likely execution of his prize breeding stock, he immediately hatched the cunning plot of throwing suspicion elsewhere. It must have seemed like a godsend. Without any reference to his own beasts, he warned Thea of what would happen, sowing the seeds in her mind, before nipping briskly over to Galton's and sowing the same seeds again.

Precisely when the slaughter happened, and how the ridgebacks were retrieved and washed clean of any evidence, was unclear. And why he so blatantly revealed their existence to Thea now, by walking them along the stretch of road almost outside Hawkhill, was equally incomprehensible. Unless – of course – *he* had got Freddy and Basil locked up somewhere, and wanted to give himself an alibi by appearing to have been calmly walking his own dogs at more or less the time they went missing. He would call Galton, tell him the murderers were safely behind bars, ready for execution at any time to suit his, Galton's, convenience.

It looked perfect at first glance, but closer

200

inspection revealed some holes. The timing would have to be extremely neat, not only on Sunday but today, with amazing luck at every turn to enable such a plan to work. The mere fact that Lister was not a likable person didn't justify accusations of such iniquity as she had been contemplating. On the other hand, was it so extraordinary for someone to try to save the reputation of their own dogs at the expense of a neighbour's? Quite possibly there was a long history of antagonism between the Angells and the Listers which could account for the man's behaviour. Perhaps he had been deliberately watching for a chance to get Cedric and his dogs into trouble.

The key lay with Galton, she realised. He must have believed Lister initially, and would be very likely to cooperate now, if indeed Lister had Freddy and Basil shut away somewhere. Or would he? Since their encounter that afternoon, the relationship had shifted. Each knew the other to be a real human being, with real feelings and preoccupations. She liked him more than she did before, and thought it was the same for him. He had ended by trying to recover his earlier prejudices, but she wasn't sure it had been effective. Would he be even half so inclined to shoot the dogs now he knew more about the person who would carry the blame?

She should phone him and try to avert any action on Lister's part. She should sow some counter propaganda against the ridgebacks.

And she would have done, if she hadn't been interrupted before she could locate the man's phone number.

It was Ariadne, her eyes staring, shoulders slumped, car slewed crookedly across the yard. She came into the house without knocking, and accosted Thea in the kitchen. 'It's Peter!' she cried, without preamble. 'They've arrested him.'

Thea saw the naked suffering, the desperate search for consolation and put her arms out to her friend. 'Hey, hey,' she crooned. 'It doesn't necessarily mean anything. When did it happen?'

Ariadne slumped into a kitchen chair, and held tightly to Thea's hands. 'Just now. They wouldn't let me go with him. He hasn't got a lawyer or anything – what's he going to *do?*'

'He'll be fine, honestly. Come on, take a deep breath and we'll talk it through.' She thought of making some more tea, but Ariadne didn't seem ready to release her grip. Confusedly, she understood that this was about more than the fact of the arrest. The fear was too acute. Ariadne was afraid of losing Peter on a more elemental level. Of finding him to be flawed, perhaps, or even of being guilty of some unforgiveable act – like murdering his own brother.

'Oh, Thea. You can't imagine how much I love him. It's like an illness, almost. I can't think about anything else. I just want him to be happy – and *with me.*'

'I know,' Thea murmured. 'It'll all be all right, you see.'

'Yes. It *has* to be, hasn't it. It isn't as if he's committed any crime. He hasn't you know.' She stared up at Thea's face, her eyes blurred with panicky tears. 'You believe that, don't you?'

'Of *course*,' said Thea stoutly. And she did. If Emily's story was accurate, then nobody could place Peter Clarke as the uncontrolled attacker. 'Of course he couldn't have done such a thing.'

Ariadne's grip loosened. 'They said they wanted to check his alibi again,' she reported. 'We heard today that they've found a will where Sam left everything to Peter. Oh, Thea – what a horrible mess. This is much worse than last time. I think they're convinced that he did it. How could he? His brother's head was totally smashed, the brains all splurging out. It must have been a *maniac* to do that.' A few more deep breaths had calmed her down to a point where she could speak coherently, and force her thoughts into some kind of order.

'The alibi – what's wrong with it?'

'That's really why I came to you. It's all down to your sister. What time *exactly* did she leave here?'

Thea gritted her teeth. 'I can't say *exactly*. It was dark, because it was raining so heavily, so I thought it must be nearly nine. But actually it can't have been as late as that. It might only have been eight. It never occurred to me to check a clock, you see. And it sounds as if she might only have been driving for ten minutes or so before – well, before she saw what she did.'

Ariadne groaned. 'So they think Peter could have had time to do the awful deed and still get to the vicarage in Cirencester for nine.'

'Surely not.' Thea's mind struggled to function. 'That's stupid. He'd have had to wash the blood

203

off, change his clothes – and act normally. Can anybody be that good at acting?'

'Not him. He's not a liar, Thea. I *know* he's not.'

Thea was still lost in the same thoughts as before. 'He'd also need to drive at a hundred miles an hour and have a clean suit lying on the bed ready. And he'd have had to get over his homicidal frenzy enough to fit into a room full of church bods.'

Ariadne giggled wildly. 'Precisely,' she said. 'God, Thea, I'd forgotten how wonderful you are. I don't know how you do it.'

'Do what?'

'Think so clearly, and put it all into words. You're so *honest*, as well. No evasions or euphemisms.'

'Oh, well,' sighed Thea. 'I suppose I'm used to it.'

'So what should I do? I feel totally helpless.'

'Not a lot you can do.' Thea let an image of Peter Clarke form in her mind, along with the unwelcome comments Phil had made about him on Monday. 'Nobody's going to take any notice of you, because they think you're blinded by passion.' She said the words ironically, but there was plainly a lot of truth behind them.

'I am,' said Ariadne mournfully. 'My wits have all gone to jelly. It's all the worse for knowing what a fool I've turned into, and not being able to help it.'

'It sounds naïve, but I honestly think that if he's innocent, they'll let him go, no harm done.'

'*If?*'

'You know what I mean. In a way it's turning

out lucky that it was my sister who was first on the scene. At least it gives you direct access to the chief witness.'

'Does it? Where is she then?'

'Well, actually – um – she's in a bit of a state, according to her husband. I guess it's because our father died so recently. Everything happening at once. She's overwhelmed.'

'She should join the club, then,' said Ariadne, and this time it was Thea who giggled.

'No, no, it isn't funny,' she asserted, sobering quickly. 'She's my big sister, never had a day's illness. It throws everybody if Emily falls apart. Now if it was *Jocelyn*, nobody would be surprised. She's the baby of the family – we're used to having to mop her up. This is altogether different.'

Ariadne had no answer for that. Thea remembered that there were only brothers in her family, which would be a whole other dynamic.

By a silent agreement to revert to something closer to normality, Thea made a pot of tea, and carried it through to the living room, where Ariadne went to the window, first to inspect the parrot on his perch, and then to observe the view beyond.

'Hawkhill used to be much bigger than this, didn't it?' Ariadne looked out of the window, as if scanning the invisible acres. 'My dad had some kind of business dealings with them here at one time. They kept pigs, years ago, and he used their boar now and then. Looks as if most of the buildings have gone now.'

'They sold off the bulk of the land, Cedric said.

There's some trouble over whether or not it can be built on.'

'As usual,' Ariadne nodded easily. 'Every new brick is cause for a massive battle around here.'

'Except it wouldn't be bricks, would it? Perfectly matched Cotswold stone has to be the only material under consideration.'

'Right. I keep waiting to be old enough to care about that sort of stuff. The campaigners are always over fifty – had you noticed? And most of them live in London from Monday to Friday. It makes you wonder what it's all about.'

'Money, obviously. Property values. If Lower Slaughter agrees to a new estate, however tasteful and tucked away, it becomes a less desirable place, and the house prices slide. Even the most whispered suggestion of new houses will start a panic. It's quite funny, really.'

'I do hate the look of new houses, just because they seem so raw and bare and cold. But they soon start to blend in, I suppose. Everything was new once.'

'It won't happen,' said Thea confidently. 'Whatever Cedric might say.'

'You're probably right.'

The diversion had been deliberate, a breathing space in the maelstrom of police arrests and crazy sisters.

'I have to feed the animals,' Thea remembered. 'At least the ones that are left.'

Ariadne gave no sign of hearing this leading remark. Thea sighed, and added, 'Do you want to help? You can do the parrot.'

'Wow – thanks. I *love* the parrot. Will he say

206

something to me?'

'Who knows? He has a mind of his own – full of some very strange material, I might add.'

'Then can we go to the pub, and decide what to do about Peter? He must be in such a state, poor bloke.'

'He has his God, hasn't he?' said Thea, knowing it was unworthy. 'It worked for Terry Waite.'

'Not enough,' said Ariadne stoutly. 'He needs us as well.'

They drove in Thea's car down to the main road, and turned left to where Ariadne knew a pub on the edge of Bourton. The bar of the Coach and Horses contained some obvious holidaymakers, with young teenage children eating chips and lasagne. The two women ordered fish pie and wine from the Specials board, Thea pointing out that this was her second pub meal of the day. 'And there was me thinking I wouldn't find any-body to go out with while I was here.'

'Can you ask Phil to keep you in the loop with what's happening to Peter?' Ariadne asked. 'He usually tells you, doesn't he?'

'Things are a trifle cool between me and Phil,' Thea reminded her. 'It all came to a bit of a head yesterday. I'm still trying to adjust.'

'Oh gosh! What happened?'

'Nothing – that's the problem. His back – I told you about his back, didn't I?'

'Oh, I get it. No rolling in the hay, as I guess they'd call it around here about a century ago, in case it goes again.'

'It was rolling in the feathers that slipped his

207

disc,' said Thea, with a shy grin. 'Don't you ever tell him I told you.'

'Poor man.'

'Yes, well, it put things to the test and it looks as if we've failed.'

'And are you upset about it?'

'A bit. I still can't quite believe it.'

'So does that mean you're on your own? I mean you can't call him if you feel lonely or scared or bored?'

'I don't know. I was just wondering the same thing when you turned up. I've got rather a crisis with the dogs. They've gone missing.'

'Oh? Is that usual?'

'Certainly not. Somebody's taken them. They might even have shot them by now. I should not be here talking to you – I should be out there searching for them.'

'But why? I mean – what's going on?'

'Never mind. First things first. We need to concentrate on your Peter.'

A look of fondness settled on Ariadne's face, a daft smile on her lips. 'My Peter,' she murmured. 'That does sound nice.'

But when they tried to focus on Peter's plight, and how they might best help him, they found little to say. 'If we could just firm up the alibi, that would settle it once and for all,' said Thea.

'And that's entirely down to your sister. She has his life in her hands.' Ariadne's tone was melo-dramatic. 'It all rests with her.'

'The police will realise that. They'll probably send somebody to check the times again with her. They'll have the log of her 999 call, of course.

They'll have worked it out from that, probably. And when they did, they'll have come to the conclusion that there could just possibly have been time for Peter to be in both places. I'm not sure they will need Emily to add anything more.'

'We could find the person who really did it,' Ariadne suggested, with a glance around the bar. 'What do we know about Sam? Can we think of a reason why somebody would want to kill him?'

'He seemed inoffensive enough when I met him,' said Thea carelessly.

'*What?*' Ariadne's screech raised heads on all sides. 'What do you mean? You never said you'd met him.' Her eyes bulged and a chip was suspended halfway to her mouth.

'Only once – at Emily's. It's nothing to get excited about. You know that Emily and her husband, Bruce – more Bruce than Em – knew him. He and Bruce went to college together. He went to their house a few times, and I was there for one of those times. It was a dinner party.'

'I hadn't realised they were really friends,' Ariadne said loudly, ignoring the people listening at the neighbouring tables. 'Don't you think that's weird?'

'Not at all. I'm sure it was just a horrible coincidence. Emily had no idea it was him. It was dark and wet and his head was crushed when she reached him. He was here to see Peter, and she was here to see me, and it just all came together in that terrible way.'

'Rubbish. Utter rubbish. If she knew him, then she must have known he was here. She probably knows who his killer was. What if she was having

209

an affair with him, and wanted to get out of it, and when he kicked up a fuss, got somebody to put him out of the way.'

'*That's* even bigger rubbish,' said Thea, suddenly angry.

'No, it isn't. It could have happened like that. She might have lured him into that layby, away from the hotel and watched while the deed was done.'

'But then she'd just have driven away. Why would she call the police?'

Ariadne paused. 'OK – what if it went further than she intended? And the sight of his mangled body snagged her conscience. After all, she might still have loved him, but felt guilty at betraying her husband.'

'Stop it,' Thea ordered. 'And stop shouting. You're saying appalling things about my sister, in a public place, and you've got to stop.'

A brief silence followed, during which they avoided each other's eye and toyed with the food. 'It's obvious that she had no idea who he was,' Thea repeated quietly. 'She would have told me when she came back here afterwards. She would have told the police, as well. They didn't get an identity for him until Sunday morning. It isn't such a wild coincidence, anyway. She and Bruce know *loads* of people. They're in a huge social network, with parties and clubs and all the rest of it. She probably knew three or four people staying at that hotel, if it comes to that.' It was a daft exaggeration, of course, which she knew even as she spoke.

'Where does she live?'

'Aylesbury.'

'Hardly local. And Sam lived in Oxford. And this is a very small village in the Cotswolds.'

'I could give you four or five true instances of much bigger coincidences than that. They sound incredible, but they're not.' She opened her mouth to tell the story of the time she knocked on a door of a B&B in Cerne Abbas and discovered a woman who'd been in the same antenatal class as herself, twelve years earlier, but closed it again. Ariadne was in no mood to be convinced.

'The clinching thing,' she went on, 'is that Emily wouldn't have called the police if she'd been in any way involved in Sam's death. Isn't that axiomatic?'

'Double bluff,' muttered Ariadne darkly. 'Oldest trick in the book.'

'You're being much too complicated about it,' Thea complained. 'Far simpler to stick with what we all thought at the start – a psycho with a baseball bat or cosh of some sort sees Sam, thinks he looks good for a few quid and works himself up into a huge frenzy before attacking him. Maybe he got some kind of blood lust, a red mist thing, and didn't know when to stop. He only came to his senses when Emily heard the noise and interrupted him. She saw him run off.'

'But she didn't describe him, did she?'

'According to Phil, she said he seemed quite small and slim and not black. She was fairly sure he wasn't black.'

'As if that matters.'

'It narrows things down a bit,' Thea said.

'It doesn't, because she can't possibly give a positive identification, even if they catch him. So it'll be down to forensics, and he's had time to get rid of every last molecule by now, hasn't he?'

'Well, this isn't helping Peter,' Ariadne sighed, after another short silence. 'And if you're not going to call Phil, then I suppose it'll have to be me. Do you want me to give him a message?'

'Tell him the dogs have been stolen, if you get the chance.'

Ariadne frowned. 'What? How could they have been stolen?'

Thea shook her head. 'Never mind. I'll call him myself. It's not your problem.'

CHAPTER SEVENTEEN

She dreamt about dogs eating the brains out of a smashed human head, and woke with a sick feeling of horror swirling in her stomach. It was Thursday, almost a week since her father's funeral, and not much over a week before she had to face the owners of Hawkhill, with whatever ghastly news there might be about their dogs – assuming her conscience didn't force her to contact them before they returned. How could she have slept at all, knowing they were out there somewhere, shut in a dark prison, or even dead already? There had to be something she could and should do, instead of passively waiting for the next thing to happen.

Phil had not responded to the message she'd left on his phone, which made her think he was sticking to his decision to keep her at a distance. It also implied that he thought it beneath him to get involved in a search for two dogs. After all, he'd decide, they came back of their own accord last time. It was probably safe to assume they'd do it again. She could think of nothing else but to return to Galton and try out her theory about the Lister man. But that did not much appeal as a strategy. The theory would be far better tested directly, she decided. If she could discover where Lister lived, she might also find Freddy and Basil.

The phone book and Google between them revealed enough of an address for her to locate the man's house. She had expected a farm, with his talk of a large compound for his ridgebacks, but it was in fact a house in a row, between Hawkhill and the centre of Lower Slaughter. She remembered the spot well, with its tetchy notices about keeping dogs off the verges.

It was an easy walk from Hawkhill. The main dilemma was whether or not to take Hepzie. It felt risky to leave her behind, where she too might be stolen away. On the other hand, if there was any trouble, she'd be a liability. Better, then, to lock her firmly in the house and hope that she and Ignatius could establish a better relationship than hitherto.

The weather was dry but overcast. There was a faint smell of woodsmoke outside and a jaded sense that summer was rapidly departing. She had always liked September, with the new school terms, new courses to attend, and the bounty of blackberries and nuts and mushrooms to collect on woodland walks. Carl had been a great enthusiast for autumn fruitfulness, organising old-fashioned family outings with capacious baskets and hooked sticks. But this was not yet September; this was August with its face still turned backwards to the summer almost over, with a feeling of time wasted. The English summer was inevitably disappointing. It never lasted for long enough, never provided the right levels of sunshine for what you wanted to do. June had been fabulous, July capricious and August a total disaster. It didn't seem much of a deal, looking back.

She tried to plot her course of action once she reached the Lister establishment. Would she creep round to the back in the hope of finding Freddy and Basil in a shed? Or would she boldly knock on the door and insist on being allowed to make a search? Neither felt very promising, as she strode down the lane towards the village. The man was sly, and he possessed two very large dogs which might be trained to attack intruders – or at the very least make a lot of noise. She needed to be sly as well. She needed to invent a story that would deceive him into giving himself away, and instantly one fell into place. She slowed her pace, rehearsing the details as they came to mind.

A woman answered her knock. 'Mrs Lister?' Thea asked, trying to seem breathless and a trifle sheepish.

'No, but I live here with Mr Lister.'

'Right. Well, I saw him yesterday afternoon, and we had a little talk. Is he in?'

'He's outside with the dogs.'

'Oh.' She feigned uncertainty. 'Then would it be all right if I waited for him to finish what he's doing? I saw the dogs yesterday, and they made me a bit nervous.'

The woman smiled. 'To tell you the truth they have that effect on me sometimes. They're not exactly lapdogs, if you know what I mean.'

'Still, they're not pit bulls, either. I don't suppose they're really aggressive.'

The woman waggled her head ambivalently. 'Not really, no. You have to keep them under firm control, animals that size, of course.'

'Right.'

'Well, come in. My name's Sharon.'

'Thea. Thea Osborne. I'm house-sitting for Mr and Mrs Angell at Hawkhill.'

'Oh?' This information had a noticeable effect on her. Her brows came together in a thoughtful frown. 'Are you indeed? So it was you who let the dogs kill Henry's sheep?'

'Er—' This was an unexpectedly full-frontal challenge. 'I don't think—'

'Come on, love, face facts. There's no doubt about it, now is there?'

'You know Mr Galton then, do you?' As questions went, this was a particularly stupid one, but she found herself floundering badly.

The withering look was all the answer she needed. Then Sharon seemed to lose interest. 'Well, I've got to be somewhere. I'll shout to Mike that you're here, and then I'm off. Though God knows why you've come. I'd have kept out of his way if it'd been me.'

Thea shrugged helplessly and said nothing more. She watched the woman go to the back door, and then tried to distract herself with a brief inspection of the house, which gave an impression of starkness. Varnished wooden floors with no rugs, no pictures on the walls, no clutter on the surfaces. She was half inclined to make an escape, but it was too late for that. She had to try and keep to her plan, and see where it got her.

Lister came in a minute or two after his partner had called him, swiping his hands together and smelling faintly of old meat. Thea had a sudden

216

nasty image of him feeding road kill to his dogs, which seemed all too plausible when she gave him a closer look. Sharon gathered a jacket and a bag and slammed quickly out of the front door leaving Thea and Lister together in the living room.

'Oh, Mr Lister,' she burst out, hoping she sounded genuine, 'I came to tell you the dogs have come back, after all. I thought you must be worrying about them.'

He ignored this, rather to her consternation. Instead of responding, he demanded, 'How did you know where to find me?'

'Um – the phone book.'

'Why not just phone me, then?' His face was the epitome of suspicion. He stared at her as if she might suddenly pull a gun on him.

'I felt like a walk.'

'What's your game?' he said, his voice suddenly loud and angry. 'What are these lies you're telling me?'

She raised her eyebrows and repeated, 'Lies, Mr Lister? What *do* you mean?'

It was like the moment when you realise you've got a word in Scrabble that not only uses all seven letters, but takes in two of the triple word scores as well. Lister was cornered. He couldn't support his accusation that she was lying without admitting that he had Freddy and Basil, or at least knew where they were. She swelled with pride at her own cleverness. She hadn't told him they were missing – so why hadn't he picked her up on that, instead of her claim that they'd come home again? It was a clear indication of his own

217

involvement, which he proceeded to embellish, albeit with a desperate turn in the conversation.

'I mean that I've seen those bloody dogs and they're dead. Dead in a ditch a mile from here.'

Thea deflated rapidly. 'They're not,' she whispered. 'They can't be.'

'I can show you, if you want. Somebody's taken the law into their own hands and done what Galton should have done days ago. So what are you playing at, telling me they've come home?' Then his eyes narrowed as he mentally back-tracked. 'You never even told me they'd gone,' he accused. 'You came here to trap me.' Small as he was, he was still substantially bigger than her, and very much stronger.

She hadn't thought it through, she realised. It was one thing to catch the man out with a clever bluff, another to deal with what happened next. She had been so intent on extracting the truth, to have something she could take to the police, that she hadn't planned the next step. But she couldn't back away now.

'You killed them,' she accused. 'You shot them and dumped them in a ditch.'

He shrugged. 'Prove it,' he challenged. But a faltering note caught her ear. Of course, he had never intended to reveal that he knew where the bodies were. He had, after all, been provoked into giving himself away by her ruse. But it was a hollow victory, if the dogs really were dead.

'Take me to where they are,' she commanded. 'I want to see them.'

'I'm buggered if I will. You go and find them for yourself. Why should I help you?'

She couldn't think of a way to force him, and sadness was beginning to engulf her bravado. She had got what she came for, up to a point, but now she couldn't see what good it could do. Nothing would bring poor innocent Freddy and Basil back, and their slaughter was all her stupid fault.

'I'll go and find them myself, then,' she said, and turned to go.

'And don't come bothering me again,' he spat at her.

She felt abandoned as she walked back to Hawkhill. Ariadne would perhaps have helped her find the dogs if she hadn't been so bound up with the arrest of her beloved Peter. Phil might have put in a word and got a constable to patrol the roadsides for a few hours, if he'd still been with her. Then she realised that a ditch could just as easily be under a field hedge, well away from the road, and take forever to find, as a result.

She badly needed a confidant, somebody who would understand her feelings of guilt and misery at what had happened. She had met so few people since coming to Lower Slaughter, and of them, one was under arrest and the other had just virtually confessed to killing the dogs in her care. Which left only one other, and some strange instinct told her that he might just turn up trumps if approached for help.

This time, she walked to the beautifully situated old farmhouse, surrounded by its huge barns and lambing sheds. She'd gone back to Hawkhill first, had coffee and released Hepzie from her confine-

219

ment with the parrot. The bird had its back turned to the room, and was concentrating on cleaning its claws. The dog was huddled in a corner of the sofa, not even getting up when Thea came into the room. There had obviously been no rapprochement between the two. Indeed, it was tempting to think the parrot had been roundly abusing the dog.

'You can come with me this time,' she told the spaniel, once the coffee was finished. 'You can't do any harm now.' She even had the vague idea that Hepzie might come in useful.

Galton was driving his tractor across a field as she walked down the track. It was a few hundred yards away and she assumed he hadn't noticed her. Finding a gateway, she went into the field and stood watching him as he pulled some sort of implement behind the tractor. It took a while for her to work out that it was spraying something onto the grass, through fine jets. 'Blimey!' she murmured. 'He's not organic then, is he!'

She waited patiently for twenty minutes, during which the man noticed her, waved, and carried on with his work. Eventually he finished the job and drove at high speed to where she stood, jerking the tractor to a bouncing halt beside her and switching the engine off.

'Is that a chemical spray?' she asked, waving at the implement.

'It is,' he nodded. 'Kills the eggs that give the sheep intestinal worms and liver fluke. What would you have me do?'

'I wouldn't presume to judge,' she said.

220

'So what can I do for you?'

She clenched her jaw against the urge to rest her head on his chest and sob. 'I came to tell you that Mr Angell's dogs are dead.' It was no good – a rogue tear trickled down her cheek before she could stop it.

'No!'

'That Lister man told me he'd seen them. He must have done it himself. He gave himself away.' The full impact of the loss of Basil and Freddy had barely hit her yet. Now she conjured their good-natured manners, their soft coats and unexciting lives and felt a wave of misery. How and why they'd died seemed less important than the fact that they were dead, wasted on some stupid man-made altar erected to sheep, of all things.

Galton sighed. 'It's nearly time to stop for some lunch. Do you want to come in and tell me the whole story?'

Without asking herself what she thought she was doing, she nodded, and he took her arm without ceremony, steering her down to the house. The spaniel trotted awkwardly behind them, pulling back occasionally to remind her mistress that she existed.

The story emerged in a handful of jumbled sentences, to which Galton listened carefully. He had given no sign of impatience for his lunch, and offered her nothing to eat or drink. 'What a bloody mess,' he said heavily when she'd finished. 'Not one of us comes out of it very well, do we?'

'Thanks for listening,' she mumbled, aware of

imposing on him.

'Well, I was always an easy touch for a damsel in distress. Story of my life,' he grinned.

He would make a brilliant friend, she decided. Unusually easy to talk to, big and amiable, but capable of vigorous action when needed – a man for every eventuality. Why had his wife deserted him, she wondered? Had he raged at her a few times too many? Had she given up competing with the sheep for his attention?

But she needed to stick to the immediate subject before exploring the man's emotional life. 'Do you think it could have been the Rhodesian ridgebacks who killed your sheep?' she asked. 'I'm sure it must have been, and he's been trying to put the blame on Freddy and Basil. Now he's gone and shot them. I suppose he'll tell people he found blood on their jaws or something.'

'He won't tell anybody anything. You've got it all wrong,' he told her. 'He'd never let those precious ridgebacks out of his sight, believe me. It couldn't have been them. And the coincidence would be too much, if your theory was right.'

'So why – I mean, what–?'

'He's always had a down on Cedric. It goes back years. That house of his – it belonged to Cedric's old uncle, thirty or forty years back, with some land attached. Lister's mother was the housekeeper there. I never quite knew the whole story, but it ended up with a scandal, and when the uncle died he left the house to old Mrs L.'

Thea followed this tale with some difficulty. 'So why the feud?'

'Cedric contested the will. He was the next of

222

kin and was expecting to get the place. He said some very damaging things, and the old lady–'

'Lister's mother?'

'Right – well, she went off her rocker with the strain of it all. She wasn't all that old, I 'spose, maybe just past sixty, but she seemed like a crone to us boys at the time. Mike Lister was a bit older, always a jack the lad, swaggering about with his gun, boasting about girls. He was a spoilt brat, youngest of three boys, came along when his mum was well past forty. Anyway, he swore he'd get revenge on Cedric and he's been doing all he could to get to him ever since. He never lets up.'

'And now he's shot the dogs simply because he doesn't like their owner? The man must be a monster.'

'He's not nice, that's for sure. And sly. But Thea – those dogs really did kill my tups. You have to face up to that. It was totally wrong of Lister to get involved, but even so, they had to go, don't you see?'

'No, I don't see,' she shouted. 'They were two fine animals, in the prime of life. They could have been sent to a new home where they'd be properly looked after. Besides, there was no blood on them.'

He heaved another sigh, even deeper than before. 'They would have licked it all off each other. They like the taste of it – it's a treat for them. It was them, I promise you. There isn't the least doubt. You've created a web of fantasy around Lister and his ridgebacks that just obscures the truth. The *simple* truth. It's possible

223

that he was worried that suspicion would fall on his own dogs, and that was why he took it on himself to shoot them – as well as being glad to get at Cedric.'

'So you're saying I should have let you do it on that first day, when you came to Hawkhill.'

He grinned ruefully. 'No, I'm not saying that. You'd never have let me. And I couldn't have done it with you watching. It isn't pleasant.'

'Have you ever shot a dog?'

He shook his head. 'But my father did, when I was twelve. I was there. It screamed. It scarred me for life, that scream.'

She looked at him, wondering at his tone. Slowly she understood that he meant what he'd said. The experience had done a damage that he permitted her to glimpse for a moment.

After a painful silence, she spoke. 'What's Cedric going to say when he gets back?'

'He won't say much, never does. Look – don't feel too badly about it. It's a strange business, sheep-worrying. Any dog's capable of it, if it gets its blood up. They just see red and act crazy for a few minutes. The minute they get a taste for it, there's no stopping them. You can't really blame them – it's in their nature. And tups are easy prey – soft things. It doesn't take much to kill them.'

She was silenced, both by his confidence that Cedric's dogs were guilty, and his surprising forgiveness.

'You're being very kind,' she said, humbly. 'After I've caused you so much trouble.' The guilt and grief remained lumpily in her midriff, tangled up with a mixture of other unpleasant emotions. Wasn't she getting her priorities upside down, agonising about a pair of dogs when a human being had been savagely killed? Somehow the three deaths merged in her mind, a confusion of violence and rage that was frightening.

He merely nodded in calm acknowledgement.

'I'd better go,' she said. 'And leave you to get on with your lunch.'

He raised his eyebrows. 'Won't you stay and have it with me?'

She looked round, seeing no sign of any food. Did he do all his own cooking, as well as house-work and running the farm?

He laughed. 'It's just cold meat and bread, and a few bits. Most days, Dave comes in and has it with me, but he's off on Thursdays. Dave's the farmhand you guessed was about somewhere, when you came yesterday. There's Eddie as well, when we're busy.' He fetched a joint of cold pork, on a large oval dish that looked like a valuable antique. Pickle, some tomatoes, crusty brown bread and a stoneware flagon of cider completed the repast. It could all have found favour with the occupants of the house a century earlier. Even the kettle was an ancient enamel object, sitting on top of the Aga.

'You like nice things, don't you?' she observed, making an effort at normality. 'I can't see any-thing made of plastic in this entire room.'

'Just like things that have some life in them,' he nodded. 'If you look after them, they'll last for ever. Mind you, I can't take the credit. Most of this stuff was here when my mum was a girl. It's like living in a museum sometimes.'

'But you keep it all so *nice*.'

He leant forward and winked comically. 'You know – I discovered a secret weapon. It's called a feather duster.'

She laughed more at his face than his words. He had somehow managed to transform himself into a Mrs Mop figure simply by doing something with his mouth, then angling his head and flicking an imaginary duster over the china on the dresser. 'You'll have to teach me,' she said. 'I've never quite got the hang of dusting.'

'It'll be that dog's fault,' he said, nodding at Hepzie who sat self-effacingly beside Thea's chair. 'They shake dry mud over everything if you let them in the house. You should have seen this kitchen when my mum had her two setters in here. There was a veneer of dust and dog hair over every blessed thing.'

What a man, she marvelled. And yet she felt no stirrings of physical attraction. He was being kind and funny and self-deprecating, but he wasn't flirting, and so neither was she. There was a comfortable atmosphere, where she found herself trusting and believing him completely. 'You know, I was really scared of you a few days ago.'

'I was a bear,' he admitted. 'I get like that. I blame the world, mainly. Things will keep going wrong.'

'So which is the real you – the bear or the pussycat?'

'Both, obviously. As the whim takes me.'

'What do the local people think of you?'

'They're cautious round me. I'll bet you Cedric Angell warned you about me – don't get the wrong side of old Galton, he'll shoot you if you do, kind of thing.'

'Something like that,' she agreed.

'Yet I've never done him any harm. I like the dopey old bugger most of the time. He can't see beneath the surface, that's the trouble. Just because I've bawled him out a few times, he thinks I'm an ogre.'

And your wife? Thea wanted to ask, simply to complete the picture. But she didn't. It would have taken them into the wrong kind of territory.

'I still need to find the dogs,' she remembered. 'Give them a decent burial, if they really are dead.' The heaviness came back, the sorrow for the animals whose lives had been so constrained and dull. 'People do such awful things to animals, don't they. It weighs me down sometimes, just thinking about it. So much suffering and exploitation. Do you think there'll ever be a time when it stops?'

He shook his head. 'It couldn't work – not with farm animals at least. If people stopped eating cows and sheep and pigs, then there'd be none left in a few years. Just a handful kept sentimentally as pets, and the odd carefully controlled so-called wild colonies on scruffy mountainsides, for the sake of the tourist trade. Look at the nonsense with wild boar going on now. Idiot people letting them run wild in the woods, and then panicking and shooting them when they get into a school playground. Seems to me you have to take the rough with the smooth. Wild animals can be aggressive. They get hungry and invade human territory, and then the same old conflicts start up again, just as they have for thousands of years. Human beings have to be in control, and their safety and property come far and away above anything else.'

She listened to this speech attentively. The underlying cynicism matched her own attitude towards much that went on. Human folly seemed to expand with every passing year, and sometimes she thought nobody could see it but her.

'Yes,' she said. 'It's just seriously bad luck to be an animal, I guess.'

This time he laughed, a booming guffaw that came from somewhere deep inside. Big men could be so *noisy*, she thought, briefly remembering Carl's slight frame, and even Phil Hollis, though tall, could hardly be described as big.

'Well, I really ought to go,' she said, after picking at the food he gave her. The knots in her stomach prevented proper eating, she discovered. 'You'll have work to do, and I'm being paid to supervise the remaining livestock at Hawkhill. Except – I do need to find those dogs. Can you suggest where I should look for them?'

'He won't have taken them far. He'll have had to use his car, probably did it late last night, and just bundled them out by the side of the road. There's plenty of quiet lanes around here with a handy ditch running alongside.'

'Do you think Sharon knew about it?' There was something awful about that thought. And yet her face when Thea introduced herself suggested awareness. 'She did, I suppose.'

Galton's face softened. 'Oh, Sharon,' he said ambiguously. 'You met her, then?'

Thea nodded.

'Did either of you mention me?'

'Yes – she did. I gather you know each other.'

'Obviously. It's a small village.' He grimaced and shook his head. 'I can't hope to explain it all to you, but let's just say that Sharon and I go back a long way.'

'Just as you and Phil Hollis do,' she remembered.

Galton laughed. 'Not *that* long,' he objected. 'Although now I think of it, she was at school with my wife for a year or so. I'd forgotten that. They both grew up in Stow.'

'I see,' said Thea, vaguely, aware that she did not really see at all. 'You're telling me that everybody knows everybody and it wouldn't be safe to make assumptions.'

'More or less, yes. But you can assume all you like about Mike Lister. I'll never work out what Sharon sees in him. He can't be a lot of fun to live with.'

She thought again of the comfortless house, and the downtrodden dogs outside. 'No,' she said. Then she collected herself. 'Well, come on, Heps, mustn't outstay our welcome.' She went ahead to the front door and turned to thank Galton for his hospitality. He wasn't behind her. 'Where did he go?' she asked the dog, who merely looked blank.

Then he reappeared, carrying a pure white sheepskin. 'Here,' he said. 'Let me give you this. I have eight or ten done every year, just because it seems such a waste not to. It makes a nice bedside rug, maybe.'

She took it in wonderment, holding the soft wool to her face. 'It's gorgeous!' she breathed. 'Surely you could sell them, rather than giving them away?'

'I don't need money,' he said, as if making a simple obvious remark. 'It was good to meet you again, Thea Osborne. I hope it's not the last time.'

Walking back to Hawkhill, she noted the way he'd used her name, as if he'd been storing it up for just the right moment. A flicker of her former fear recurred. Henry Galton was clever, mercurial and powerful. He had threatened her with his gun, fed her a classic country lunch and given her a sheepskin rug. What next, she asked herself.

CHAPTER EIGHTEEN

She had neglected to take her mobile with her to Galton's, and when she went into the kitchen, it caught her eye. Picking it up, the little symbol told her there was a message, and she listened guiltily to Phil's voice. *Thea? Why aren't you answering? I only got your message late last night. You left it on the wrong phone. What's the matter? It's all about those dogs again, apparently. Call me on this number* – and he slowly dictated the digits.

'What does he mean, the wrong phone?' Thea muttered. Then she remembered that he had recently made a more concerted effort to keep work and home separate, explaining rather tediously that it was disruptive to let the two merge too closely. She had called the home number, a mobile he kept for personal matters – and which he only bothered to check every second or third day, it seemed.

'Well, I don't need you any more,' she added in a louder mutter. 'I can get along quite nicely as I am.'

But Phil Hollis must have felt otherwise, because within ten minutes his car was sweeping down into the Hawkhill yard. She stood in the doorway watching him getting out, still stiff and careful from the bad back. He was simultaneously dreadfully familiar and painfully distant. She found herself rehearsing how she should be with him, not frosty, but not too affectionate, either. It was horrible, and she felt slightly sick.

'I didn't come because of your phonecall,' he said quickly. 'It's something else.'

The nausea was replaced by anxiety, something cold and even more unwelcome. 'What is it?' she demanded. It could only be to do with the murder of Sam Webster and the involvement of her sister. And Peter Clarke and Bruce and a shattered skull.

'Come into the house,' he ordered. 'I haven't got very much time.'

His urgency irritated her. 'You're lucky I'm here at all,' she said. 'I've been out for most of the day.'

'Without your phone. Yes, I know,' he said. He was doing his headmaster act, pulling rank, very much the grown-up. She had to fight to quell the mulish adolescent response that rose from the depths.

'Listen,' he said. 'We've got Peter Clarke, the vicar chap, under arrest. When we had a closer look at the timing, it made it just feasible that he could have been in that layby at eight fifteen or so.'

'Yes, I know,' she said, coolly repeating his own words. 'I've seen Ariadne. It's old news, anyway – if you don't charge him soon you'll have to let him go.'

'We won't be charging him. There's nothing concrete to put him in the frame. Though I don't believe half of what he's saying. He's going to hurt that girl, that's for sure.'

'So – what's so urgent?'

'Emily. I assume you know she's had some kind of breakdown. Her husband wouldn't let our officer see her this morning. We need her to firm up the timings – there's a gap that doesn't make much sense. And we need you to say precisely when she left here on Saturday evening.'

'Yes, I know all that as well. Ariadne wanted me to say the same thing. And I can't – not precisely. I've already told you, I thought at the time it must be nearly nine. It was fairly dark, but of course it was raining. She went off in a rush, not wanting to get wet, and I shut the door behind her for the same reason. I didn't watch her drive away. I didn't look at a clock. But it can't have been as late as I thought. I remember noticing when it was ten, and that was a lot more than an hour after she left.'

'Did you put the telly or radio on?'

'No. I tidied up a bit in the kitchen, and did some jigsaw and just sort of mooched about, thinking about Emily and Dad and the stuff she'd come to talk about. It didn't really matter to me what time it was. I know it was half past eleven when she came back.'

'And that's odd, too. Why did she come back to you? Why not go home?'

'She said she was too shaky to drive that far. And I suppose she wanted to tell me the whole story, face to face.'

'She called for an ambulance at eight forty-three. If she left here at eight fifteen, say, and the accident was only a mile away, what was happening in that half hour?'

'She got lost. And maybe she was too horrified

233

at first to work her phone. And I didn't *say* it was eight fifteen. I said I didn't know what time it was.'

Her response was automatic, instinctive. It had little or nothing to do with any idea of protecting Emily, simply the provision of a neat and credible explanation for something muddled and irrational. The police preferred the former, as Thea had discovered.

'Well, don't go for me, but I still think there's a chance she knew the attacker. It strikes me she could have had time to actually talk to Webster and the mystery man, and be more of a witness than she's letting on.'

'Phil, that's quite wrong. Emily doesn't know any crazed psychopaths, capable of so much violence. Do you think she'd just stand there and let it all happen? And why would she tell lies about it?'

'To save her own skin. If she was up to something, and didn't want you or her husband to know, she'd have to lie to the police as well as you – she'd have to stick to the same story with everybody.'

Thea shook her head emphatically. 'It's just not her,' she said. 'Emily's too fastidious, too much in control, to get caught up in anything so chaotic. And I don't believe she'd have been able to fool me when she came back afterwards, if she'd known who the dead man was. She'd have been far more upset. It wasn't until Monday evening, according to Bruce, that she really went into a spin, when you told her it was Sam. She did a normal day's work, and then fell apart.'

'Chaotic,' he repeated sceptically. 'Didn't it all get damned chaotic anyway?'

'Yes, but not because of anything *she* did. She dealt with it pretty well, from the sound of it. She didn't panic or run away pretending nothing had happened.'

'No,' he agreed. 'But I'm still puzzled by that time lapse. I don't suppose there's any chance she knows Peter Clarke, is there?'

'I'm sure she doesn't. He's been in Africa for years, after all. Oh, by the way – there's something I should confess to you about him.'

'Oh?'

'I let slip to Ariadne that I'd met Webster. I expect it would have been better to keep quiet about that, wouldn't it?'

It obviously wasn't the confession Phil had been expecting to hear. He gave it some consideration, absently rubbing the damaged disc in his back as he ruminated. 'I can't see what difference that would make,' he said at last. 'Clarke probably knew that already, anyway.' He rubbed harder. 'All three of them were there at that hotel, or close by, at the same time. We know that much. Webster knew Emily, but his brother didn't. Where does that get us?' he finished with a groan.

'Have you found the murder weapon?' The change of subject seemed politic to her, a safer topic to discuss.

'That's another thing.' He willingly followed her lead. 'It's not easy to work out what it could have been. Heavy rubber-soled boots would fit much of the damage, according to Pathology. But

235

Emily talked about a stick of some sort. It must have been something unusually broad – like a cricket bat. And yet there's nothing on the man's body to suggest blows from a weapon. The only injuries are to the head.'

'Nasty.'

'Yes, and a bit weird, only kicking his head. Most people aim for the ribs at some point, as well.'

'Surely not always. If the intention was to kill him, from the start, the head's the best thing to concentrate on.'

'Well, he did that all right. Stamped down with all his weight, or so it seems.'

'I'm assuming you haven't found heavy blood-stained boots in Peter's house?'

'Right.'

Thea suddenly thought of Henry Galton – a big weighty man, with rubber boots part of his daily apparel, inclined to great rages. But she shook away the thought. The killer was somebody she had never met, *would* never meet. A psychopath who had escaped back to his lair, leaving no useful clues.

'Peter's not really *big* enough, is he? I mean, you'd have to stamp down pretty hard to crack a skull.'

'Once he was unconscious, and unresisting, it wouldn't be so difficult. And if there was some sort of weapon, even quite a small person could have hit him hard enough to do the damage. It's just–' he sighed. 'Just that it feels weird,' he said again.

'So, listen,' she urged him, needing to change the subject even further. 'Now you're here I'll

236

have to tell you about the dogs. It is a police matter, if somebody shoots someone else's animals, isn't it? It must be.'

He nodded cautiously. 'Normally that would be against the law, yes.'

'Well, you remember I told you about a man called Mike Lister?'

'Vaguely.'

'The thing is, he lives just this side of Lower Slaughter and he's got a breeding pair of Rhodesian ridgebacks–'

'Nice,' approved Phil. 'Lovely creatures.'

'Yes, well, I don't think he's very kind to them. They seem horribly cowed and miserable. Anyway, he was the one who saw me a few minutes after my dogs ran off. He told me Henry would shoot them if he caught them near his sheep.'

'Henry?' The jealous male that had always been buried quite deep in Phil's breast stirred and flicked an enquiring tongue at this casual use of the man's first name.

'Yes, Henry,' she repeated impatiently. 'I've seen him a couple of times yesterday and today. Anyway, I saw Lister as well, this morning. I went to his house, and pretended the dogs had come home–'

'My God, Thea, what on earth have you been playing at?'

'Never mind, just listen. I tricked him into admitting the dogs had disappeared, and he said he'd seen them dead in a ditch. But he wouldn't say exactly where, so now I've got to try and find them,' she finished sadly.

'So what does *Henry* think about all this?'

She ignored the tone. 'He says Freddy and Basil definitely did kill his rams, but he didn't shoot them, and Lister's been in a feud with Cedric for decades and never misses a chance to do something horrible. So he took his chance and murdered the poor dogs.'

'Who would have had to be put down anyway if they were worrying sheep.'

'Not if it couldn't be proved. You know,' she added with a wretched expression, 'I think this is why the Angells decided to get a house-sitter in the first place. They wanted somebody to keep their dogs safe. So I've totally failed them.'

'Seems as if you have,' he said unsympathetically. 'But you also walked into a messy situation without knowing the facts. And it wasn't altogether your fault that the dogs slipped their leads and ran off. You were actually trying to keep them under control, if I understand it right.'

'Thanks,' she muttered. 'I did have one of them on a lead, yes. Cedric said that would be all right.'

'Well, then. You didn't disobey orders, after all.'

'Strictly speaking, that's true. I suppose I could manage to take that as a very small consolation.'

Nothing was said for a few moments, giving them both time to realise that they'd reverted to a former mode, where they could talk easily, their minds following similar tracks, any arguments readily resolved. Except that Phil's manifestation of jealousy where Henry Galton was concerned seemed worthy of notice. In the circumstances, it appeared inappropriate, even irrelevant, and Thea was inclined to ignore it as an aberration.

But she found it gave her a little glow of satisfaction that was equally inappropriate. Presumably, she told herself, a relationship never really
ended as smoothly and instantly as this one had
seemed to. There would be ragged edges,
nostalgic moments, changes of heart and panicky
feelings of abandonment. If Phil thought she had
gone directly into the arms of another man, he
could hardly fail to find this painful.

'I'll have to be off,' he said. 'Though I'd like to
tell you about the Cirencester bloke, if I had time.'

'The one who gave Peter his alibi?'

'The very one. Plus eight or ten others to back
it up. What a piece of work, though! You'd have
thought I'd come to ask him to confess to the
killing himself, he was so defensive.'

'You went yourself? Wasn't that a bit unusual?'

'I do get out sometimes,' he reproached her.
'It's called keeping in touch. Nobody's above a
bit of gentle interviewing.'

'I bet the Chief Constable is,' she argued.

'OK, but that's because he's too busy with
other things. I'm part of the team, and as such I
lend a hand. Anyway, I'm only saying I didn't
take to that vicar.'

'And what about Peter Clarke? Have you met
him yet? Have you *interviewed* him?'

'Not directly, but I've watched the tapes. He's –
complicated.'

'You misjudged him,' she accused. 'Admit it. His
daughter's fine with his mother, and his relationship with his brother wasn't the least bit sinister.'

'We'll see,' was all Phil Hollis would reply to
that.

CHAPTER NINETEEN

'On our own again, then,' Thea said to her spaniel, when Phil had gone. 'Lock the doors,' muttered Ignatius, who had seemed subdued all day. 'Don't you get poorly on me,' Thea warned him. 'I have no idea how to cope with a sick parrot.'

'Frankly, my dear...' the bird attempted, before fading into silence.

Thea had a long evening ahead, and felt torn between a hope that it could be spent in quiet idleness, and a desire to be kept in close touch with outside events. Nobody had offered to help her find Freddy and Basil, which was a constant worry. What if they weren't dead at all, but locked up somewhere dark and stuffy with no water? That would be difficult, she told herself. They would bark and howl and someone would hear them. But would that someone react? It was normal enough to hear dogs barking, even all through the night, and do absolutely nothing about it. She, Thea, ought to be out there, combing the countryside with ears attuned for any such sounds.

She would make it a priority for the next morning, she decided. One way or another, she would find them. If necessary she'd bury their bodies. She had learnt from previous experience that it was part of a house-sitter's remit to deal with pets who fell ill or died, and that included using a fair bit of initiative at times.

It would be nice if Ariadne would drop in, and at every small sound outside, she found herself wishing a knock on the door would follow. Hepzie picked up on this alertness and yapped sporadically at stirrings that only she could hear. It all made for a restless unsettling few hours.

When the mobile warbled, she snatched it with an urgency that surprised her. What was she expecting?

'Thea?' It was her mother. She suppressed a feeling of impatience, as if this might be blocking a more important call. She wasn't sure she had any energy to spare for her parent, if the call made demands on her reserves of kindness and sympathy.

'Hi, Mum. How are you?'

'I'm all right.' The voice was firm and business-like. 'I'm phoning about Emily. I've just been speaking to Bruce, and wondered whether you knew what was going on.'

'In what way? What did Bruce say?'

'He says she's ill. Some sort of emotional thing. Was she like that at the weekend, and you kept it from me? Is it about Daddy, or what?'

'I think it's about everything. She was very upset about Daddy, and then this – accident – happened, and she was involved with the police and everything, and I suppose it's all been a bit much for her.'

'But *Emily*.'

Thea relaxed, finding herself glad to be sharing her mother's worries, after all. 'I know. She's not usually the type to get overwhelmed, is she? We wouldn't be half so surprised if it was Jocelyn.'

'Thea, I know my daughters. I know Emily especially. If she's in enough of a state to make Bruce sound as he did, then there is something very badly wrong. Did the police bully her? Did they accuse her of anything? You know how fair-minded she always is. She hates anything to be unjust. Nobody will tell me what exactly happened. That's why I'm ringing you. I want you to tell me the whole story.'

Seeing no reason to prevaricate any longer, Thea did just that: the rainy night, the shouting and kicking, the smashed skull and police questions. 'She had no idea it was anybody she knew until the next day,' she finished. 'And that's when she got really upset, according to Bruce. She phoned me and sounded a bit hysterical, but nothing too bad. It all seems to have got worse from then on.'

'But the poor girl – fancy seeing something so horrible. Such awful violence! And if she couldn't help the police, she'd feel badly about that.'

'She's not helping them at all at the moment, apparently. Bruce has told them she's too ill to be interviewed again. They've got somebody under arrest, and it's really all down to Emily to establish whether his alibi is credible. It's the timing, mainly. And I suppose she might remember a bit more about what the man looked like.'

'She must be terrified. What if the murderer thinks she saw his face, and could identify him? She might be in danger – he might track her down and attack her.' Mrs Johnstone's voice rose in alarm. 'Good God, Thea – no wonder she's in such a state.'

'I have thought of that, of course. It might explain why she won't go out. But somehow it sounds more complicated than that.'

'Oh, rubbish! Well, I'm going over there first thing tomorrow, and I'm staying with her until this is all sorted out. If the murderer is the sort of madman you describe, surely they'll soon catch him.'

'We'll have to hope so,' said Thea, feeling oddly reassured by her mother's brisk attitude.

She found she was in no hurry to wake up and start the day on Friday. The sun still hadn't broken through the thick August clouds, and although not raining, it looked uninviting outside her window. The prospect of roaming the local lanes, peering into brambly ditches for the bodies of two dogs did not appeal in the slightest. She had little idea of where to start, and the image of what she might find was more repellent every time she revisited it.

The ferrets mewed at her in a friendly fashion, and she wondered whether she'd ever gather the nerve to catch one and take it out. Cedric had assured her that they were quite tame and enjoyed some human contact. But after her failure with the dogs, it seemed much too rash to attempt. Instead she simply stroked them as they ate, enjoying the sinuous bodies under her fingers and wondering idly whether they were included in Henry Galton's gloomy prognostications for farm animals. She could only assume that the arcane practice of rabbit-hunting with the use of ferrets had a very limited future, and the animals themselves could not expect a long and prolific destiny. There was already something old-fashioned about them, a hint of barbarity and secret male cruelties out in the unobserved fields and woods.

Ignatius appeared much as usual. When she took his night-time cover off, and produced a handful of sunflower seeds, he shifted rhythmically from one clawed foot to the other on his perch, as if dancing gently, and muttered, 'That's a very nice hat, Mrs Smithers,' in a low voice, which was nonetheless perfectly clear and articulate.

'Why thank you,' said Thea. 'It's good of you to say so.'

'We aim to please,' added the parrot casually, and slowly winked one eye, with a dry blue-tinged eyelid. Thea found it hard to believe he was a real animate creature, as she watched his antics. It was more like a very clever toy, operated by batteries and containing a tiny digital tape of utterances.

Outside, in the silence and stillness that was the gap where the dogs should be, Hepzie seemed restless, sniffing the air and trotting in and out of the shed that had been Freddy and Basil's home. 'Stop it,' Thea ordered. 'You're just making it worse.'

There was no sign of the cats when she left them some milk and biscuits, but their food kept disappearing, and Thea assumed they were around, getting on with their usual routines.

A car engine approaching was her first inkling that there was another visitor on the way. *Let it be Ariadne, and please not Mike Lister, the dog killer,* she prayed in the few seconds before the vehicle came into view.

It was Henry Galton, who up to that point had always walked the short distance from his farm to Hawkhill. Now he was in a large Toyota truck, its body high off the ground. He looked down at her through the open window, and said, 'Found your dogs. They're in the back.'

She went without hesitation for a look, remembering in an uncontrollable flash the body of her father in his coffin, viewed only a week earlier. This time it was a jumble of muddy hair, snarling teeth and a lot of stiff-looking legs. Galton had laid one on top of the other, with a sack which must have been over their heads, but which had slipped off during the drive. They lay in the bed of the truck, which was almost too high for Thea to peer into. There was matted blood on both chests.

'Shot them all right,' Galton said, coming to stand beside her. 'He's a good enough aim not to make a mess of it, if that's any consolation.'

The sound of the passenger door closing sent Thea whirling round to see who else had been in the truck. Sharon, partner of Mike Lister, was stepping down from the vehicle. 'Hello,' she said softly.

'Why are you here?' Thea asked rudely.

'She showed me where to find the dogs,' Galton said quickly. 'She's come to help us bury them.'

Thea shook her head, and let her gaze return to

the tangled bodies. 'It's so *wrong,*' she mourned. 'So cruel. Even if he was the best shot in the world, he'd have to do first one, then the other.' Her voice choked. 'The second one would have known what was coming.'

'They'd both know,' said Galton grimly. 'These dogs knew all about what a gun could do.'

It was too much. She sagged against him, tears welling furiously. 'How could he?' she sniffed. 'How could anybody do that? He's got dogs of his own, he must understand how terrible it was.'

'I was all for doing it myself,' he reminded her, with a kind of nobility. 'You have to be ready for a lot of killing if you live on the land.'

Sharon approached tentatively, putting a hand lightly on Thea's arm. 'It was very quick,' she said. 'And he did it for the best, you know. He wanted to save a lot of dithering, and decided to take the law into his own hands. Sometimes that is the best way.'

'Is it?' Thea rounded on her. 'What about the Angells? What are they going to think, when they come back?' She put a hand to her head. 'Damn it, I'll have to phone them and tell them, won't I? Now we know for sure what's happened.' She cast a pleading look at Galton, as if hoping he might make the phonecall for her.

He made no such offer, but shrugged gently and said, 'Wasn't it you who told me that bad news can wait?'

'Was it? Well, I'm not sure I was right. What time is it in Hong Kong, anyway?'

'Mid-evening – something like that.' He squared his shoulders. 'I don't like to rush you, but I do need to get on. First, though – have you got a camera?'

She stared at him. 'Pardon?'

'A camera – and not just the one in your phone. We ought to record their injuries, just in case. Cedric might want see the evidence.'

'In the car. I've got a camera in the car.' She went to get it, and turned away while Galton took eight or ten shots, turning the bodies over, and bending in close. Sharon stood to one side, and Thea wondered exactly why she had come. Did she really mean to defend Lister? Why did it matter to her what Thea thought of him?

'OK – let's do it,' said Galton, pulling down the rear flap of his truck. 'Where's best, do you think?'

She had no idea where Cedric and Babs might choose to bury their dogs, but a small square of neglected lawn lay between some large shrubs, set back from the main garden, and Thea selected that. 'This is very kind of you,' she said.

He shrugged, and the knowledge that big men were meant to be kind seemed to flow between the two of them. Big men came to the rescue of small women, perhaps less now than in earlier times, but still it could happen. She had been so overcome for a moment that she had actually rested her head on his chest and let tears fall onto it. His reaction had been one of easy acceptance, as if he knew that was the main purpose of such a broad accommodating torso. He ought to be a doctor or a fireman or an Air and Sea Rescue person, his arm encircling the half drowned or the distraught. And perhaps he was, she thought.

Anybody could be a part-time fireman, after all.

The magnitude of his helpfulness had not fully dawned on her, until she stood watching him dig. Now she didn't have to go and search for the dogs herself. The awful task had been taken from her by a man she had first encountered in a towering rage, brandishing a threatening gun.

For a few minutes it felt as if there were no real worries left. She would have the dreadful task of telling the Angells about their dogs, but she wasn't going to do it until the end of the day, at the earliest. The presence of Sharon was a distraction, creating an uncomfortable triangle with Galton, forcing Thea onto the outer edge as the uncomprehending stranger. The woman seemed to want to include her, though.

'It wasn't really your fault,' she said, as they stood over the finished grave. 'It was bound to happen sooner or later. Mike's obsessed with the worry that our dogs will do the same thing one of these days.'

'So he keeps them cooped up in that compound,' Thea accused.

'They don't mind. They play together and he takes them out for walks now and then. And Boris goes to the shows two or three times a year. He got Best in Breed last year.'

'What – at Cruft's?' Thea's eyes widened.

Sharon laughed. 'No, no. Only a regional thing – but it looks good on the pedigrees. Breeding dogs is quite a business these days, you know.'

'I can imagine,' said Thea. 'But I still feel wretched about Freddy and Basil.'

'They were called Ben and Jack, actually,' said

Sharon. 'Didn't Cedric tell you?'

Thea felt weak and foolish. 'No,' she said. 'He never did. I thought they didn't have names.'

Galton snorted, beside Thea. 'All dogs have names,' he said, as if intoning some great mystical secret. She half expected him to embark on a legend about the power of naming, with Cedric withholding the information lest Thea steal his animals' affection. Instead he merely tossed his spade back into the truck, and stamped the soil from his boots. 'Better get on,' he said, cocking his head at Sharon. 'Coming?'

With a lingering glance at Thea, Sharon climbed into the passenger seat, and the truck departed. Only then did Thea wonder how come Lister's partner was riding with Galton back to his farm.

CHAPTER TWENTY

Hepzie obviously knew what a grave was. She returned to the burial place of Freddy and Basil time and again, sniffing the edges of the raw earth, and whining. 'Leave it alone,' Thea told her, worrying that the bodies were not deep enough and foxes or badgers would come and dig them up again. She would suggest to Cedric that he pile stones on top, to make sure there was no disturbance.

Eventually she felt forced to take the spaniel out for distraction. 'We'll go and see how Ariadne's getting on,' she said. 'And she'll have to put up with you this time as well.'

By now, Peter Clarke must surely have either been released or charged, and the latter seemed highly unlikely. It would be diverting, at the very least, to hear about his experiences as a murder suspect. And she wanted a chance to compare him to Galton, to check her own reactions to the two very different men. If he was there at Ariadne's cottage, that would be a bonus, even if they did regard her as an intruder on their romantic idyll.

But there was nobody at the Cold Aston cottage. It had the indefinable air of an empty house, even in broad daylight when lights would not be on. Thea tried the front door, which was locked, and then went round to the back, where there was no sign of life. 'Drat!' she muttered. 'Now what are we going to do?' The day stretched ahead, blank and uninviting.

Across the village street was a house still owned by Phil, despite his intention to sell it, nine months earlier. She suspected that he had nursed a secret plan to move into it himself when he retired, perhaps taking Thea with him. Meanwhile, he had found tenants for it, and there were toys and a battered Fiesta in the front garden. A dramatic change from its chilly darkness last November when Thea and Phil had stayed there together, sorting through Aunt Helen's possessions and unpleasantly embroiled in the killing of a young woman not far away.

They had never discussed the distant future, never made firm commitments to each other, but now that it all seemed to be over, Thea found herself regretting the possible scenario that had been lurking at the back of her mind. It would have been nice to live in the big old house, in the unassuming village, with a retired police detective.

One of the hazards of house-sitting was that it left far too much time for introspection. As a strategy for surviving Carl's death, she had trained herself to live in the present moment, not allowing fears for the future to intrude, and not giving too much rein to nostalgic visions of the past. It worked extremely well, but was hard to sustain. People would persist in asking what she intended to do, where she thought she would be in five years' time, how long she would keep up this ridiculous house-sitting business. She wondered now whether this habit had been destructive in her relationship with Phil. Had it made him feel somehow temporary? Did he think he was a kind of stop gap while she pulled herself together and found a new career, new home, new *life?* Maybe he had, but it seemed unlikely now that she'd ever be able to ask him.

And now, this morning, she very much needed to *do* something. She needed to take control, and not just sit around waiting for people to come and visit her – even though that had worked unexpectedly well for much of the week. Now they'd all wandered off on their own affairs and she was forgotten. It was a Friday thing, she realised. Friday was the day when nobody sent a friendly email or made a sociable visit. On Fridays they were all holding their breath and counting the minutes to the weekend.

Except vicars, she presumed. Vicars had to work at the weekend. They had to visit their parishioners and preside over garden fêtes and jumble sales on Saturdays and hold a scrambled succession of church services on Sundays, rushing from village to village, doing the work that three or four would once have done.

She got back in the car where Hepzie was resignedly curled on the passenger seat and opted for a circuitous drive northwards, taking the B4068 through Naunton, simply because Naunton was so spectacularly beautiful that it could cheer the glummest heart. It worked brilliantly, as she let the car crawl over the lovely old bridge by the church, and then curve around into the main street where the houses still managed to suggest a medieval style of living, with their low windows and stone mellowed from yellow into grey. Tourists seldom discovered Naunton on its unambitious little B road that led from nowhere to nowhere, simply a long loop off the much faster and straighter A436. It passed to the north of Upper Slaughter, and finally emerged at Stow, at a junction where its humble status was emphasised by a set of traffic lights which gave it such low priority that you could wait many minutes before being allowed to proceed.

Numerous villages laid claim to being the most typically Cotswold – the stone buildings, the rolling hills, the crooked little lanes, the characterful churches – and there were certainly several to choose from. But Thea had not yet seen one that could compete with the perfection of Naunton. It had none of the self-consciousness of the Slaughters, none of the deserted preserved-in-aspic air of the Duntisbournes. Naunton had real people living in it, a shop and a Post Office, pubs and the glorious river Windrush. Naunton, in short, had everything, and just to get a five-minute fix of it, from a slow drive-through, was enough to raise anybody's spirits.

'That's better, isn't it,' she said to the dog beside her. But Hepzie was unmoved by handsome buildings or living history. She wagged her tail in a brief acknowledgement, but showed no sign that her own spirits had lifted at all.

They drove back through Upper Slaughter, passing the impossibly fairytale Manor Hotel and the layby where Sam Webster had died, and presumably the ditch where Cedric's dogs had been dumped, as well. She found herself wondering precisely where Galton had found them, realising that it had to be somewhere alarmingly close to the scene of the murder. Another nagging coincidence, she thought. There was no possible connection between the two killings, and yet the bodies had lain within the same quarter-mile stretch of road. And of course there *was* a connection: Thea herself. She was the pivot at the centre of events, the one person who knew and cared about all three deaths.

Unless bloody Mike Lister had killed Sam Webster as well, of course.

The sky was clearer, and small patches of blue were appearing, almost for the first time all week. 'Another few days and we might be able to do a bit of sunbathing,' she told the dog. She had acquired a pleasing tan during June, in Temple Guiting, where the sun had blazed down all day every day, and she and Phil had been together to enjoy it. But now her skin was turning pale again, and those glorious days were a distant memory.

Hawkhill had a creeper growing up part of its facade, untrimmed and pushing into the crevices between the fascia and the roof. Already a few of its leaves had turned red, signalling the imminence of autumn. It was a pretty house, Thea conceded, as she drove slowly down the track towards it. The air of untidiness in the objects scattered about the yard and the straggling weeds in the garden had a certain appeal. It looked real and used, unlike many Cotswold houses. Why could she not simply settle down and enjoy some quiet days with the jigsaw and TV and Ignatius, letting the hours float by without having anything to show for them? That had been her vision when she first began house-sitting. She would walk her dog and read a lot of improving fiction, and play games on her computer and feel smug that she was being paid to be so lazy. It had not worked out like that. From the very first day, the outside world had intruded, and she as a stranger in their midst had been quick to observe the cracks and conflicts going on in a seemingly serene little village.

She made herself a small snack lunch, barely even sitting down to eat it. The radio was on, tuned to the local station, and she listened to the bland music being played, interspersed with weather forecasts and interviews with people who had complaints against the Council. Then came a news update, which began with the latest on the Upper Slaughter murder.

'Upper Slaughter slaughter,' muttered Thea wryly.

'Police have released from custody the Reverend Peter Clarke, who has been helping them with their enquiries,' the man read, as if barely registering the sense of the words. 'The deceased man, Doctor Samuel Webster, suffered very severe head injuries during an attack near the Manor Hotel in Upper Slaughter, where he had been staying as a guest on the evening of last Saturday. Reverend Clarke is his half-brother. The police are appealing for anybody who saw a man with blood on his clothes, on Saturday evening, to come forward with information to help with their enquiries.'

'Who writes this stuff?' thought Thea. She thought of her daughter Jessica's impatience with the news media, and the careless way they disclosed guesses as if they were facts. In Jessica's opinion, police work would be greatly simplified if all reporting of murders was banned completely. Thea disagreed. 'You don't understand how useful they can be,' she had argued. 'The police can't function unless they have the active participation of the people. You'll learn that eventually.'

It had been a back-to-front argument, but Jessica had been new to police work at the time, and had experienced only the more obstructive and misleading side of the general population thus far in her career.

At least Peter Clarke was free again. That came as little surprise, but was nonetheless a relief. He and Ariadne were probably celebrating somewhere, he pouring out the horrors of his incarceration and she soothing his fretting brow.

It would be interesting to see him again, and find out how the questioning had been conducted. His seemingly impeccable alibi must have stood up, after all. The Cirencester clergy must carry enough status to satisfy any detective, and if Clarke had turned up to the post-dinner get-together clean and calm and devout, then this alone would weigh in his favour. Hard to imagine that someone who had just come from committing an act of such intense violence could disguise the fact. Unless he was a real Jekyll and

Hyde, a skilled master of concealment and suppressor of emotion.

It was possible, of course. Case histories abounded of men and women who had recently savagely killed a close relative, only to appear convincingly innocent on the television, appealing for the killer to give himself up. People were very clever at dissembling. The trick, she supposed, was that they could first convince *themselves*. If they could believe their own lies, then anything was possible.

She thought again of Mike Lister, the wiry little man who was at ease with raw meat and large dogs and guns. A man who could kill an animal without flinching – would he be able to stamp down on a man's skull, hard enough to shatter it? He'd probably done it enough times to rats and even perhaps foxes – but a human victim was something altogether different. With a foolish feeling of regret, she dismissed him as a suspect. That would be too great a coincidence, even if he did live barely a mile away, and had dumped the dead dogs almost on the very spot where the murder had taken place. Besides, there was Sharon speaking up for him, trying to explain that he had no sinister motives for what he had done. Thea had not been entirely convinced, but she no longer regarded him with quite such revulsion as before.

The thread running behind all her musings was one she persistently tried to ignore. Phil had said things on Sunday morning that she had not examined at all in the ensuing days. Emily, he had suggested, could have known both the victim and the perpetrator, in the ghastly scene she had witnessed. Thea had assured herself that her sister had not recognised Webster in the rain, with his head impossibly mangled. The horror in her voice when she phoned on Monday could not have been an act. With what Bruce had said of her condition since the phone call, she had created a theory in which Emily blamed herself for not successfully saving Sam from his fate, for not being braver or quicker in some way.

But there were also discrepancies in Emily's explanation of where she had parked the car, and Bruce's account of her sounding the horn to scare away the attacker had not come up in the version Thea had heard on Saturday night. It would be a sensible thing to do, effective and safe – a very *Emily* thing to do. And it ought to be quite easy to verify. People in surrounding houses would have heard it, even though they'd be unlikely to go out in the rain to investigate.

She gave it up. What she needed was another person to talk it through with, and the only candidate for that role was Phil Hollis, who was no longer prepared to sit cosily with her in a strange house discussing the details of violent deaths and suspicious characters. He was talking it through with Detective Inspector Jeremy Higgins, and other colleagues. A team of officers would be calling on all the houses in the area, asking whether they had heard or seen anything; did they remember a bloodstained man running through the rain, and if so what time was this sighting?

Not a very promising investigation, then.

258

Random, irrational, frenzied – the sort of killing where careful assessment of motive, means and opportunity meant nothing. If Emily had not been there, it would have been no more difficult to resolve. Emily added almost nothing to their knowledge of what had taken place, apart from a fairly accurate idea of the time it all happened. She blinked – there was something wrong with that thought, some odd logic, that she couldn't identify. She shook her head and forced her thoughts onto something else.

Men. Peter Clarke, Henry Galton and Phil Hollis provided plenty of material for fantasy, ample opportunity for comparisons and wry might-have-beens. She sat at the kitchen table, sorting out jigsaw pieces into different heaps, and indulged in half an hour of these and similar thoughts.

CHAPTER TWENTY-ONE

Friday had continued to be far too quiet and uneventful. Much too much thinking time had led to sentimental memories of her father, a painful acceptance that he was gone for ever, gloomy musings on the inexorable passage of time, which brought only oblivion and pointlessness. She had gone to bed early only to find the thoughts impossible to turn off. She finally fell asleep past midnight, wishing she had some excitingly energetic plan prepared for the next morning.

Saturday was almost sunny. The clouds were semi-transparent, the blue sky behind them a reminder that fine weather was still a possibility. A morning for being outside, where she might have romped with Freddy and Basil – she couldn't think of them as Ben and Jack – if an alternative destiny had permitted them to live. As it was, their demise continued to cast a pall over the whole property; the grave, though out of sight, impossible to forget.

She deferred for a third time the phonecall to Hong Kong. What would she say? The more she thought about it, the more unnecessary it seemed to spoil a holiday with unhappy news. There was nothing Cedric or Babs could do from such a distance, no sense in upsetting them. Undoubtedly she ought to tell them, in her capacity as paid house-sitter. But she was more and more sure that the humane thing to do was to leave it until they got back.

The chores were conscientiously performed, including cleaning out the ferret cage and giving them a generous layer of fresh wood shavings from a large bale in their shed. The ferrets were the aristocrats of the Angell household, she suspected. Ignatius was a novelty, the cats employed for their rodent-catching skills, but the ferrets probably earned money and status for Cedric. Quite where the dogs had fitted into the picture, she was resigned to never fully understanding.

Shopping was becoming an urgent priority, with the milk all gone and no fresh food in the cupboard. She would get a salad, some good bread and cheese – and a bottle of wine. Perhaps *two* bottles, in the hope that someone would eventually come to visit her, and she could offer them some decent hospitality when that happened.

There was a reasonable choice of good food shops in Stow, and by eleven she and Hepzibah were in the car heading north.

Phil saw her before she saw him. She supposed he was trained to recognise cars at a glance, but even after he flashed his lights at her, and tooted the horn, she was still asking herself what was going on. This was embarrassing, she knew, after seeing his car about two hundred times over the past year. It ought to have registered on her memory as quickly as hers clearly had on his. She drew up by the side of the road, waiting for him

261

to run back to her. They were on a straight section, but not especially wide; traffic had to slow down and skirt round her in a way many drivers obviously found irritating.

'Don't stop there!' Phil shouted, as she put her head out of the window to greet him. 'Drive on to the next layby and I'll come and find you.'

The next layby was nearly two miles away, as it turned out. What a drama, she grumbled to herself. What annoying things cars could be, not to mention the men who drove them. What did he want that was so important, anyway?

He was behind her almost before she'd switched the engine off. His face looked red and she could feel rumblings of confused emotions in her belly: a repeat of the uncertainty as to how to behave with him, sadness at their changed relationship and worry about what he might have to say. She had completely forgotten how it felt to meet an ex, how all that shared history got in the way and prevented you from just being two normal people together, ever again.

'Thea – I was coming to see you,' he began, superfluously.

'Get in the car,' she invited, before heaving the spaniel over into the back seat. The passenger seat was only slightly muddy, she noted. Anything that got onto Phil's trousers would soon brush off again.

He wasted no time in coming to the point. 'We haven't given up on Peter Clarke,' he began. 'Jeremy's done more checking up on him, and frankly, he's little more than a conman. I'd like to warn Mary–'

'You mean Ariadne,' Thea corrected him automatically.

'Yes, whatever. The thing is, she might well be in danger from him. We think that's what could have happened with his brother – he threatened to expose him for what he was, and got killed for his trouble.'

'So why have you let him go?'

'Lack of evidence, as usual.'

'Oh, no.' She leant away from him as if he'd waved something horrible under her nose. 'I'm not going to act as a decoy for you. You want me to do something sneaky, I can hear it in your voice.'

'Not at all. When have I ever asked anything like that of you?' His tone was injured, reproachful.

'What, then?'

'Just try and spend some time with them. Try to get Mary – Ariadne – to see him for what he is. And be there for her, when she finally gets the message. She doesn't deserve a bastard like him.'

'Phil–' Her face was pinched with utter resistance to what he was saying. 'Are you *sure* you've got this right? He seems so *nice*. And why would he go to the trouble of seducing Ariadne if he doesn't really like her? It doesn't make any sense.'

'I never said he didn't like her. That part might even be genuine. But he won't stay.'

'No, because you'll have him locked away for thirty years, convicted of murder.'

'I hope so,' he nodded emphatically. 'I don't mind admitting that's my best case scenario.'

'So are you going to tell me what awful things Jeremy discovered about him? Worse than what you told me last time, which I'm pretty sure turned out to be not even halfway true? Did it?'

He shifted awkwardly, trying to look at her face, but afraid to twist his back too far. 'It's not a matter of provable facts, true or otherwise. There's no single revelation, just a long list of small deceptions and lies. Absolutely not what you'd expect from a clergyman.'

'But he *is* a real vicar, is he?'

'So it seems. He's in Crockford.'

'And he hasn't been abusing small children?'

'Not as far as we know.'

'And he really did spend ten years or so in Africa?'

'Yes, yes – those things are true. They're too big to lie about. But we've interviewed former neighbours and colleagues. Nobody likes him or trusts him. Obviously they didn't want to slander him, but they've said enough to ring any number of bells.'

Thea shook her head. 'It sounds very feeble to me. Lots of people these days don't like vicars. And when they look like him, you can just imagine what high emotions might be raging.'

'What do you mean?'

'Phil, the man is *beautiful*. Those eyes are fantastic. I agree with you that he shouldn't be a vicar, but not for the same reasons. Temptation must have been a constant hassle for him, women throwing themselves at his feet. I think it was very clever of him to go to Africa, where white skin and blue eyes probably don't arouse the same passions.'

'Well, it all adds up to a picture of a man nobody trusts. Combined with his connection to Webster, we'd be negligent to leave him to his own devices.'

'But you arrested him and questioned him for two days. It sounds as if you're at risk of persecuting the poor man.'

Phil heaved a sigh. 'I can see you're not going to be of much help, if you feel like that. Think of your sister, for God's sake. The trauma of what she saw has sent her into a real spin – doesn't she deserve for the killer to be caught?'

'Don't give me that. Of course the killer must be caught. And I haven't said I won't help you. I'm just exercising my rights to express an opinion based on what I've seen of Peter Clarke.'

He gave a mock shudder at her severity. 'OK, then, thanks,' he said. 'Well, that's not actually the main thing I wanted to talk about.'

'Oh?'

'We think it might help to stage a reconstruction of the killing – this evening. It's exactly a week since it happened.'

'But – you'll need Emily. Has she said she'll do it?'

'That's the problem. Her husband won't even let us speak to her. He says she's still too ill. So–'

'Oh no! I know where this is going. For heaven's sake, Phil, I don't look anything like her.'

'That doesn't matter. It's just to jog people's memories. All we need is a woman in a car in that gateway, two men skirmishing in the layby, and the woman walking along to see what's going on.'

'Doesn't seem worth the bother, if you ask me. Won't you have to keep doing it over and over, because you're not sure of the time?'

'Two or three times, maybe. I thought you'd be keen to get involved, actually.'

She laughed scornfully at this. 'I might if I thought it would help. But you're assuming there'll be people who pass by that same spot at the same time every Saturday. Besides, the weather's completely different today.'

'You'd be surprised how many people live by a rigid routine. Hotel staff coming and going, for a start. They've been totally unable to come up with anything useful so far. It's as if they're ashamed that something so unpleasant could happen practically on their grounds. And Saturday has its own routines. We're not terribly hopeful, I admit, but it's worth a try.'

'Aren't there any other witnesses at all? At that time in the evening, people must have been out and about.'

'Nobody heard anything or saw anything until the flashing blue lights appeared at the layby. That in itself is odd. Webster walked through the foyer of the hotel at seven fifty-five, a few minutes after his brother left, and went out of the main door. They think he was going for a smoke. He had cigarettes in his pocket.'

'Poor chap – having to go out in the rain to satisfy his habit.'

Phil ignored this opening onto one of their perennial arguments, in which Thea, a lifelong non-smoker, defended the right of people to do what they liked with their own bodies. Instead, he stuck to his account. 'Somehow, for some reason, he walked down to the road, and turned left into the layby. In the rain.'

'Was he wearing a mac?'

'Not a mac, but a light anorak. With a hood.'

She gave him a thoughtful look. 'Was it up?'

'Pardon?'

'The hood – was it over his head when he was attacked?'

'Um–' he narrowed his eyes and stared at the dashboard. 'I don't know.' A thought visibly occurred. 'It was covered with blood and brain tissue. It had filled up, like a bag. I don't think it's possible to know for sure where it was at the time of the attack.'

'It would have marks all over it,' she argued. 'Footprints.'

He sighed. 'Thea, everything was covered with mud and blood – it was a hopeless mess. Besides, I can't see why it matters whether the hood was up or down.'

'Surely it makes some sort of difference, don't you think? It changes the image of him as victim. Not a middle-aged professor, but a type of hoodie. A faceless male person, that's all.'

'He was a don, not a professor,' he corrected her pedantically. She resisted the urge to challenge him to explain the difference.

'Well, if you ask me the killer is bound to be someone from out of the area, with no reason to choose Sam Webster, and who's five hundred miles away by now.'

'Possibly,' he nodded irritably. 'But you know as well as I do that such bogeymen are pretty rare. There's always got to be a reason, especially for such a level of violence.'

'Maybe. Emily did say he was shouting as he kicked poor Sam. A lot of bad language, she said.'

'Did she?' He frowned. 'I don't remember that.'

'Did she tell you the bit about honking the car horn to frighten the man away?' As soon as she'd spoken, Thea wondered why she couldn't keep her mouth shut. Phil was suspicious enough without adding more discrepancies to the story.

'Oh yes,' he said, to her great relief. 'She made quite a thing of that. We couldn't work out where the car had been, but she cleared that up. When she got out to inspect the scratch, she heard the attack–'

'And the shouting,' Thea supplied.

'Maybe. Anyway, she says she sounded the horn as a way of driving him off. Though it's a bit funny that nobody remembers hearing it. Then she left the car where it was and walked the thirty yards or so to where it was all happening in the layby.'

'Right. And the car was still in the gateway when the police and the ambulance arrived.'

'Yes, it was. They offered to help her push it free, before we took her to Cirencester to be interviewed, but it wasn't stuck, as it turned out.'

'Did she ever say it was?'

He scratched his head. 'I don't think she did. We just somehow assumed it was, from the odd angle, and all the mud everywhere.'

They lapsed into a silent contemplation of the increasing complexities of the death of Sam Webster. Then Thea remembered what she had promised to do that evening. 'We should at least have a car the same as Emily's,' she said. 'For the re-enactment or whatever you call it.'

'No problem.'

'I can't really refuse to do it, can I? What time do you want me?'

'We'll collect you at seven thirty.'

'It'll pass the time, I suppose,' she said grudgingly.

'Thanks,' he nodded. She expected him to make a move, but instead he still seemed to be working down a mental list of things he had to say. 'Now, what about those dogs? Are we still meant to be helping you to find them?'

'Not necessary. They're buried in the garden at Hawkhill, poor things.'

'Oh? What happened?'

She gave a quick account of the final stages of the story, surprised at the way he went tense at the mention of Galton. 'And you believed him?' he blurted, incredulously. 'Good God, Thea, that's the oldest trick in the book. There's no evidence at all against Lister, is there? Don't you think it's all a bit neat, the way Galton explains it?'

'I don't understand what you're saying.'

'Well, from my objective viewpoint, it sounds to me as if Galton's been very clever in shifting the blame onto Lister, just as Lister was clever in blaming your dogs for the worrying. They've both got what they wanted, anyhow, at your expense.'

She puzzled it through, trying to test the probabilities all over again. 'That's crazy,' she concluded. 'Sharon was there as well – defending Lister. It was *definitely* him. There's no more to be said about it. Henry was kind and sweet about it. You just don't like him for some reason. I suppose he got better marks than you in his A-levels.'

Phil snorted at this. 'He didn't, as it happens. But he did steal Hilary Tomkins from me.'

'Aha! I knew there was something,' she crowed.

'It was a bitterly fought battle,' he recalled. 'But in the end she married Roger Rowlands, which served us both right, I suppose.'

'Well, you have to take my word for it that Lister shot the dogs. He wouldn't even deny it, if you asked him. My only worry now is how I'm going to tell their owners.'

'They could turn nasty,' he warned. 'Refuse to pay you, and press charges against their killer.'

She sighed. 'I refuse to even think about it any more. Freddy and Basil were dear sweet dogs, but they did kill those sheep – Henry convinced me of that. They didn't mean any harm, but it was an awful thing, all the same. They couldn't have stayed here, whatever happened. It just goes to show,' she ended vaguely.

'What does it go to show?'

'Oh – I don't know. The way things can turn out, I suppose. I was so sure they were innocent, at the beginning of the week.'

They were both uncomfortable, with each other and with the way the conversation had gone. 'Well, let's focus on the layby killing,' said Phil. 'I just wish we had a bit more hard evidence.'

'Evidence,' she repeated. 'That's what it all comes down to, isn't it. With all this DNA and CCTV and satellite surveillance, we still don't have any evidence for this killing.'

'We might have done if the rules had been properly observed.'

'What?'

'The way Webster's body was handled was pretty dodgy. Human nature reared its ugly head, I'm afraid.'

'In what way?'

'It was raining hard, you remember. Nobody likes to squat in a mud puddle with rain pouring down their neck staring at the contents of a man's crushed head. So they didn't take very good note of how the body was lying before it was moved. The police doctor certified life extinct, and that was about it. Then the post-mortem was a joke. The way the skull was broken was consistent with heavy pressure from above, end of story. Large person jumped violently onto victim's cranium and caused massive trauma to the brain in several places.'

'That sounds clear enough to me.'

'Except your sister mentioned a stick or cudgel or some such thing. She talked of kicks to the body. She couldn't account for forty-five minutes in the middle of the whole episode. She knew Webster. It would be nice to have supporting evidence to explain away these niggles.'

'You don't believe anybody, do you? Emily, Galton, Peter – they're all liars in your eyes.'

'Well, *somebody* killed that man. Until we find who it was, it doesn't make much sense to trust anybody.'

It felt like going over stale old ground, and Thea gave up her questioning. She wanted him to get out of the car and go away. There was too much feeling flowing between them for comfort. Sensing the hiatus, Hepzie pushed her way between the seats and pawed at Phil's sleeve.

271

'Hello, old girl,' he said, fondling one of her long ears just the way she loved. 'How are you getting on with that nasty parrot, then?'

Thus encouraged, the dog came all the way through and flopped down on his lap, staring at him adoringly. 'Stop it, Heps,' muttered Thea, realising for the first time that if Phil and his two dogs went out of their lives for good, the spaniel would feel the loss.

It seemed Phil was having similar thoughts. He lifted the dog off himself, and opened the car door. 'Well, that's it, then,' he said. 'Stay there, Hepzie, there's a good dog.' He looked quickly at Thea. 'I can't give you any more guidance on what to do, but if only for your sister's sake, I think you'd do well to try and help.'

She gave him a look that contained none of the bridling resentment that most women would manifest. The look was soft and sad, and very slightly reproachful. 'We all want the same thing, I suppose,' she said calmly. 'I'll do what I can, for us all. And that includes poor Ariadne.' Then she thought back over the past year. 'You don't seem very concerned for my safety,' she added. 'If you're right that Peter did do that to Sam Webster, it wouldn't take much to finish me off, if he wanted to.'

Phil winced, as he straightened up – whether from his back or her words, she couldn't be sure.

'I gave up telling you to be careful some time ago,' he said. 'I'm assuming you won't provoke him or threaten him or go off alone with him into dark deserted country lanes.'

'With those beautiful blue eyes, there's no

knowing what I might do,' she said, starting the car engine. It was more than she had intended to allow herself, but the satisfaction was considerable, as she drove away.

She indulged herself in the shops of Stow, where expensive gourmet food was the norm – cheese, bread, organic vegetables – and it all ate up money. If the Angells decided to withhold part of her payment, due to the loss of their dogs, she was going to be significantly out of pocket. But Thea Osborne had never been one to worry about financial matters, mainly because she had little interest in buying things. Her laptop computer had been the single biggest purchase for the past two years, and now Phil had gone off her, the prospect of a surprise holiday in Greece or Morocco had disappeared. She might as well eat and drink lavishly, she decided – and added a bottle of locally made wine to the basket.

The town was not crowded, but there were plenty of people on the pavements, stopping to chat to friends, many of them with old-fashioned baskets on their arms. Thea suspected that most of them did their main shopping at a big supermarket somewhere, but topped up with chutney and olives and organic ice cream in a deliberate effort to keep the small local shops in business. She would silently converse with Carl at times like this, keeping him informed of the way society was going, highlighting anything that confirmed his passionate interest in environmental matters. Now things were apparently over with Phil, she found herself reverting more and more to Carl as her companion.

Is this healthy? she asked herself, wondering why there had to be a man, even a dead one, in her life.

She watched the faces approaching her, hoping to see someone familiar. She had met a number of local people over the past fifteen months – it wasn't unreasonable to hope to meet one of them here in the main town of the area on a Saturday.

But nobody emerged from the crowd. She bought her extravagant provisions and went back to the car, where her dog waited patiently for her. She had found a space quite close to the main square, on the kerbside, Stow being unusually capacious when it came to parking places. A man was standing unnaturally close to her vehicle, his face pressed to the front passenger window, the dog barking hysterically inside, jumping at the glass. 'Hey!' Thea called. 'What do you think you're doing?'

She'd known who it was from twenty paces away. The man who had given far more cause for suspicion than Peter Clarke or Henry Galton. A man who seemed to relish causing worry and pain. A nasty little man she would have preferred never to see again.

Mike Lister slowly lifted his head and grinned at her. 'Just amusing your dog,' he said easily. 'You shouldn't leave her in a hot car like that.'

'It's in the shade,' she pointed out. 'She's perfectly all right.'

'If you say so.' Something about his sly expression made her quiver inwardly. A knowing look, suggesting a secret that would shake her to the core if she knew it. Taking a deep breath, she reminded herself that some people adopted this sort of look simply to make themselves feel superior. It was a learnt trick, amply reinforced by the anxiety it caused in other people. What could he possibly know that would worry her? What more could he do to her, now that Freddy and Basil were dead?

'Your sister—' he said. 'I hear she's the one who found that dead man.'

She shook her head impatiently. 'That's old news now. So what if it was her? What's it to do with you?'

'It just seems odd, that's all.'

'It isn't remotely odd, you stupid man. Why shouldn't it be Emily as well as anybody else?'

She had gone too far. It was like the moment when the miller's daughter guessed the name of Rumpelstiltskin. Lister actually stamped his foot, albeit lightly, at being called stupid. 'You're going to be sorry you said that,' he threatened. 'I've heard things that would be bad for your sister if they came out.'

'Don't be ridiculous. If you really know any-thing about it, you should tell the police. Emily and I have nothing to fear. In fact we both want nothing more than to find who killed Sam. It's horrible to think there's such a violent killer out there, roaming free.' She gave him a very direct look, hoping he could read her implication that the killer might be somebody very like himself.

He grinned again, his rage successfully bat-tened down. 'Not so many as there were a week ago, thanks to me,' he said. Thea took a few seconds to understand him.

'You mean Freddy and Basil,' she gasped. 'You want to gloat about killing them.' She remembered Sharon's efforts to justify Lister's actions, and wondered why she'd gone to the trouble.

'Had to be done,' he said.

'So why do you have to go over it all again?'

'You're right,' he nodded carelessly. 'Far more important to discover who killed that Oxford bloke.'

'I don't believe you know anything about it.' Thea held his gaze, finally staring him down. He took a step away from her, and said nothing. 'Do you?' she insisted.

'I know one thing,' he hissed. 'You are one stuck-up piece of work, thinking you're so much cleverer than everybody else. Always knowing better, aren't you? Well, maybe you ought to have listened to me last weekend.'

'What difference would that have made? By the time I met you, the dogs had escaped. And you were *glad*. I could see it in your face. You didn't want them caught and kept safe. You saw it as a chance to get at poor Cedric.'

'Oh – aye. Been talking to friend Henry, I see.' He narrowed his eyes, and Thea remembered the way Sharon had so casually ridden away in Galton's truck. Something else going on there, she suspected.

But it was none of her business, and she felt weary of village scandal. 'Goodbye, Mr Lister. As you say, it's warm in the car and I should make sure my dog's all right.' Brushing past him, she unlocked the car and got in, without giving him another glance.

CHAPTER TWENTY-TWO

Hepzie took some time to calm down, jumping all over Thea and whining, preventing her from starting the car and driving away. 'It's all right,' she soothed the dog. 'Poor old you. This isn't much fun, is it? No decent walks, nobody to play with. Not what we expected at all, as far as you're concerned.'

The long silken ears flapped as the spaniel expressed her pent-up feelings with continuing vigour. The soft coat, which was overdue for a trim, brushed Thea's face. The undocked tail, with its curly fronds, wagged frantically. 'Hey, hey, put me down,' Thea laughed, hugging the animal tightly. 'Let's get back to the ranch and have some lunch – OK? Then we'll go for a walk, I promise.'

Honouring her promise, and trying to forget all about Phil Hollis, Mike Lister and everybody else who made her feel anxious, which included her elder sister, she set out with Hepzie on a lead, just before two o'clock. The sun had broken through, and a light breeze was blowing. Perfect for a lengthy stroll, she decided. They'd stay out for most of the afternoon, exploring the country-side and recapturing what was most lovely about the Cotswolds. Plenty of time to forget the crime reconstruction that evening, and the anxiety it threatened to cause within her.

Not being entirely confident of her map reading ability, she opted to use the big well-marked footpaths that converged on the Slaughters. The Macmillan Way became Monarch's Way and then Heart of England Way. Covering a distance of three or four miles it struck northwards through Upper and Lower Swell, and Thea aimed to get as far as Upper Swell before turning back. A close examination of the map revealed a short path skirting Lower Slaughter to the south, although it was going to be necessary to traverse part of the village itself, before heading into open country.

The rhythm of walking was conducive to peaceful thoughts, nothing forced or uncomfortable. She tried to remain alert to the beauties all around her: the undulating ground, the glimpses of the river Dikler, the patches of woodland and occasional old house blending effortlessly into the scenery. It was a privilege, she acknowledged, to have the time and freedom to spend an afternoon in such a way. Once out of Lower Slaughter, she released Hepzie from the lead, knowing the dog would keep her in sight, sniffing cheerily into rabbit holes and other points of interest. She could not permit the disaster of Freddie and Basil to affect the way she treated the spaniel. The footpath was well away from any roads until it reached Lower Swell. Nothing bad was going to happen on such a lovely day.

Regular consultations of the map ensured that she stayed on the correct path. Away to the right she could see the tower of the church in Stow, and she realised she had walked almost the same distance as she had driven that morning, which came as quite a surprise. An hour and a half had passed in easy calm reflection, walking at an unhurried pace, recovering her spirits after the turbulence of the past two weeks.

She had encountered precisely three other walkers during the afternoon: a couple in late middle age, with walking sticks and sensible boots, striding out competitively; and a young man with a rucksack and a haunted look in his eye. Walking had become an end in itself, an activity that just about everybody claimed to find interesting. No longer a simple means of moving from one point to another, but a virtuous practice that made you slim and fit and somehow superior. Thea hated to be thought part of this odd business – she was unashamedly aimless in her walking, unless it was to exercise her dog – but she was at least taking the time to appreciate the landscape.

Every few minutes, this landscape altered. At one moment it would be framed between large trees, the glitter of water completing the picture of patchwork fields and jumbled elevations; the next there'd be a broad uphill sweep with a handsome wood breaking the line of the hedges. The map showed three long barrows, a disused quarry and two tumuli within a single square mile – all of them evidence of human habitation and activity going back into the distant mists of time. The thing about the Cotswolds, she explained to herself, was that they combined a sense of space and sparse habitation with a tightly packed history that added rich significance to every single feature. Long before the Romans made their own particular mark on the region, there had been people living and working and dying here. She slowed her pace even further, to examine the edges of the path, trying to imagine how many millions of feet had passed over the identical stretch, since the dawn of time.

It would be better, she thought, to find a different route back. A circular walk was always preferable to a straight there-and-back. But it seemed from the map that the only viable alternative was to use roads, and however quiet they might be, the constant need for vigilance for traffic did not appeal to her. She'd have to stick to the same footpaths she came on, and watch out for different vistas and landmarks on the return.

But the prospect of another ninety minutes or so without a drink was a worry. She had forgotten, as she usually did, to bring a bottle of water with her. There was a pub marked on the map, in Lower Swell, but whether it would be open at four in the afternoon was doubtful. Otherwise, she could see nothing until she reached Lower Slaughter.

The Golden Ball pub had an instant appeal. It was on the main road, clearly open and moderately busy, to judge from the vehicles in the car park. By Cotswold standards it seemed slightly down market, which suited Thea perfectly. She and Hepzie went in, with nothing on their minds but the need to slake their thirst.

She ordered lemonade and lime for herself and a bowl of water for the dog, both of which were provided without question. A man standing at the bar looked down at the eagerly lapping spaniel and said, 'Best not let her drink too much at once. It'll give her colic.'

'Do you think so?' smiled Thea, wondering how she was going to stop the process without her dog feeling hard done by.

Before the man could elaborate on his theory, there was a diversion.

'You're following us, aren't you,' came an accusing voice, from a table by the window. More heads than Thea's turned towards the speaker.

Ariadne and Peter were looking at her unsmilingly.

Thea picked up her drink, and leaving the dog to her own devices, crossed the room to her friend. 'I promise you I'm not,' she said. 'I've been walking all afternoon and got thirsty, that's all. This seems to be the only place to get a drink for quite a distance.'

Peter Clarke was slumped on the wooden bench, looking tired or even possibly ill. Ariadne laid a hand on his arm, a look of pain on her face.

'What's the matter?' Thea asked her. 'Is there something wrong with him?' She thought of malaria, or sleeping sickness or even, despite his denials, AIDS. People brought all kinds of sickness back from Africa with them, the atavistic taint of the Dark Continent, even now.

'His brother is dead,' Ariadne said, in a low angry voice. 'And he's under suspicion of killing him. Isn't that enough?'

Thea wasn't sure that it was enough. The man had seemed to bear up well enough a few days ago. 'Has something else happened?' she asked,

281

only then remembering that Phil Hollis had asked her to spy on this couple, to report anything significant about them. It was as if by some magic he had engineered this very encounter, entirely against her own will.

'Like what?'

'I don't know.' She reminded herself that she did not know Ariadne very well, when it came to it. In the solitary experience of house-sitting, they might have seemed like best friends, but the truth was quite otherwise. They had spent a week together, the previous year, in the middle of a murder investigation, sharing the feeling of being tossed on an uncontrollable wave of shock and bewilderment, during which they'd exchanged a few personal facts, and talked about life and death and the point of it all. Ariadne was inclined to anger, she remembered, especially when Phil Hollis forgot her new name.

'Leave us alone, OK,' Ariadne said. 'We wanted some space, that's all. Don't you go reporting to Phil Hollis that you've seen us acting suspiciously.'

The accuracy of this instruction struck home, and Thea backed away, one leg getting entangled in the spaniel standing right behind her. 'I'm sorry,' she said. 'I honestly had no idea that you'd be here.' She looked again at Peter, hoping for a glimpse of the blue eyes and one of his smiles. 'Cheer up,' she told him. 'As I understand it, there's absolutely no evidence against you.'

It was a betrayal, of course. She had revealed police information, when Phil had trusted her not to. The fact that it was a negative, nothing more than an absence of something, was a mitigation, but to a guilty man it would come as huge encouragement.

It was Ariadne who seized it as a gift. 'Really?' she said eagerly. 'Is that right?'

'Of course it is,' snapped Clarke, looking up at last. 'How could there be evidence of something I haven't done? Be sensible, will you.'

Ariadne forced a laugh, and pressed his arm again. 'I never was much good at logic,' she giggled. To Thea it looked like someone clinging desperately to an inadequate stick as the waves of reality burst over her. This man did not love this woman, she felt sure. He found her irritating, annoying, perhaps useful but not the object of his love. Poor Ariadne, she thought. She's going to be so miserable when she has to admit the truth. The loss of dignity and self-respect had to be the greatest peril, for someone who had always struggled to maintain both. Not afraid to be different, outspoken and solitary, Ariadne was a cruel choice for a man to exploit.

A young man at another table was watching them with interest. 'We're causing a spectacle,' said Thea, still hoping to raise a smile, at least in Ariadne.

'What's new?' said the woman with a sigh. 'People always seem to be staring at us these days.'

'I'll have to go,' said Peter Clarke abruptly. 'I've got things to do.'

'Services tomorrow, I suppose?' said Thea brightly, still trying to locate the friendly, open man she'd met a week ago. 'Got to write your sermon?'

'I don't do sermons,' he said frostily. 'Ari, you'll have to come with me, if you don't want to walk home.'

'Oh, yes, all right. Sorry, Thea. You caught us at a bad time. Are you all right to walk back?'

The concern was at least a suggestion that they were still friends, and Thea smiled confidently. 'I'll be fine,' she assured Ariadne. 'It was nice to see you. Look – I'll ring you. I'm only here another week, and it would be great if we could meet up again, properly.' She glanced at Peter Clarke, hoping he understood that she was offering Ariadne a supportive shoulder, for the inevitable moment when he broke her heart.

There was more to be said, but not in front of Peter. 'I've got to go to the loo,' said Ariadne. 'I'll just be a minute.'

'I'll be in the car, then,' he said. 'Don't be long.'

Ariadne turned back as soon as he was out of sight, confirming Thea's suspicion that there had been a deliberate ploy to get rid of Peter. 'It's not what you think, you know,' she said in a low voice.

'Isn't it?'

'He's under a terrible strain. He isn't like this at all, usually. But he thinks his whole life has fallen apart – again. It's brought up everything about his wife and the trouble there was years ago, with the Bishop. I suppose Phil's told you about that?'

'I don't know,' said Thea softly, dodging the question. 'He's like two different people. That's never a good sign, in my experience. It makes it so hard to trust him.'

'Careful,' Ariadne warned. 'I know you and

284

your habit of stepping over the line. I'm not asking for your advice.'

'So what *are* you asking?'

'For you to understand. Give him some leeway. You can't judge a person by the way they behave in such an extreme situation.'

'Wrong, Ariadne,' said Thea, with more force. 'That's exactly when you *can* judge them. That's when the real person shows through. Peter's being horrible to you, when all you're trying to do is help him. You must be able to see it.'

Ariadne shook her head. 'You weren't there this morning, when I snapped back at him. He went all to pieces. That's why we came here, away from everybody and everything. He was *crying*, Thea, saying he didn't know where he'd be without me. He *needs* me.' She said the last words with an air of wonder, as if unsure of what they meant, exactly. 'And I need him. We're committed, for better or worse. This is it for me, whatever happens.'

Thea stepped away, hands held up in surrender. 'OK, OK – I get the message. And I'm honestly not trying to knock it. I really hope it works out and you can make each other happy, if that's what you want. Just–'

'What?'

'Just don't take too much bullshit from him. Don't giggle when he says something patronising or rude. Make him see he can't get away with it.'

Ariadne laughed. There was relief in the sound. 'Oh, Thea, you're wonderful, you really are. You trample all over the biggest no-go area there is, and still manage to make me feel better.'

'We aim to please,' said Thea, not sure who she was quoting, for a moment. 'And I meant what I said about phoning you.'

'Good,' said Ariadne, before striding off to where Peter was impatiently revving the car engine.

CHAPTER TWENTY-THREE

The walk back seemed much longer than the outward leg. Hepzie was tired, and jogged along at Thea's heels with no dashing off to the side or scrabbling at mysterious holes in the hedge. It was almost six when they finally reached Hawkhill, and the animals were waiting to be fed. The cats showed their faces in the barn doorway, and Ignatius greeted them with 'Here's a fine kettle of fish,' as soon as they got through the door.

It was difficult to resist the conclusion that something had happened, and the bird was warning her about it. Quickly she went from room to room, checking that things were as she'd left them, finding nothing untoward. She was weary and still thirsty, as was her dog. After drinking the contents of the water bowl in the kitchen, Hepzie flopped down on the grubby rug in front of the Aga and fell into a deep sleep. Thea drank a glass full of tap water, and thought wistfully of bedtime and the chance of a long dreamless night. But first, she remembered, she was participating in a police reconstruction of a vicious murder. Slumped on the sofa, she tried to imagine how it would be.

There was something almost superstitious about the mere fact of replaying events, keeping them as closely identical to the original as possible. It might conjure something unexpected.

287

The murderer himself might materialise – indeed that was one of the best hopes of the police. If it was somebody who always passed that point on that day, then he just might be doing it again a week later, even though he'd committed such a ghastly act there. A certain sort of criminal would be careful to allay suspicion by behaving normally. If the murder had been less irrational and psychotic than it seemed, the man's cunning might be in full working order. If it was a barman from the hotel or a local lorry driver, he might take a quiet satisfaction in standing idly by and watching events in all their clumsy drama. There would be mistakes and wrong assumptions that would make him quietly chuckle.

She knew, deep down, that everything she had done that afternoon had been designed, at least partly, to distract herself from the one thing she ought to be thinking about. Something she felt she was dodging to a degree that was almost immoral. Her sister, whose husband had reported as being ill, obviously wanted help from her, and what had she done about it? Precisely nothing.

She looked at the big old clock on the wall, which kept perfect time. Six thirty-five, and she had not yet fed the ferrets or cats. Heaving herself up, she did the job in five minutes flat. Hepzie never even noticed her leaving the house and coming back again. Ignatius said 'We aim to please,' four times, which she interpreted as a call for some supper of his own. His feeding times had not been given as precisely as the others. 'Just give him a handful of seed when the bowl's empty,' Babs had told her. 'And pick him some stuff from the garden – anything that's got nuts or seeds on it.' So far she had overlooked this part of the bird's diet, worried that she might give him something poisonous.

Then she phoned Emily.

It was a relief when her sister answered, sounding more or less normal, if a trifle flat. 'Oh, hi,' she greeted Thea. 'How's things?'

'All right. What about you? I've been hearing all kinds of dire reports about you.'

'What do you mean?'

Almost too late, Thea realised that Bruce might well not have mentioned his lunchtime rendez-vous with Thea. 'Oh, Mum. She phoned and said you weren't very well.'

Emily groaned softly. 'Yes, she's here, making a fuss of me. It's very sweet of her, but I'm not *ill*. I just had a bit of a funny turn. I'd rather not talk about it now, if that's OK. I'll be all right by Monday.'

It seemed an odd thing to say. 'Why Monday?'

'For work, of course. I have to get back to work.'

'I see. But Em – Bruce told the police you weren't well enough to come to their re-enact-ment this evening. That's why I'm phoning. I wanted to check a few details. I've got to be you, you see.'

'Re-enactment?' Her voice was suddenly hollow, as if all the breath had left her body. 'Is that what you said?'

'Yes.' Thea was losing patience. 'Or recon-struction – I think that's what they call it. I suppose Bruce didn't want to tell you, in case it upset you. I suppose I wasn't meant to, either. Well, sorry, but I think we all need to face up to things. We're grown up people, after all. What is there to be scared of?'

'He didn't tell me.' It was almost a whisper. 'But you're right, of course you are. Trust Thea Osborne to rub everybody's nose in it. I can see you're never going to let me forget about it. Fifty years from now, you'll be saying, "Remember that night when you saw a man die in a layby?" Won't you?'

'I might,' said Thea, defiantly. 'If I haven't lost my own memory by then.'

'They think it'll help catch the man, do they? If they play the whole thing over again. Is that what you're telling me?'

'They think it could jog the memory of somebody who was passing at the time.'

'Nobody passed,' said Emily, with such emphasis that Thea believed her. 'The whole thing's utterly pointless.'

'Oh, well–' she didn't know what to say to that. 'I suppose they think it's worth a try.'

'I'm glad Bruce told them I couldn't do it. It would be *disgusting*.' Emily's voice rose on this word, and then she went silent for several seconds. 'And I can hardly leave Mum now she's decided I need to be cossetted, can I? Besides – it isn't raining today. That makes all the difference in the world.'

'That's what I said,' said Thea.

The police came for her as promised, in a car the

same colour and model as Emily's. Thea sat in the back thinking it was a lot earlier than the time Emily had left, the previous week. In the front seats were two uniformed policemen, who had introduced themselves familiarly as Jamie and Chaz. The sky was still entirely light. Given that the nights were closing in earlier each evening, this seemed significant. 'I'm sure it was later than this when she left here,' she said.

'Don't forget it was darker because of the rain,' said Chaz wearily, as if he'd already said the same thing many times. 'Sunset was eight twenty-four last Saturday. It's eight-ten tonight.'

'How depressing,' said Thea, thinking of the dreadful days in January when it was dark at four.

It seemed to take mere seconds to reach Emily's gateway. The policeman carefully reversed the car until it was off the road, and then both officers got out. 'All yours,' said Chaz, who'd been driving.

She opened the door carefully, trying not to bang it against the gatepost that was only eighteen inches away. It was a squeeze to get out and move to the driver's seat. 'Is this where she got the scratch?' she said, knowing it had to be.

'That's right. Look.' The policeman indicated an abrasion on the post, at about knee level. 'There was paint from your sister's car just here. That's about the only part of the story we can confirm with forensics. It all matches perfectly.'

'You examined her car? I thought she said you didn't.'

'Not at the time. But we had someone from Bucks go and have a look, on Monday. Just to get the whole picture.'

291

'Right.' This chap was very clued up, she thought. Probably trying for promotion to CID, acquainting himself with all the details in the hope of making an impression. Well, good luck to him. He seemed pleasant enough, with a look of intelligence that was all too rare in the average cop. When her daughter had insisted on going onto the Force, Thea's first response had been, 'But you're far too bright for that.'

'So what next?' she asked.

'Wait until you hear shouts from the layby, and come walking – or running, as you think fit – to see what's going on. Then shout until the attacker runs off.'

'When do I sound the horn?'

'Pardon?'

'Emily says she sounded the horn.'

He rubbed his earlobe reflectively. 'Did she? I guess it must have been when she first heard the shouting. Seems an odd thing to do, though, before you even know what's going on. You can't see anything from here, the way the road curves.'

It *was* odd, Thea had to agree. 'She could have come back afterwards and done it then. She probably left her phone in the car and had to come for that.'

'Possibly. But isn't it just as odd to do it *then*? After the bloke's disappeared into the bushes? What would be the point?'

'I suppose people do funny things. She must have wanted to make sure he wouldn't come back. That would make sense.'

'Maybe,' he said doubtfully. 'Which doesn't answer your question, does it? Plus, nobody we've spoken to has said anything about hearing a car horn.'

'We ought to do it, though. It's exactly the kind of thing that jogs people's memories.'

'Hmm,' he said. 'OK – well, do it afterwards. Come back for your phone and do it then.'

'Is Phil here?' she asked, trying to work out the whole setup.

'DS Hollis? No. The DI is, though.'

'Jeremy? Right.' Jeremy Higgins was a friendly man, but somehow lacking a dimension. Phil spoke of him more as a piece of equipment than a human being, and when she met him Thea could see how that might happen. Inconspicuous, uncontroversial, obliging – DI Higgins was an ideal detective in many ways.

'He'll be over the road, watching what happens. We're trying not to be intrusive, obviously. But we need to be very alert. It's not just jogging memories, you see. It's figuring out exactly what must have happened.'

Thea frowned. 'Surely you've done that already?'

Chaz shrugged. 'Can't do it too many times.'

He went ahead of her up the road, and she was left to get into role, imagining herself to be Emily, cross about the scratched wing on the car, annoyed at the incessant rain, embarrassed at being lost. Into all that, the shouts of men fighting would have seemed the final straw. Or would it have been a minor background noise, something she needn't worry about in the more urgent concern for the car? As she stood there, she heard shouts.

Inarticulate cries floated down the road, deep-throated roars of aggression. Beneath them were feebler cries that were barely audible. It was loud, but in pouring rain might not be enough to attract curiosity. It was in any case something that any sensible woman would ignore. She would get back in her car and lock the doors. And *then* she might sound the horn. That at least began to make some sense. It even felt like quite a clever thing to do.

But Emily had told everybody that she walked up to the layby to investigate. So Thea did the same. She strode briskly, and was soon in sight of what was going on. The layby was quite deep – the sort of place people would stop to consult a map, or eat their picnic, or even turn their car around. In the fading light it looked as if it had been created by accident – a natural bend in the lane where a heap of gravel might have been positioned, in those days when such heaps regularly appeared. Or it could have been an ad hoc sheep enclosure, in even earlier times. There was a low bank separating it from the road, leaving openings at either end for cars to enter and exit. A bank apparently much more recently constructed, perhaps, as a deterrence to the dreaded New Age travellers of the nineteen-eighties, now long forgotten. As laybys went, it was a pleasing one, with a view of a rising hill across the road and a handsome oak tree close by.

The two men were against the hedge, as far as possible from the road. Still shouting, one was standing upright, pumping a leg as if inflating a car tyre with a foot pump. Not until she had got right off the road did Thea see the second man lying prone. 'Hey!' she called, feeling intensely self-conscious. 'What's going on?'

The upright man lifted his head and looked at her. Then he gave a final pretend kick to his victim, and turned to run away. But where should he run? To obey a natural instinct to leave Thea/Emily as far as possible behind, he would have to go up the road towards the hotel. Across the road was a substantial hedge that even a determined goat would hesitate to try to penetrate. If he came back, past the interfering woman, she would get a good look at his face, which was not a good idea.

The fourth option was to get over the hedge into the field beyond the layby. Beside the oak tree there was a gap, with nothing more than a few strands of wire fencing blocking it. With a thoroughly out-of-role slump of the shoulders, he made towards it, looking as if he hoped somebody would stop him before he had to climb over. He and Thea both knew that there were watching police officers at various points, but not one was visible.

Thea left him to it and walked hesitantly towards the figure on the ground. 'Hello? Are you all right?' she stammered. His head was imaginatively draped with a bright red piece of cloth. 'Oh, my God!' she squawked. 'Help! Oh, God. Where's my phone? Listen – can you hear me? I'll go and phone for help.'

She knew she ought to kneel down and touch him, turn him over, listen to his final gasps, but she could not bring herself to do it.

She hovered for a few more moments, expecting instructions that never came. Then she went back to the car at a trot, remembering to sound the horn. Except the horn only worked if the engine was turned on, and that seemed too big an effort, in the circumstances. She waited uncertainly, with little idea of what she ought to do next. Not a single car had passed since the role-playing began. The whole exercise began to seem futile at best and a stupid waste of time at worst.

Her policeman rejoined her. 'Very good!' he approved. 'Except you didn't sound the horn.'

'No – because it seems to me now that she'd have done it early on, if at all. When she very first got out of the car and heard the shouting. She'd be in too much of a hurry afterwards. You have to turn the ignition on for it to work.'

'Ah!' he said, with an intelligent little nod. 'That's very helpful in itself.'

'Is it?' she said, feeling strangely alarmed.

'So – what else seemed peculiar to you? I noticed you didn't actually kneel down by the body. Your sister certainly did. Next time, I must ask you to do it.'

'Next time?' She'd known there'd be a repeat, but she quite badly didn't want to do it again.

'In twenty or thirty minutes, yes. But first, have you got any feedback?'

'Well – there didn't seem to be anywhere for him to run, did there? Which way does Emily say he went?'

'She didn't. She said he just ran off into the dark. She says she didn't watch him go.'

'It wasn't dark enough just now. I said it wasn't, before we started,' she accused. 'We've been wasting our time.'

'I don't think so. I think it's all going very well, actually. The DI's going to be very pleased.'

'That's all right then,' she said with a flicker of sarcasm. She was realising how very much she was not enjoying herself.

'So why didn't you kneel down?'

'Well, I didn't want to get dirty,' she said feebly.

'Right. And last week, that whole area where he's lying was a mud puddle about an inch deep. Your sister's clothes had more mud on them than blood.'

'So I imagine. I guess when it's the real thing, you don't worry about anything like that.'

He smiled understandingly. 'We can put something down for you to kneel on. And while you're there, have a look round, as if searching for help, OK? In the hope that there'll be a car coming along soon.'

As he spoke, a car did finally appear, the sound of its engine warning of its approach some seconds ahead. The driver, a young man, glanced curiously at the two people standing by the car in the gateway, but barely slowed down.

'In the dark, people probably wouldn't notice us,' Thea said. 'Or the car.'

'Who can say?' He smiled again, infuriatingly serene.

The second time, she sounded the horn earlier in the proceedings, and then knelt by the body, laying a hand on its shoulder and trying to

297

imagine how it would have been in reality. Terrifying, she concluded. The killer might not actually have run away at all; he might be right behind her, ready to shatter her skull as well. It was much darker this time, shadows thickening into swathes of dense black in the lee of the hedge. With something close to genuine panic, she looked wildly around for assistance, only to realise that the road was not visible from where she crouched. The intervening bank shielded them from the road completely. Even if a car had passed, she would scarcely have had time to stand up and attract its attention. Emily had said nothing about a torch, nothing to make herself visible. And it had been bloody *raining*.

It was well past nine o'clock when Jeremy finally joined her in the gateway, and thanked her for her trouble. He carried a notebook in which she could see he had made a lot of jottings. 'Has that taken things any further forward?' she asked him.

Before he could respond, another car could be heard, its engine sounding low and powerful. This time the driver came to a sudden halt just past the gateway, and stuck his head out of the window. In the murky twilight, Thea could not see his face. But she knew who it was. Henry Galton.

'Problems?' he said.

Chaz interposed himself. 'Good evening, sir. I wonder whether I could ask you a few questions?'

'Fire away,' Galton invited.

'Are you local, sir?'

'About as local as you can get. I live a mile from here.'

'And were you by any chance passing this point at the same time last Saturday evening?'

'Oh – I get it. How slow of me. You're talking about the killing. No, no. I was nowhere near here last Saturday, officer. In fact, I've already been asked that question, some days ago. You'll find my alibi is all in order.'

'Could I have your name and address, sir, just for the record.'

Galton gave it, his tone and manner steadfastly relaxed. Then he said, 'Do you mind if I have a word with Mrs Osborne now?'

Chaz stepped aside slowly. Thea wanted to assure him that Galton would never have killed Sam Webster, that he had never been a candidate for the role of murderer. Even without knowing he had an alibi, she could not begin to believe it of him. *How odd*, she thought now, realising the idea had never taken root, despite his size and demonstrable capacity for rage.

'When will you be finished here?' he asked her.

'I think we're done,' she said. 'Aren't we Chaz?'

'Well–' the constable looked at the Detective Inspector, who was chewing the end of his pencil and staring at the sky where a few stars had just appeared. 'Sir?'

'What? Oh, sorry. Mrs Osborne, thank you again for all your help. I've got a great deal to think about, now. Shall we say ten tomorrow, at the station, for a proper debriefing?'

She blinked at him. 'Debriefing?'

'That's right. I need to know how it felt, what you noticed. We could do it now, if you'd prefer, while it's fresh in your mind. But–' he glanced at

Galton, 'if you're busy...'

'Tomorrow's fine,' she said. 'I don't think I'm likely to forget anything.'

'Do you need a ride back to the farm?'

She looked at Galton, still with his head and elbow hanging out of the car window. 'I think I've got one, thanks.' *How presumptuous,* she thought. He could be going off to see a lady friend or to join a group of men for some serious drinking.

'You have,' he confirmed. 'Get in.'

CHAPTER TWENTY-FOUR

She never found out where Galton had been going. He turned round in the layby, a deft sweep in one end and out the other, and headed back towards Hawkhill. 'Your place or mine?' he asked, as he drew level with the entrance.

She giggled, never for a moment thinking he was suggesting the usual practice behind that line. 'Yours, if you like,' she said. 'It's a much nicer house.'

'Won't your dog miss you?'

'Yes, but she'll manage. So long as I'm home by midnight.'

'That's a promise,' he said, still almost alarmingly relaxed. And yet she was not alarmed. She trusted him to be offering nothing more than a listening ear and a glass or two of wine. There was something unhurried about Henry Galton, and although she had seen his capacity for passionate rage, she somehow knew his other passions were dormant, and it would take more effort than she was inclined to make to awaken them.

She hadn't meant to talk about dark laybys and dead men, but it was all too fresh in her mind to ignore. Besides, Jeremy had wanted her to hold onto the details until the next morning, and wouldn't that be easier if she talked them through now, to anchor them in her memory?

Only later did she permit herself to see that she had been using Galton as if he'd been Phil Hollis.

She was supplied with a glass of rich red wine, and a bowl of interesting nibbles that turned out to be spicy broad beans, coated in some sort of crisp brown powder. 'I'd never have guessed,' she laughed. 'Where do they come from?'

'Some outfit over the border in Herefordshire. They started with potato crisps and branched out into this sort of thing.'

'Locally grown, of course.'

'Actually, no. They came from Singapore.'

She pouted sceptically. 'Tut tut – isn't that an air mile problem?'

Galton raised an eyebrow. 'I should have known you'd be an eco-freak. Actually, I agree with you. I'm wondering whether to turn some of my land over to growing beans and peas. Everything's changing so fast, and there's no money in sheep any more. But it would cost a fortune to set it all up, and the marketing's a nightmare.'

'You'd relish the challenge, I bet.'

'I might,' he admitted.

She sipped the wine and felt a slow relaxation flow through her. The sofa was leather, creased and squishy and old. She thought it might be one of the three most comfortable sofas she'd ever encountered.

'Where were you going?' she asked, aware that she had aborted whatever plans he might have had.

'Sorry?'

'When you passed the layby and saw me and the police. You must have been going somewhere.'

'Where does a divorced forty-something man go on an August Saturday evening? I'll let you guess.'

'The pub, I suppose.'

'Right. Nobody's going to miss me. You saved me from a few hours of tedium.'

'You are so different from when I first saw you,' she blurted. 'I still can't get used to it. Red in the face and shouting, waving that gun about. You were terrifying.'

'All part of a farmer's repertoire,' he said, quite seriously. 'You can take my word for it that just about anyone with sheep would present exactly as I did, under the same circumstances.'

Present? What a surprising word to use. As if he'd trained in psychotherapy or personnel management. 'Oh,' she said.

'So – did they solve the mystery? Do they know who killed that Oxford bloke?'

'I doubt it. It was all a waste of time, as far as I can see. The weather being so different made it pointless from the start.'

'I have to confess I haven't been following the story. I never read the papers, and try to avoid the news as much as I can. But I do know your sister's involved, and the dead man was the vicar's brother. Coincidences all round, in fact.'

'And the police hate coincidences.'

'I can imagine. How do you tell a coincidence from a clue?' He blew out his cheeks to suggest it was too large a puzzle for him.

'It isn't so strange when you boil it down to basics. The only real surprise is that Emily knew Sam Webster, who happened to be staying the night in a hotel a mile away from where I'm house-sitting. And Emily knows hundreds of people, so even that isn't as odd as it might seem.'

'And why wasn't Emily there this evening?'

'She's too upset to face it. According to her husband and our mother, she's going through some kind of breakdown – if that's what they call it these days. I think it's because our father has just died. She came here last Saturday to talk to me about him. Then she got lost trying to get home again, and ended up witnessing a murder.'

He looked at her with an expression she'd seen in his eyes before. It took some moments to remember that it had been when he told her that Freddy and Basil almost certainly had been guilty of sheep-worrying. It was a look of patient sympathy, a look that told her that he knew more than she did, and she wasn't going to like it when the knowledge was shared.

'What?' she demanded. 'Why are you looking at me like that?'

He gave himself a little shake, and smiled. 'Oh, nothing. What do I know about it? As I said, I haven't even been following it in the news.'

'There's hardly been anything to follow,' she said, a little too loudly. 'Just that they arrested Peter Clarke and then let him go again.'

'Poor bloke. I don't suppose that was much fun.'

'Do you know him?'

Galton shook his head. 'Never met him. He's not been here long, I gather. I rather tend to steer clear of vicars. They carry disagreeable associations for me.'

She assumed he meant his wedding to the incomprehensible wife who had deserted him, when she ought to have counted her blessings every day of her life. 'I don't expect you'd like him,' she said. 'Phil doesn't.'

'So tell me about the reconstruction of the crime, if that's not breaking police confidentiality.'

She went through it slowly, aware that this was a practice run for her debriefing the next morning. It made a short and simple story, a piece of drastic violence in the Cotswold countryside, which was, when it came to it, no stranger to slaughterings of every kind.

'There was mud and blood all over everything when it actually happened. I had to try to imagine it this evening – they wrapped a red cloth round the pretend victim's head. It worked quite well, oddly enough. I couldn't bring myself to kneel down and touch him, the first time we did it.'

'Your sister was probably very wise to duck out of it. I don't expect they have the power to force her to take part, even if she wasn't too – *upset*.'

'She really is in a state,' Thea assured him. 'Her husband's quite worried about her. Not that it takes much to worry him. He's one of those men who like life to stay predictable and calm.'

'I know a few women like that, as well,' he said, mildly reproachful.

'Oh, yes. Emily's the same, of course. She lost her first baby, and I guess that's made her excessively protective and controlling of the ones she's got.'

'How many's that?'

'Three boys, thirteen, fourteen and sixteen. They're turning out rather well, considering. I'd have expected them to stage spectacular rebellions by now, but they seem to be toeing the line perfectly happily so far. Except that the big one wants to get his nipple pierced. Emily wouldn't stand for that.'

Galton winced. 'Give them time. They might leave it until they go away to college, if she's that rigid. But it'll definitely happen eventually. It has to, you see, if they're to achieve any sort of maturity.'

'You sound as if you know a lot about it.'

He tipped his head in a small bow of submission. 'I thought you'd catch me out eventually.'

She put her fingers over her mouth, sifting out the clues. 'No, I'm not there,' she said, giving up. 'Tell me.'

'I'm a counsellor for Relate. I finished the training five years ago. I do six sessions a week, which isn't as much as they'd like, but I'm a bit busy here, as you can imagine.'

'Good Lord. I'd never have guessed.' But she might have done, she realised, with only a few more clues. 'Although I don't think I've ever met a counsellor before, so I wouldn't know what to look for.'

'They're pretty much the same as everybody else. But my special interest is in the formative years of life, and how parents behave with their babies. I read research reports like other people read novels.'

She could think of nothing to say that sounded

even remotely intelligent. She knew nothing about the latest theories of baby management, and cared hardly at all. 'My sister's got five children,' she offered, daftly. 'The other sister, that is.'

'Aha – don't tell me – you're the middle one.'

She nodded, showing no surprise at what felt like a party game in the making. 'Except there's an older brother at the top.'

'Poor chap – three younger sisters.'

'Mm.'

To his credit, he quickly detected her lack of interest in his favourite subject. Just as he detected a cooling generally. 'Uh – oh,' he said.

She smiled wistfully. 'I should go. I expect I'll be able to see to walk. It isn't far.'

'Don't be stupid. I'll come with you. After all, isn't there a crazed killer on the loose out there?'

'I don't expect there is, is there?' she said. 'Not after a whole week.'

'Well, I'll come with you anyway. I like walking at night, especially this time of year. I can scare away a few foxes, and watch out for barn owls. Funny, the way we celebrate some predators and abhor others.'

Everything he said felt loaded with meaning. She knew she should be playing his game, working out what he was trying to tell her, seeing the world through his eyes. But she didn't want to. She did not want to spend time with somebody who saw layers and layers of significance in every small remark. She did not want to talk about how she felt all the time, or make uncomfortable connections with the way her mother had once given Jocelyn two sweets and her only one. She did not want to be constantly struggling to catch up, to understand something that he already knew and was patiently waiting for her to grasp. No wonder his wretched wife had left him.

But what she was really running away from was that look in his eyes. The look that said the unthinkable is actually perfectly thinkable, that guilt and suspicion are everywhere, with very good reason. Freddy and Basil were guilty, all along. Mike Lister was an opportunist, seizing his chance to get back at Cedric Angell for some old injury. And police reconstructions might turn up much less acceptable results than she had bargained for.

CHAPTER TWENTY-FIVE

The night walk turned out to be an unexpected enchantment. To his credit, Galton switched into a whole new mode, pointing out things that ought to have been invisible. They passed by a large group of sheep lying scattered across a field, breathing noisily, smelling of fermenting grass and damp. A few got up, and Thea regretted the disturbance to their slumbers. 'They never really sleep,' said Galton. 'They're still too scared of wolves, after all these centuries.'

'With good reason,' said Thea unhappily, thinking of the mangled tups.

'Nature's natural victims,' he agreed. 'Magpies, buzzards, foxes, badgers – they'll all have a go at a sick sheep, long before it's dead.'

And then, as if by magic, a pale shadow crossed silently just in front of them. It disappeared across the field, only to return, slightly further away. 'What's that?' Thea whispered.

'A barn owl. That's the first I've seen for months. Isn't it magnificent!'

'I hardly saw it. It seemed very big.'

'They're a fair size. And the numbers are increasing, around here. I think they're glorious.'

'And do they attack sheep as well?'

He snorted his amusement. 'Definitely not. They like the thrill of the hunt. A sheep wouldn't be nearly enough of a challenge.'

'That's a relief,' she said.

He left her at the front door of Hawkhill, and went striding off with minimal ceremony. She watched him for a moment, full of jumbled regretful thoughts. On the other side of the door, her dog was scrabbling, desperate to greet her after such a long confinement.

Ignatius was asleep, even without his night-time cover. It was almost eleven, and Thea crawled up to bed, surprised at how tired she felt. Hepzie followed her closely, nudging the backs of her legs as if to assure herself the return of her mistress was real.

Jeremy had not given a precise time for the Cirencester debriefing. Nor had he offered a lift. What would happen if she just stayed where she was and tried to forget the whole business? They'd send Phil, she decided. Even if he told them how things were between Thea and him, they'd still assume he must be the one for the job. Or Chaz. She'd got on well with him, in a detached sort of way.

But they would all know her for a conscientious, law-abiding citizen. She'd taken part in the re-enactment, hadn't she? She obviously wanted to find Webster's killer as much as they did. Why wouldn't she present herself as required, without any prompting?

It was Sunday – a day that felt less and less special with every passing month. Thea was too young to have experienced the full shut-down of the Sabbath – the taboos against certain activities, the slow pace and general habit of sleeping through much of the day. Her father had described the way his own father had always spent Sunday afternoons in bed, catching up on sleep from his busy farming life. There had been books and magazines that were proscribed on a Sunday, even though it was far from a religious household. You were supposed to wear nice clothes, and brush your hair properly, even if you weren't going to see anybody. God, everybody still vaguely believed, was watching you a lot more attentively on a Sunday than on any other day of the week.

And how could Thea note the day without also calling to mind the Reverend Peter Clarke? He would be busy conducting services, and she found herself wondering what sort of a job he made of it. She had almost never been to a standard church service that was not a wedding or a funeral or a Carol Service. The mysteries of the Prayer Book and the Collect remained entirely closed to her. The fundamental *point* of it was ever harder to grasp. Listening to a man speak lines made meaningless by repetition, answering automatically and equally meaning-lessly – it surely required a major effort of will to gain any succour from it?

It might, though, seem very different to others – Ariadne, for example. She was a practising pagan, in the sense that she led ceremonies and rituals designed to bring to mind the essential importance of the seasons, the realities of birth and decay, the interdependence of different forms of life. It probably wasn't a very big step from all that to an Anglican service. She'd have some of the necessary conditioning, at least.

All this went through her mind as she fed the animals, then herself, deliberately not hurrying. It was well past ten when she finally got in the car and drove south to Cirencester. She knew exactly where the police station was, thanks to her association with Det Supt Hollis. She knew the man on the front desk by sight, and he knew her. He pointed her down the corridor to the room where DI Jeremy Higgins was waiting for her. And no, DS Hollis wasn't in this morning.

It was all quite calm, at least on the surface. There was coffee and remarks about the weather and a few words about the joys of house-sitting in somewhere as lovely as Lower Slaughter. And then it began. 'So – what did you make of the reconstruction, then?' he asked, abruptly, as she was sipping her coffee.

'I'm still not convinced of its usefulness,' she said. 'After all, nobody passed by except Henry Galton.'

'That's true,' he nodded. 'It would have been nice to have a few more people to quiz, I agree.'

Thea remembered all over again that her sister had been the sole and solitary witness to the events of that Saturday evening. The single voice speaking up as testimony to what had happened. She too would surely have appreciated a supporting informant to confirm her story. But it wasn't crucial. 'Well, it looked as if Emily gave a good account of it all,' she asserted. 'It all held together pretty well, I thought.'

'Did you? Did you really?'

'Of course. The gateway and the layby and the mud – it was all as she said.'

'Oh yes, they were all where she said they were. And there were flakes of paint from her car on that gatepost, as well.'

'So?' She was resisting so intensely that her back began to ache. The worst thing was the half-hidden look of pity in Jeremy's eyes.

She had never taken much notice of Jeremy. He was always polite, almost deferential, when she'd been with Phil. He had a big round head and a thick neck to support it. But his shoulders were disproportionately narrow, which made him look like a baby. Not especially tall, his hair a very English light brown, he gave no cause for undue attention.

'Mrs Osborne – Thea – I'm going to ask you to do something for us.'

'Something *else*, you mean,' she flashed.

'Yes, that's right. Although I think this is something you'd want to be included in, anyway.'

'Go on.'

'Will you come with us this morning to Aylesbury?'

She spoke quickly, needing words to fill the sudden hollow inside her. 'To Emily's house, you mean? What for?' But she knew. Somewhere far away in her bones, she knew.

'We need to take her in for questioning,' he said, not meeting her eye.

It wasn't strictly orthodox, she supposed, to take the suspect's sister along when you went to arrest her. It was a special dispensation because of who she was, and her involvement in the case from the start. From *before* the start, she reminded herself miserably.

But still the inner resistance was strong. She argued relentlessly throughout most of the drive, repeating herself over and over, getting no satisfactory answers from Jeremy. 'But how can she *possibly* be involved? She's far too respectable. She doesn't know anyone who'd commit such a terrible crime.' Because she had assumed that Emily was in the spotlight Phil's initial suspicion that she knew the killer had somehow returned with bells on. That somehow the reconstruction had demonstrated the probability of this, because how could the killer have run away so completely unless Emily had aided him? Why had she behaved in such a fearless way unless it had been somebody she could rely on not to attack her as well?

Jeremy had begged her to stop. 'I can't say anything that might influence you,' he said. 'I want you to think it through for yourself.'

'But she's my *sister*,' she persisted. 'I'm not going to do or say anything that'll get her into trouble, am I? I don't think I'm going to be of any use to you at all. You're hoping I'll lure her into a confession, aren't you? Why would I? Where do you think my loyalties lie?'

He had looked at her then, in the bright August light that filled the car. 'I know you well enough, Thea Osborne, to trust you to do what's right.'

That had frightened her more than anything that had happened thus far. It finally silenced her, for the last ten miles of the journey.

314

Bruce answered the door, looking tousled and startled and generally out of control. There were bags under his eyes and stubble on his chin. An alternative Sunday stereotype, Thea thought wildly. The morning after the Saturday night before.

Jeremy had a female police constable with him, a stout woman who had not spoken a word during the drive from Cirencester. Thea had wanted to stay in the car, but the DI had politely and firmly asked her to come to the door with them.

'Mr Peterson, we'd like to speak to your wife, please. Might we come in, do you think?'

Bruce then conformed to a different stereotype, glancing anxiously up and down the street to check that no neighbours had observed the visit-ation. Some hope, thought Thea, certain she could see at least three twitching net curtains already. The stout PC's uniform was a real give-away.

Emily was huddled into a corner of their expensive cream corduroy sofa, which Thea had cause to loathe because Hepzie had once com-mitted the appalling sin of jumping up onto it, and been smacked for her offence. The familiar room took on a sinister atmosphere with two police officers in it. Both Jeremy and the PC seemed to give off intimidating vibrations that sent Emily even deeper into the cushions.

And their mother was also in the room, sitting very upright on the edge of an armchair, as if braced for any eventuality. 'Thea,' she said, in

315

only the mildest surprise. 'Thank goodness.'

Automatically, she went to her mother, reaching down to take her hand. 'Still here, then?' she said, feeling as if somehow they'd slipped back in time to the days following her father's death. Those gentle days when they had all been so careful with each other, exchanging ruefully intimate glances, sharing the sense of being on a tiny island of bereavement that only they – the immediate relatives – could experience.

'They want Emily, do they?' said Mrs Johnstone.

'That's right. They need her to help them a bit more.'

'I see. Well, she'd better go, then.' She directed her gaze at her eldest daughter. 'Emily, you must go with them. Get up, darling. Thea's going with you.' When Emily made no move, the tone sharpened. 'Go on now. Think of your father – what he would have wanted.'

It was a cruelly powerful thrust and Emily flinched. 'Thea?' she said, having taken a strangely long time to recognise her sister. 'Is Phil coming as well?'

'No, it's just us. How are you, Em? You look pretty grim, I must say.'

'Bruce made me go to the doctor, and they put me on some pills. They've made me all woozy.' And it was true that her voice was slurred, her eyes barely focused. Thea wanted to pummel the DI on the chest and tell him to go away and leave well alone. What good did he think he could do, bullying a woman in this condition?

'We have to ask you some more questions, I'm

316

afraid,' he said, stepping forward. 'We'd like you to come with us, back to the police station.'

Bruce cleared his throat, but his voice still emerged as a squeak. 'What for?' he asked. 'And why is Thea with you?'

'Do you mean the Aylesbury police station?' Emily wondered. 'Do you mean *now?* I'm not dressed, look.' She stroked the blue dressing gown that enveloped her. 'I can't go like this, can I? Where are the boys? Bruce, where are they?'

'Two are still in bed and the other one's on the computer. Don't worry about them.'

'Come along, then,' said the policewoman. 'We can wait for you to put some clothes on. We'll have to go to Cirencester, you see.'

Emily closed her eyes, and Thea wanted to go and put her arms around her, shielding her from the cruel power of the enforcers of the law. She wanted to shout, 'Leave her alone, will you? The man's dead, isn't he? All this isn't going to bring him back to life.' Instead she went and perched on the other end of the sofa, and tried to speak soothingly to her sister.

'It'll be all right,' she said. 'They only want to get the full story. They want to catch the man who did that terrible thing, that's all. Think of poor Sam, who never did anybody any harm. Doesn't he deserve your help to settle what really happened to him?'

Emily stared at her, eyes wide and wild. 'If only you knew how stupid you sound,' she said flatly, hopelessly.

Thea recoiled. Emily had called her stupid on a daily basis for about ten years, a detail she had

317

forgotten completely until now. Emily was her clever big sister who got three Grade As at A-level, at a time when that was an almost unimaginable achievement. Thea got a B and two Ds. She was therefore manifestly stupid, and Emily had been right all along. Now she was stupid all over again and her brain closed down accordingly. 'Sorry,' she muttered, which seemed an even more stupid thing to say.

Bruce made a bleating sound, not attempting to help his wife. Thea caught him giving Emily a look that bordered on dislike. Instinctively, Thea adopted a sisterly protectiveness. This was *Emily* in the kind of trouble that never happened to normal people. Somehow she had stepped across a line, and like it or not, her family had to go across it with her. And that included Bruce. 'What are you going to do to her?' The question came from their mother, still sitting rigidly on the chair, hands clasped tightly over the upholstered arms.

The DI cast a pained glance around the room. 'Just ask a few questions,' he said ponderously.

'Can Bruce come as well?' asked Thea, more for her brother-in-law's benefit than anything else. She already knew there wouldn't be space for him in the car.

'Sorry,' said the DI. But the purpose had been served. Bruce lifted his head and sighed, as he was forced to acknowledge his rightful place in the picture.

'When will you bring her back?' he asked.

'Can't say, sir, I'm afraid. I expect Mrs Osborne will keep you informed.'

The drive seemed to last much longer than the identical outward journey. Emily sat silently, watching the countryside flow by, apparently in a state of suspended animation. When Thea managed to glimpse her face, there was no sign of deep thought or naked emotion. It appeared that her sister was simply waiting for whatever would happen next.

Thea felt as if she was thinking for both of them. Emily's accusation of stupidity had not been a random piece of habitual sibling sniping: she really did think that Thea was being stupid. She had got something idiotically wrong, and she tried to remember exactly what she'd said. *Sam Webster never did anybody any harm* – was that it? Was it the case that Webster had somehow injured Bruce or Emily, and deserved no sympathy for his fate? Knowing Emily, it could even be that she blamed him for getting himself killed, and dragging her into something so unpleasant. And yet, the degree of trauma during the past days suggested that her personal feelings had been deeply stirred by whatever it was that had happened.

It would be a mistake to overlook sheer squeamishness, of course. The sight of another human being's head split open and leaking its contents onto your clothes might easily suffice to explain a severe case of hysterics afterwards. Bad dreams, inability to concentrate, self-pity – they were all quite acceptably normal, under the circumstances. And they wouldn't be entirely surprising in Emily's case. Doggedly, Thea repeated these thoughts to herself, insisting that there was no real cause for concern, nothing to account for the frantic roiling and griping of her own stomach as her body drew conclusions that her mind refused to face.

Jeremy spoke to somebody on his mobile, estimating times and muttering about 'positions'. They were not going to Cirencester, it seemed, but to the Slaughters. They were yet again revisiting the scene of the crime. Only when they turned off the A429 did Emily's eyes widen and her head jerk round in suspicious recognition. 'Where are we going?' she asked.

Where do you think? Thea wanted to reply. 'The place where it happened, I suppose,' was her actual muted answer.

'What for?'

Thea merely shrugged.

Jeremy turned round in his seat, unsmiling. 'There are a few discrepancies, you see,' he said. 'We're hoping you can sort them out for us.'

Emily shrank into the corner of the back seat. 'I can't,' she whimpered. 'I can't bear to think about it any more.'

'Well, you'll have to,' said Thea. She wanted to adjure her sister to be grown up, to behave responsibly, to pull herself together. But you didn't address your older sister like that, even when you were both over forty. At least, you didn't do it repeatedly, she corrected, thinking back over some of the sharper remarks she'd made in the past week. She regretted them now, seeing the misery on Emily's crumpled face. Misery and fear and a vestigial seam of defiance were all apparent, and Thea knew better than to say anything that could bring about any further collapse.

'Here we are,' the driver announced, drawing into the layby itself.

'No, no, I didn't park here,' Emily cried. 'This isn't right.' She gazed tremulously out of the front windscreen. 'It looks completely different,' she said, as if this realisation gave her some reassurance.

'That's good,' said Thea. 'It might not upset you as much as you think, then.'

'I can't believe it's the same place. It was so wet and dark.' She seemed to be focused on the far end of the layby, and more animated than she had been thus far. 'It rejoins the road up there, does it? I mean, you can just drive in this end and out the other? I never realised that.'

'You thought it had a dead end, did you?' Jeremy's voice held a sharp note of interest. 'That you needed to turn round to get out again?'

She retreated back into herself. 'I never thought about it,' she mumbled.

'I see,' he said, with a severity that struck Thea as unnecessary.

'So what now?' Thea asked.

'Bear with me a minute.' He too was looking fixedly at the far end of the layby. Suddenly a familiar uniformed officer came into view. It was Chaz, and he made a thumbs-up signal at the car.

'OK,' Jeremy said to his driver, who started the engine, and began to make an odd manoeuvre, sweeping first towards the field hedge, and then sharply left towards the bank between the layby and the road. The width of the layby was insufficient to permit a turn in one go. He had to reverse again, and still couldn't get round on the next forward leg. 'Nasty place to try to turn,' said Jeremy, his eyes on Emily's face. 'Especially in the pouring rain, and the dark.'

'I didn't,' she said. 'I was in the gateway. I scraped the car on the gatepost.'

'Yes you did,' he agreed. 'You most certainly did. We'll talk about that in a little while.'

'Wait!' cried Thea in sudden alarm. 'There's somebody behind us. You'll hit him.'

Emily erupted into life. With a strangled scream, she wrenched open the car door and half fell out. Before anybody could get to grips with what she was doing, she had begun running, to the end of the layby and out into the road. A car horn sounded, and then the squealing of tyres as a vehicle braked horribly hard.

'Shit,' said Jeremy flatly. 'That's the last thing we need.'

Thea felt herself frozen to the seat. She could not get out and walk back to see if her sister was sprawled dead on the road. She struggled to move, to be the one to cradle the dying Emily on her lap, but something had withered inside her. It was too much. There were policemen on all sides – let them take care of it. But the paralysis departed as quickly as it had come, and ten seconds later she was wrenching at the handle of the car door to let herself out.

Everybody was running to the spot, several yards ahead of her, and she listened closely for evidence that everything was all right, for Emily's own voice apologising for her folly. It was like the moment after a baby has been born, when everyone holds their breath until the new infant splutters into life. People were talking, and somewhere near by a dog was barking crazily. But the paralysis was back, and she found herself rooted to the ground, still in the layby, fighting to prepare herself for whatever she might have to see in a few seconds' time.

Then a large body was holding her tight against its chest, murmuring soothing nothings, persuading her that everything was all right.

For a few seconds, it was her father, and she was five years old again. But this person was softer, and smelt entirely different. With an embarrassed giggle, she pulled away and looked up to meet Ariadne's gaze. 'Is Emily all right?' she said.

'She will be,' she said. 'I've got good brakes.'

'You! It was you?'

'She ran out in front of me.'

'Yes.'

'I left her to the police and came to find you. Phil's just behind me, as well.'

'That was kind of you, to look for me, I mean.'

'Not really.'

She tried to work out exactly what had happened. 'How did you know I was here?'

Ariadne laughed. 'They told me. The policewoman said you might need a friendly face.'

'Too right,' said Thea shakily. 'It's all been a bit—'

'So I see. That's your sister, then. She doesn't

look like you.'

The whole assembly had moved into the layby, including a white-faced but ambulant Emily. Jeremy followed her, looking grim. Thea found herself acutely aware of all the implications and dilemmas crowding the poor man's head. His witness had thrown herself into the path of an oncoming car rather than face his questions. She ought to be thoroughly cross-examined and challenged – but she was clearly in an even worse state than before.

'So, what's going on?' Ariadne wanted to know.

'Good question,' said Thea.

CHAPTER TWENTY-SIX

Phil materialised and took charge effortlessly after a quick briefing from Jeremy. The Detective Inspector seemed reluctant to abandon his plan, simply because his chief witness had sustained a few bruises. 'We'll take her to the hotel for a bit,' Phil decided. 'That's the nearest place. Everyone can take a bit of a breather.'

'Something was just about to happen,' Thea said. 'A man was behind the car. That's what sent her off.'

Ariadne looked all around in confusion. 'It just looks chaotic to me. Why's that car at such a weird angle?'

'He was turning it round.'

'Why?'

Thea shook her head. 'I'm not sure, really. I suppose he was testing a theory.'

Ariadne put a firm hand on Thea's arm. 'Well I want to know what that theory is. It *matters*, Thea, in case you've forgotten. I thought all along that the key to the whole thing lay with your sister. Now she's here and I want to know exactly what she saw.'

Thea had a sense of waters closing over her head, or the lights going out inexorably, leaving her in a dark and dreadful place. 'I know,' she muttered. 'I understand.'

'What? What do you understand?'

But Thea merely shook her head again.

Raggedly, the whole party made its way to the hotel, Jeremy Higgins running ahead to warn the staff that a quiet room would be required, and some cups of tea and coffee. Thea found herself wondering how such a select establishment would regard the motley party that had insisted on invading their elegant sanctum. They must already be wishing they'd never had such a guest as Mr Sam Webster, whose death had put them in the headlines.

Thea walked beside Ariadne, who clearly assumed she had a rightful place in the group. Emily was folded back into the police car, which Chaz drove up the long drive to the hotel's imposing front door. The sense of disorganisation was strong. The policewoman seemed to have little idea of where she ought to be, missing a ride because she had been overseeing the relocation of Ariadne's vehicle to a safe spot in the layby. She walked stolidly behind Thea and Ariadne, like a redundant sheepdog.

It was her presence which prevented any meaningful conversation between the two friends. That, and a burgeoning reluctance in Thea's breast to consider the implications of what had just taken place. In an effort to divert her thoughts from Emily and what she had done, she found herself thinking yet again of Freddy and Basil, the guilty innocents, the blameless killers – but that was little comfort. Somehow the dogs became entangled with her sister, and ghastly parallels began to arise in her mind.

It took some time, but eventually everybody was settled in a small sitting room furnished with pristine mock regency objects – two-seater settees, uncomfortable chairs, low glass-topped tables. Emily was brought in, still white-faced, but with little sign of physical damage. The WPC took charge of her, sitting beside her on one of the fragile-looking two-seaters. Ariadne stared malevolently at her, plainly wanting to hurl accusations and reproaches, but just managing to keep a grip on her tongue. Instead she challenged Phil, her old comrade.

'The car in the layby,' she began, her voice low and slightly breathless. 'Why were you turning it round there, when you can just drive in one end and out the other?'

Phil barely hesitated before answering. 'Because we had a hunch that's what had happened. We found some marks on the bank which made us wonder. Mrs Peterson has admitted she thought it was a dead end.'

Slowly Ariadne looked first at Jeremy, then Emily, then Thea. 'I get it,' she said. 'Bloody hell – it's obvious, isn't it. *Nobody* stamped on that bloke's head. Not Peter, not some crazy psycho on the loose. That's not what happened to him at all, is it?'

'What?' Thea asked, but got no reply. Jeremy was holding Ariadne's gaze, with acute interest.

'*She* killed him herself. It was your sister all the time,' she pushed her face towards Thea with an expression of triumph mixed with indignation. 'Wasn't it?' she turned to challenge Emily.

'No!' moaned Emily. 'I parked in the gateway,

327

and walked up here. It was muddy and dark, and I couldn't see properly. There was a man lying there, with his head in a mess. I shouted and another man ran away.'

It sounded like a badly spoken speech in a play. Words from which the meaning had drained away through too much repetition. But that didn't mean it was untrue.

Thea had been involved in enough murder cases to know that nothing could be settled without evidence. She assumed that Emily knew that, too, by this time. She'd had a whole week to think about it, after all. But then, so had everybody else, including Ariadne Fletcher.

'That's enough,' said Phil, appearing to remember his official role. Thea felt a flash of acute sympathy for him. Here he was, in the presence of two women who knew him intimately – knew his body, his family, and his life history. Easy enough, then, to slip from professional police detective to ordinary man, and muddle the two. 'You two – you can go as soon as you're ready.' Thea and Ariadne looked at each other, eyebrows raised. Were they being *dismissed*?

'But what about Emily?' Thea asked. 'I need to stay with her.'

'We'll look after her,' he said gently. 'She's in our custody now, you see.' He turned to Emily, and with scarcely any alteration of tone, recited the standard police caution to her.

The effect was devastating, not only on Emily, but on Thea and Ariadne as well. All three emitted squeals or moans, as the import of the words sank in. Thea spoke first. 'You can't!' she protested. 'This is my *sister* you're accusing.'

'Yes!' Ariadne rounded on her. 'And a few days ago it was my *boyfriend*. Maybe you know what it feels like now.'

Thea looked at Emily, who was still white-faced and withdrawn, but with a different look in her eye. A cornered animal, eyes darting from one corner of the room to another, desperate for a line of escape. And then, as Thea watched, the look turned to despair, a plain giving up in the face of such opposition. 'Em?' she said hoarsely.

'I want Mum,' her sister whimpered. 'And Bruce.'

'They'll be here soon,' Thea promised, thinking of the grim family gathering in store for them, under the gaze of uncaring police officers, with Emily confined to a temporary cell before the court hearing there was bound to be next day.

And still, more than half her mind was shying away from a full reconstruction of what must have happened.

Ariadne stood up. 'I need to find Peter,' she said. 'Tell him the good news.' She threw an apologetic little smile at Thea. 'Sorry,' she added. 'But you know what I mean.'

'No. I don't,' Thea insisted. Still she was expecting it all to come right, for Phil to suddenly smile and assure her that he could straighten it all out for her. She looked into his face expectantly.

'Go with Mary,' he said. 'She seems to have got the picture. She'll explain it all to you. We have to keep your sister with us now. She'll have to be questioned again when she's feeling better.'

Nobody corrected his habitual use of Ariadne's

former name, the name he had known her by in his youth.

And so Thea permitted herself to be walked back down the long drive, and into Ariadne's car, and driven back to Hawkhill where Hepzie was reproachful and subdued, and the parrot was silent, and the world seemed grey and foreboding.

Before getting out of the car, Ariadne made a call on her mobile. 'He'll be here in twenty minutes,' she said to Thea's back.

They sat in the kitchen, neither of them risking the distraction of tea or other refreshment. Thea shivered like a dog waiting to be whipped. 'Get on with it, then,' she said. 'Explain.'

Ariadne took her hand, and Thea remembered again the broad receptive breast on which she had laid her head only an hour before. Ariadne could be relied on; she was kind. Why then did Thea feel as if she was about to be very badly hurt?

'I think you can work it out for yourself,' Ariadne began. 'But I can see it needs to be put into words. It's all very simple, really. There never was a murder at all. Sam was behind your sister's car when she was turning it round in the layby. She can't have seen him, and knocked him over in the mud, crushing his head under one of the wheels. An accident.'

'But – why did she *lie* about it then?'

Ariadne shrugged. 'Panic, I presume. She might have been afraid she'd be charged with dangerous driving. You know her better than I do – what would she be most afraid of?'

'Public criticism,' Thea said slowly. 'Scorn. Bruce thinking badly of her. Being tainted in some way. Losing her self-esteem.' She looked up from the corner of the half-finished jigsaw that she'd been staring at blindly. 'That sort of thing.'

'Right,' nodded Ariadne.

'After all, she *did* kill him. She must have been utterly horrified, although I'm sure she had no idea who he was, until the police told her.'

'Not so horrified that she couldn't invent a convincing story to cover herself.' Ariadne spoke less gently. 'Which meant innocent people fell under suspicion.'

'That explains the missing time,' Thea realised. 'She must have sat there working out what to say. Then she drove the car into that gateway and deliberately hit the post to make a scratch on the wing. Obstructing the course of justice,' she concluded. 'She'll go to prison for that, as well as manslaughter.'

Ariadne tilted her head. 'Very likely she will, but not for long. Not if she can convince the court it was an accident.'

'She was a fool. She called me stupid, but I'd never have been such an idiot as she's been. And what about my *mother?*' she suddenly remembered. 'This is going to be so terrible for her.'

There was no reply to that, and in the silence, they both heard a car engine approaching, and then the slamming of a car door. Ariadne got up and went out, coming back a moment later with the Reverend Peter Clarke. He smiled briefly at Thea, and she met the blue eyes with indifference.

'Ari thought I might be able to help,' he said softly. 'But I'm not sure she's right there.'

331

'No,' said Thea. 'I don't really see–' Then she remembered who he was. 'Oh God – he was your brother. My sister *killed* your brother. I am *so* sorry.' It seemed hopelessly inadequate. What possible script could there be for such a situation?

'Yes,' he said. 'So I understand. But it had nothing to do with you. You don't share her guilt. You've done the right thing from first to last.'

'Have I, though?' She struggled to examine her conscience. Hadn't she been brusque to people who'd deserved more sympathy? Hadn't she cared as much about two dogs as she had about the slaughtered Sam Webster? 'I'm not sure.'

They both remained quiet, standing close together, united in a warm bubble of relief and concern. They could afford to be gentle with her, now, in their liberation from suspicion and anxiety.

'But she's innocent, isn't she?' Thea went on. 'I mean, she didn't do anything really bad, apart from telling lies after the event. She never meant to hurt anybody.' She blinked. 'Like the dogs, I suppose. The slaughters were all committed by innocents. What would the church have to say about it, I wonder?'

Peter shook his head slowly. 'Dogs?' he asked.

Thea explained clumsily, looking to Ariadne to elaborate. 'I see,' said Peter finally. 'I'm not sure there's a suitable Biblical text to cover all that – it's more a matter of the Buddhist doctrine of *mindfulness*, I suspect.'

Thea sighed. 'You mean that Emily and I should both have been more careful. The crime of carelessness. I think my father would agree with you.'

There were a lot of questions lying unanswered,

but they addressed only a few of them. 'Why do you think he got behind the car like that?' Thea wondered.

'My guess is that he recognised Emily, and was trying to attract her attention,' said Peter. 'Maybe he waved and shouted, but she didn't see him. Or thought he was going to attack her.'

'Maybe she skidded in the mud. Maybe he'd already fallen over and she couldn't hope to see him lying behind the car,' Ariadne suggested.

Thea sighed. 'It doesn't really matter, does it?' she realised. 'All that matters now is that Emily tells the whole truth, and faces up to whatever the law decides to do with her.' She winced. 'She's going to be so appallingly *embarrassed* about it all.'

The expressions on both faces made her smile a little. 'I know,' she said. 'It's meant to be far worse than embarrassing, and it will be, I'm sure. It's just that for Emily, that's almost the worst thing of all.'

'Shame? Humiliation? Remorse?' Ariadne supplied.

'Oh yes,' Thea nodded miserably. 'Yes, yes and yes.'

Thea phoned her mother as soon as Peter and Ariadne had left, wondering how much she should tell her. But of course it was Bruce who picked up the phone, demanding explanations. 'Bruce – I'm sure Emily will call you any minute now. Do you mind if I speak to Mum first? There's something I really need to say to her.'

With surprising grace, he complied, and her mother came on the line. 'Thea?' she asked.

'Mum, I want you to come here, and spend the

333

next few days with me. Things are looking bad for Emily – they're questioning her now, but the whole story has come out, really. I can't talk about it on the phone–' her voice thickened as she imagined the effect of the truth on the whole extended family. 'But we'll deal with it together. And, Mum–'

'Yes, yes,' interrupted Mrs Johnston energetically. 'I understand. I'll come as soon as I can. You'll have to give me directions, of course. I don't think I've ever been to Lower Slaughter.'

The echoes of Emily, the weekend before, were too acute to ignore. 'Just come to the middle of the village, and I'll be waiting for you,' she said weakly. 'And – thanks, Mum.'

It was true, she realised, as she ended the call. Together, the family would survive this crisis, because people always did survive. Worse things had happened, after all.

In need of comfort before her mother arrived, she fetched the sheepskin that Henry Galton had given her, and laid it on the sofa. Inviting Hepzie to join her, she curled up on the warm wool, and thought about Emily and Bruce and Sam Webster and how Emily's lies had made no real difference to anything. And would she see Phil again sometime soon? Probably, she concluded. He too would need a degree of debriefing, after a misguided murder investigation that had turned out to be so close to him personally. Precisely where it would leave their relationship remained to be seen.

'Lock the doors, Daddy!' shouted Ignatius. 'Lock the doors.'

The publishers hope that this book has given you enjoyable reading. Large Print Books are especially designed to be as easy to see and hold as possible. If you wish a complete list of our books please ask at your local library or write directly to:

Magna Large Print Books
Magna House, Long Preston,
Skipton, North Yorkshire.
BD23 4ND